Bounty Calls

Markus Matthews

Bounty Calls
Copyright © 2020 by Markus Matthews

Tellwell Talent
www.tellwell.ca

ISBN
978-0-2288-2785-6 (Hardcover)
978-0-2288-2783-2 (Paperback)
978-0-2288-2784-9 (eBook)

**To the fans of this series,
thank you for making this happen!**

Zombies for the win!

Tuesday, May 29

"**B**ored. So bored," said Olivia as she wandered aimlessly around the living room.

I couldn't disagree with my fanged friend. Since taking down the Acolytes a few weeks ago, things had been a little scarce bounty-wise. At first I'd welcomed the downtime, as it gave me a chance to deal with their deaths. We hadn't killed them—that was the so-called Master who controlled and financed the group, but those deaths had weighed heavily on me, especially at night when I was trying to sleep. We'd spent that first week doing everything we could to find the Master, but he was in the wind and we couldn't find a trace of him.

We had gotten used to taking down six- and seven-figure bounties, but in the last few weeks we'd not taken down a single one.

Liv wasn't talking so much about our business lull but more about the here and now. It was the night of the full moon, which meant Bree, our Werepanther, was out with the Barrie pack running through a forest in her beast form with other Weres. Bree was Liv's usual nighttime companion. I was just filling in while she was away.

Keeping Liv company was more like babysitting, though. We'd all decided that since last month's full moon kitchen incident, where we'd all left Liv unsupervised, it was a bad idea. I still couldn't figure out what a blood-drinking vampire was doing trying her hand at cooking at three in the morning. Trying to explain to the fire department why there was a live cow in our smoldering kitchen wasn't an experience I wanted to repeat. Especially since Animal Control still hadn't finished their investigation.

It also might be a little odd that a twenty-one-year-old vampire needed supervision, but as much as I loved her, Liv was a bit crazy. That was probably why I loved her—she certainly kept things interesting.

I watched in horror as Liv picked up my prized 1/72 scale B-25 Mitchell model from the display shelf and examined it. I prayed that if real B-25s could take '30 seconds over Tokyo' that my model could take a few seconds of vampire attention. I exhaled in relief when she put it back on the shelf. I swear the only thing scarier than a vampire in full bloodlust is a bored one.

My attention was pulled back to the chess game I was playing with our pixie companion. I cursed under my breath as Alteea, with a flutter of her wings, moved her bishop, taking the knight I'd left exposed. Normally I was better than this, but Liv was distracting me from the game.

"Why don't you watch a movie on Netflix?" I suggested to her as I pondered my next chess move.

"I checked; there's nothing I want to watch …"

I moved my queen up and pinned Alteea's bishop, putting her in check at the same time. She frowned, and her gossamer wings beat slowly as she contemplated her next move.

"What about something we have on Blu-ray?"

"We have movies on Blu-ray?" asked Liv.

I rolled my eyes and said, "Check the bottom drawer."

There were at least one hundred movies in that drawer, and I hoped maybe one would appeal to her. In a blur of movement, she darted over to the cabinet under the large flat-screen TV. Liv bent over and began rummaging. The view of her shapely figure in those tight-fitting yoga pants made me more distracted than I already was.

"We could have sex?" I suggested with a grin.

"Yeah, but after those two fun-filled minutes, I'd be bored again," said Liv without even looking up.

Ouch. Bored vampires are snarky vampires.

Alteea moved her queen in front of her king, offering a queen-for-queen trade. Normally I would have taken it, but being down a knight, I couldn't afford to trade piece for piece. I took the bishop instead. Alteea brought out her knight and threatened my queen.

"Don't you have any good movies?" said Liv as she continued poking around the drawer.

I was about to argue about the quality of my movies when my iPhone rang. I picked it up and saw 'R. Quinn' on the display. Rob was my best friend and a Hamilton police officer. As it was after midnight, I assumed this call was probably police-related rather than a social call.

I answered it and he said, "Hey, Hurricane," which confirmed for me that this was a business call. For ten years, I patrolled the city as the

Hamilton Hurricane, using my elemental powers of Air and Electricity to keep the city safe. I'd retired from the hero business six years ago when I took up bounty hunting full time. My official status was reserve, which meant I could still be called upon during emergencies. If Rob had been calling for social reasons, he would have called me 'Zack' or 'Airhead,' depending on his mood.

"I'm currently at the Hamilton Cemetery and there are a couple hundred zombies trying to break down the main gate."

"YES!" said Olivia, who blurred out of the room and came back not a second later with her sword in her hand.

I shook my head in amazement at her vampire hearing and asked, "Where's SWAT and EIRT?"

"SWAT is tied up in a hostage situation in Stoney Creek. The three nearest EIRT teams are busy; two are dealing with rogue Weres and the other is dealing with a troll. It's a full moon after all … so, can you get your team down here or not?"

The Hamilton SWAT team was usually the first line of defense in cases like this, but they were only a stopgap measure until EIRT—the Enhanced Individual Response Team—could arrive on scene. They were Canada's federal anti-monster teams. They were made up of six officers and usually one or two of them were Enhanced Individuals.

If there was one night you could almost guarantee monster activity, it was during a full moon. The fact that Weres were forced to change was one reason, but even without Weres, full moons tended to be the night crazy stuff happened. Police and emergency services would always schedule extra personnel on the night of a full moon due to this.

"Are they shamblers or sprinters?" I asked

"Shamblers."

There were two types of Zombies: shamblers were the slow-moving kind, and the easiest to deal with. They moved at a slow shuffle and almost anybody could outrun them. They were only really dangerous in large numbers, or if you got trapped in a confined space with them.

Sprinters sucked. They moved fast and never got tired. Both kinds, though, were a concern. Anyone they killed would rise and join the zombie hoard. It was important to take them down quickly so their numbers didn't grow.

"I don't know; I am currently enjoying a rousing game of chess …"

Liv swatted me with the sheath-covered end of her sword, and Rob said, "Really?" in the most sarcastic tone ever.

"Okay, we'll be down there shortly."

"Sooner than later would be good. I'm not sure how long the gates will hold."

"You eat too many donuts this week and can't run fast enough to stay ahead of shamblers?" I teased.

"Har-har. Just get your ass down here, okay?"

"On my way."

I hung up and got to my feet. I kicked around the idea of waking up Blue and Stella. Blue's shadow-travelling abilities could transport all of us down there in seconds. Stella could transform herself into an almost-indestructible Hyde form, which would have no problem stomping a couple hundred zombies. One look at Liv, who was practically bouncing with excitement at the thought of carving her way through some shambling zombies, and I decided to let our other teammates sleep.

Less than a minute later, the three of us were out in the front yard. May this year had been stupid hot, but tonight was a nice mild eighteen degrees Celsius. The full moon was big and bright in the sky and there wasn't a cloud to be seen.

Liv snuggled up to me and Alteea grabbed on to the back of my T-shirt collar. I called on my Air power and lifted us all into the night sky. Hamilton Cemetery was on York Boulevard in downtown Hamilton near the edge of Burlington. I lived on Hamilton Mountain, on the rural edge of the city. If we were driving, it would probably take fifteen to twenty minutes to get there, depending on traffic. Flying through the air at close to 140 kilometers per hour, we got there in less than five minutes.

From the air it was easy to find. There had to be at least twenty police cruisers with their lights going in front of the cemetery. They'd blocked off both ends of York Street and the rest of the cruisers were parked nose to tail back from the front gate, a second line of defense if the gates gave way. The officers stood behind the line of cruisers with their weapons drawn, eyeing the straining iron gates warily.

I didn't know why they were so concerned. The gates should hold, unless a lot more zombies showed up. The gates groaned as the silent undead hoard pushed up against them, trying to reach the tasty humans on the other side. The gates were supposed to be able to hold the entire cemetery's worth of zombies, according to the Official Cemetery Act of 1946. On the other hand, this was an old cemetery, so there was a good chance these gates had been here since 1946, and things did wear out over time.

The Act had come into being after the Winnipeg Massacre of 1945 when a bunch of zombies were called forth from their graves by a necromancer. They wandered into the city, and in short order, hundreds of people were infected. The army had to be called in to put them down. The final death toll for the night was close to 500 people. To stop this from happening again, the Cemetery Act was passed. It had three parts to it. One, all cemeteries would be required to have ten-foot walls and a gated entrance that was to be locked at sundown each night. Two, from then on the government would pay for cremations in the hope that people would choose cremation over burial. And three, raising zombies for any reason was deemed an offence punishable by death.

Rob spotted us and we moved over to him.

"Thanks for coming so quickly," he said. "There are a couple hundred ..."

As Rob was talking, the slight breeze shifted, and I got a whiff of decay from our undead friends who were about twenty feet away behind the straining gates. I held up my hand to cut him off. I inhaled theatrically. "Smell that bouquet? A mild stench of decomposition with peaty, earthy undertones and a hint of formaldehyde; they can only be circa 1900; a very good year."

I was only sort of joking. Hamilton Cemetery was an older one, and I didn't think anyone new had been interned here in years. Most of its residents were buried in the late-nineteenth and early twentieth centuries. The zombies didn't smell as bad as fresher ones would have.

Rob rolled his eyes at me.

Olivia snickered and then said, "Less talky-talky, more choppy-choppy!"

I nodded and said, "I'll push them back. You hop the gate and take them down, okay?"

Liv drew her sword and said, "Hear that, Mr. Slicey? We get to have fun."

A few cops looked at Liv like she was insane as she spoke to her sword, but nobody said anything. I called on my powers and used my

Air powers to float myself over the protective line of cruisers, landing about ten feet from the straining gate.

I was impressed at the well-dressed group in front of me. Considering the clothes were over a hundred years old, they'd held up better than I would have expected. The corpses themselves were in pretty good condition too, considering their age. They were now mostly skeletons with blackened and dried skin. They were a quiet bunch, as their vocal chords and tongues had decayed.

I called my Air power to me and built up a hefty charge. I released a powerful gust of wind a few seconds later. The zombies tumbled back from the gate like leaves in a gusty fall storm. A couple of stubborn ones clung to the gate, even as they were picked up by the wind and blown horizontal to the ground. I narrowed my focus and hit each of them with a more precise and powerful gust. One by one they flew off the gate and deeper into the cemetery.

The gate now cleared, I turned off the wind. I spotted Liv's black and red aura flash by as she leapt effortlessly over the iron gates.

"Come get some!" said Liv from the other side of the gates at the pile of undead slowly getting to their feet.

I used my Air power again, flying to the top of the wall on the righthand side of the gate and sat down atop it. Alteea landed beside me. She was invisible due to her glamour being up but her small rainbow aura ensured that I could see her.

Liv swung her silver-edged sword in confident strokes and three headless Zombies tumbled to the ground and went still. She moved deeper into the mass and more zombies dropped.

"Master?" asked Alteea, "Aren't we going to help Mistress Liv?"

I smiled and shook my head, "We are helping; we're moral support." I yelled out like a proud dad at a soccer game, "You get them, girl! You're doing great!"

More zombies fell, burying Liv under a pile of them. A moment later, zombies flew in all directions as she got back to her feet.

"No biting!" yelled Liv as she cut one male Zombie in half vertically.

The two halves dropped to the ground but both pieces were still moving.

"Cut side to side; you need to remove the heads!" I yelled down to her.

She flipped me the bird with her free hand and sliced off the head of a large female Zombie in an ornate black dress.

Alteea gasped as Liv got dogpiled again and went under the mass of bodies yet again.

"Master, are you sure she doesn't need our help?"

"She's fine; zombies only eat brains—so she has nothing they'd even be interested in."

Alteea let out a small giggle beside me and said, "Master, you're terrible."

"The only terrible thing is that I forgot to bring popcorn for this show," I said, watching as more zombies went flying again.

Liv did look a little worse for wear. She had a few bite marks that were bleeding and the right knee of her black yoga pants was torn, as was a small section of her white tube top.

"Those were my favorite pants, fuckers!" said Liv while swinging her katana; three more headless zombies dropped to the ground.

She got faster, and her sword whirled like a blender. Heads, arms, and other body parts shot off in all directions.

Out of the corner of my eye, I spotted a flash of silver from the back of the graveyard. I turned my attention to it, but it was gone in an instant.

"Did you see that?" I asked.

"See what, Master?"

"A flash of silver over there," I said, pointing in the direction I spotted it.

"I didn't see anything, Master."

I wondered if I had imagined it, but I really thought I saw a camera flash going off. My stomach knotted at the thought of someone taking pictures from inside the graveyard. If some stupid civilian was there taking pictures, it would be my luck that they got bit. If that happened, they would turn in less than twenty-four hours and we'd have another zombie outbreak. And this time it wouldn't be in a secure, enclosed space.

"Stay here and keep an eye on Liv. Shoot up a fireball if she gets in trouble and I'll come running, okay?"

"Yes, Master."

I took to the air and flew over to the back of the cemetery, looking for the possible photographer. It was a large place, but I made it to the back of the grounds in mere seconds. I hovered over the area and searched for any sign of the silver flash. The graves in this area were disturbed, which meant this was the spot the zombies had been raised. The area was quiet now, and nothing moved. The street on the other side of the aging brick wall was also deserted.

I'd been sure I'd seen something, but now I started to doubt myself. Maybe the flash had been from a phone in the window of one of the nearby houses, or maybe it was just moonlight reflecting off something. I shrugged and did another slow rotation in the air just to make sure I wasn't missing anything. When my search came up empty, I flew back to my perch on the wall beside Alteea.

Liv had been busy; there were more zombies down on the ground now than standing. She had a few more rips and tears in her clothing and a couple new bite marks, but her earlier bites had healed already thanks to her vampire healing abilities.

Liv got buried under another mass of zombies but came up swinging and cursing a few moments later.

"You sure she doesn't need help, Master?" asked Alteea in an anxious tone.

I shook my head and watched as another two zombies lost their heads to Mr. Slicey. Liv was the perfect solution to this problem. She was stronger and faster than zombies. She could quickly heal whatever damage they did to her. They weren't carrying wooden stakes or fire, so unless they could somehow gnaw her head off or remove her heart, there was no way they could kill her. Lastly, and most importantly, she couldn't get infected by the zombies, as her vampire blood somehow neutralized the virus.

"Hey, can the Fae be turned into zombies?" I asked my pixie companion.

"I don't think so, Master. I've never heard of it happening before."

I wasn't surprised at her answer. I knew the Fae were immune to things like human colds and flu, so it made sense that whatever virus or pathogen that caused humans to be transformed into zombies wouldn't work with the Fae. I was also relieved; the idea of something like a zombie ogre sent a chill through me. Ogres were scary enough; a zombie one that didn't feel pain was downright terrifying.

I pulled out my phone to snap a few pictures of my own. This would help with the bounty claim later. There wasn't a posted bounty on the UN bounty website for this particular group of zombies, but there were set rates for jobs like this. Zombies would be worth $500 US each at standard rates. If they were sprinters instead of shamblers that rate would jump to $1,500 US. Even at $500, tonight's work would be a nice payday. There were at least 200 zombies when we started, which meant we'd be looking at more than a $100,000 for a couple hours work.

"Oh my God! Look at that dress!" said Liv in an almost giddy tone.

I glanced over and shook my head in distress as Liv sheathed her sword and pulled out her phone from her top. Liv had her eyes on a female zombie in a formal, flowing emerald green dress. Liv grabbed a handful of the zombie's long, grey hair to prevent it from biting her. The zombie lunged forward, snapping at Liv. The hair fell away from the zombie's head and it almost managed to bite Liv, but she jumped back a few feet.

"Gross," said Liv as she brushed the clump of hair from her hands.

Undeterred, Liv stepped closer to the zombie and grabbed it by the neck with her free hand. She kicked another zombie that approached her. "Don't be rude; I'll get to you in a moment …" It flew back and crashed into a couple of others that were about ten feet away.

The zombie in the green dress kept trying to bite Liv but couldn't get close due to the grip Liv had on its throat. Liv held up the phone and said, "Say 'Brains!'" and the flash on the phone went off as she took a selfie. Liv kicked another couple of zombies back and took a few more pictures before tucking her phone back into her top.

She'd just gotten her other hand back on the handle of her sword when the zombies surged, and she went under again in a writhing pile of corpses.

I got a bit more worried as time ticked by and she didn't resurface. A good twenty seconds later, she exploded from the pile with her sword out and swinging. Body parts and whole zombies flew in all directions. My eyes widened; Liv was now topless and her left butt cheek was exposed from where the Zombies had ripped away her yoga pants.

Liv looked down at her bare chest and screamed, "My phone!" She dove back to the ground and disappeared into the pile of zombies again.

I caught a couple catcalls from the cops at the gate and laughed to myself. Only Liv would be more concerned about her phone than the topless show she was giving Hamilton's finest at this moment. In the same situation, Bree would have been mortified. On the other hand, Bree wouldn't have stopped in the middle of a fight to take selfies.

Liv shot out of the pile with her phone clutched in one hand triumphantly and her sword in the other. The beaming smile on her face probably meant her phone was okay. I raised my phone and took a couple of shots of the semi-nude vampire. Mainly because it was hot, but I knew the rest of the team would find this whole thing amusing.

Less than an hour later, the zombies were down, and Liv had done a couple of walkthroughs of the cemetery to make sure there were no stragglers.

I groaned as I gazed over the bodies and parts on the ground; the paperwork on this one was going to be a bitch. The problem was that the bounty claim was per zombie, which meant that each zombie would need to be photographed as proof and have its own claim form. I smiled to myself when it occurred to me that I could probably pass this off to Stella and Blue to do tomorrow. I'd take the pictures, get the federal bounty claim number for this incident but the two of them could submit the paperwork.

"What's next?" yelled Liv from below.

"We'll come down. We need pictures for the bounty claim."

"Crap," said Liv as she realized how long that was going to take.

Alteea and I landed beside Liv. I gave her a onceover to make sure she was okay. All her bites were healed but judging by the bloodstains covering her, she'd taken several of them.

"Stop checking out my tits!" said Liv.

I shook my head and said, "I wasn't … alright I wasn't *just* checking them out. You okay? You took a lot of bites …"

I stripped off my T-shirt and handed it to her.

"Thanks. I'm fine but could use a pick-me-up," she answered with a gleam in her green eyes.

I sighed. I knew what she wanted. I still wasn't a big fan of her feeding off me, but tonight she had done most of the work and I owed her for that. "Okay, but just a little. I still need to fly us home."

Liv stepped closer to me and we embraced. She softly kissed my neck. I felt a brief pinch as her fangs pierced my skin. Liv moaned in pleasure as she drank from me.

Ten seconds later, her tongue licked the area where she had been feeding from to heal me. Vampire saliva had healing properties; if I checked the area later in the mirror, it would be hard to find exactly where she had fed from me.

Her mouth came up to my ear and she whispered, "Thank you. I love how you taste …"

"You're welcome. Now shall we get back to work?"

She nodded and let go of me. I walked over to the gate and told Rob the coast was clear. He unlocked the gate with a master key. Officers slowly and cautiously entered the grounds, most carrying flashlights and shotguns.

Rob looked at me and said, "Guys, this pale one is with us and not a zombie, so don't shoot him by mistake, okay?"

I rolled my eyes at him but grinned at him for scoring a verbal point.

I had to admit that my pasty, exposed upper body could have used a bit of sun. It had been hotter than usual this May and most people by now had tanned more than I had. I'd been hiding during the day in the air conditioning. I'd been outside a lot this month but mostly at night for Blue's team physical training exercises, which were always at night because of Olivia.

The three of us walked around with cops as they made sure the scene was secure. Liv still had her sword out in case anything jumped out at us, and I had the air around me thickened to prevent any zombie turning me into a Zack snack. I'd already fed my one undead companion and that was my quota for this evening.

The tour took twenty minutes, but Olivia had done a great job and there wasn't a single twitching zombie that needed to be dispatched. Most of the officers left after that. It was still a full moon and there was a backlog of calls they needed to respond to. Rob and five officers stayed on scene. Two were posted at the gate while the rest stayed close to us as I began taking pictures for the bounty claim.

"How's Ian doing?" I asked as my phone flashed. Ian was Rob's new infant son who was born last month.

"He is doing great. Annette and I, however, could do with some more sleep," said Rob with a yawn. "For a little guy, he has an impressive set of lungs on him."

I laughed and said, "Enjoy these years; I'm sure it won't be too long before he is wrecking your car and needing you to bail him out of jail."

"At least then I'd probably get some sleep …"

We made a slow circle around the entire area where the zombies had fallen, and I kept taking pictures. We reached the one Liv had cut in half vertically before she'd chopped off its head. "Do think we could claim this one twice?" I asked.

Rob laughed and said, "You could try, but I doubt you'll be successful."

Rob yawned and that set me off with a yawn of my own. By my phone, it was just coming up on 4 a.m. This had been a long night and it was catching up on me. That also meant the sun would be up in less than two hours, so I needed to get Olivia home soon. Thankfully we were almost wrapped up.

Rob was waiting for a Hazmat team, an EIRT team, and the crime scene techs to arrive. The last part about the techs reminded me that this was a crime scene. Zombies don't raise themselves; someone or something called them from their slumber. "The zombies were raised from the back corner but when I checked it out earlier, I don't remember seeing any blood, animal or human sacrifices ..."

Rob frowned and the whole party walked over to the disturbed graves. We searched the area for a bit but came up empty. There were no signs of a ritual to be found. That meant whoever did this either cleaned up immediately after or didn't need the usual blood rites to raise them. I hoped it was the former and not the latter. Most necromancers needed a blood sacrifice to call the undead but there were things out there that didn't—scary things that made for much bigger problems. There were rumors that some older vampires could call the undead to their service but to acquire that type of skill, the vampire would need to be at least 500 years old. Gods and demons could do it too. A lich would also have that ability. None of those things were something I wanted to get near.

I'd cross my fingers and hope that we had a tidy amateur necromancer and that this was a one-time thing. An amateur would make more sense. Why raise a couple hundred when there were thousands in this graveyard? Unless this had just been a test to see if their power worked or not. Also, if it were one of the more powerful things like a lich or demon, they'd have busted the gates open to spread the chaos.

I yawned again and asked, "Do you need us for anything else?"

Rob shook his head and said, "No, we have this covered. EIRT will be here shortly. Go home and get some sleep. And thanks for your help."

Olivia snuggled up to me and I spotted Alteea's aura on Liv's shoulder. I called on my Air power and headed home.

The moment we got in the door, Liv said, "I need a shower," and blurred off upstairs before I could say anything. Alteea flew up the stairs after her and I assumed our pixie was going to join her. Alteea loved playing in the rain or the shower.

I entered the kitchen and made a beeline for the fridge. I kicked around having a beer but settled on a glass of milk. I found a package of cookies in the cupboard and helped myself to a couple. Normally I wouldn't be snacking this late at night, but I needed a bit of sugar to help with the blood loss from Liv's feeding.

As I finished my late-night snack, my phone vibrated in my pocket. I pulled it out and there was a text from Rob with the bounty claim number. I left my phone and a note on the kitchen counter for Stella and Blue, asking them to start on the paperwork. I left another note on the counter for Olivia wishing her a good night and telling her not to burn down the kitchen tonight.

I'd played with the idea of staying up another hour until the sun came up, but I couldn't stop yawning and figured even Olivia couldn't destroy the place in an hour.

The night hadn't gone like I'd pictured it, but at least tonight's work broke the slump we'd been in bounty-wise. A six-figure bounty was a good start to getting back on track.

When does the hurting stop?

Wednesday, May 30

Stella

It wasn't even 7 a.m. and I could already feel the humidity in the air. The steady hum of the air conditioner as it tried to keep up with the heat was another clue today was going to be hot one. The extremes of Canadian weather never ceased to amaze me; the bone-chilling cold and sweltering heat made it easy to miss my native England. If it was this hot in May what would July and August be like? At least if it got too bad, Blue could transport us both to our secret underground lab in London.

Blue was already up; her bed made. She was probably getting in a workout to start the day.

I perked up as I took a gander at the notes I'd made for a new project Blue and I discussed yesterday. I had been so excited that rather than going to sleep last night, I stayed up and made a list of all the parts we'd require.

I was probably more enthusiastic about this project than I should be. Since taking down the Acolytes, business had been slow. It was my role to find bounties for the team and the pickings had been slim. I felt I was letting them down. Zack assured me that it wasn't my fault, and that lulls like this were just how the business worked. I took his word for it, but it still chaffed that I'd hadn't found a good bounty for us.

My dress was wrinkled from sleeping in it, so I quickly changed to my Hyde form and back. A quick check in the mirror reassured me that my dress was restored to its original pristine state. I sighed as the image staring back at me was exactly the same as it had been for over a hundred years. I'd be over the moon to see a pimple appear. At least that would mean I was hitting puberty.

I grabbed my list from my bedside table. A cup of tea and a light breakfast with Blue and we'd be off to Home Depot, Best Buy, and a couple of other places to get the items on my list.

Blue raised a questioning eyebrow at the pad of paper in my hands when I entered the kitchen. "I got excited about your idea to make the training area more active and made a list of supplies."

Blue nodded approvingly at me and said, "It is a shame that we have to make the traps non-lethal; how are people supposed to learn if there is no risk?"

I stopped in my tracks at that. I loved Blue, but there were times when she truly scared me. Most times I forgot she was raised in an alien world that had very different morals and values than we did. She grew up training to be a warrior in a society that was harsh and unforgiving. To her, training with lethal consequences was normal.

Sensing that she was dismayed about the lack of risk, I decided to appeal to her sense of mischief, "Just because we can't kill anyone doesn't mean that we can't have fun. Sure, a flamethrower trap in the training area would be exciting, but if we get creative, we can make the same point." Blue frowned at this and I added, "Instead of something that shoots flames, what about flour? Think of how cheesed off the others will be when they are covered in flour."

Blue's tail began moving in rapid circles, which meant my idea pleased her. I continued, "So we can't use poison darts to fire at them; paintball pellets will make the same point. Those things sting when they hit and will splatter them with paint."

Blue's pointy-toothed smile appeared, and she said, "Pain is a great teacher."

"We'll go shopping for supplies after breakfast," I said.

I spotted Zack's phone and note on the counter. Blue saw what had caught my attention and added, "It seems Olivia and Zack were busy last night—they took down a bunch of zombies, so the shopping trip will have to wait, we have paperwork to do first."

I sighed. Zombies were a pain to process for bounty claims, as each zombie needed its own claim form. Hopefully it wouldn't be that bad. I opened Zack's phone and thumbed through the photos, groaning to myself as picture after picture showed multiple headless corpses. At the end, there was a picture of Olivia, topless, battling a bunch of zombies. I rolled my eyes at Zack being a pervert again and deleted it to protect Olivia's modesty.

Also, judging by the pictures, Blue's statement about Zack and Olivia being busy was incorrect. Since all the zombies had been beheaded, and none were blackened and fried due to lightning, it looked like Olivia had done all the work last night. I wasn't sure if Zack had been lazy or was just being safety conscious; Olivia couldn't be infected by zombies like Zack could.

I cheered myself up as I ran the numbers in my head. At $500 each, there had to be $100,000 worth of zombies here. I kept the books for the company, and this would certainly help our bottom line, which hadn't seen any revenue in over a fortnight now.

After our tea and a light breakfast, Blue and I got cracking.

It took all morning, but we had all the bounty paperwork done and filled online. The final count was 207 zombies for a grand total of $103,500.

Finally done with our paperwork, Blue opened a shadow portal and we stepped through.

"Bloody hell! It's as hot as Hades out here!" I exclaimed as the wave of heat hit us as we stepped out from the shadows. We were in the shade behind the Home Depot and it was still insanely warm. Blue hit a button on the bracelet on her wrist and the tall blue alien was replaced by a tall, heavy-set elderly man. That hologram technology had cost us a pretty penny, but it was worth it. We didn't get any stares or whispered comments at Blue's unusual appearance. Blue just looked like an old man out with his granddaughter.

Without a word, we both headed around the building to get out of the heat. I sighed in relief as we entered the air-conditioned store.

As the cart filled up with supplies, it got harder to push due the wonky front wheel. I grunted with effort but got it moving again.

We were having a good time right up until we entered the lumber aisle.

Bloody hell! I thought as an overwhelming pain slammed into me. I screamed, as it felt like my entire body was burning. Without even a thought, I changed into Hyde to protect myself. This had to be the first time ever that changing into Hyde improved my thought process. Usually my brain felt like it was in a fog while I was in my Hyde form. The fog was still there but it was an improvement over the pain my human form was experiencing.

Blue was on the floor in the fetal position, screaming in agony.

Friend in pain ... must smash! roared my alter ego in our shared mind.

I forced my will over my Hyde side to stop it from going on a rampage. I looked around and tried to deduce what was causing this. Further down the aisle there was a pregnant woman on the floor, shrieking in pain, and at the end of the row an older man in a Home Depot smock was doing the same thing. My anger grew at seeing these people suffer.

I scooped up Blue and ran. I stopped at the pregnant woman and carefully picked her up in my other arm. She was in so much pain that I don't think she even realized she'd been moved from the floor.

No carry. Smash! Hyde growled in our mind.

Save friend and innocent lady then smash, I thought back at it.

It grunted unhappily in response and I turned for the exit. In each aisle there were people on the ground writhing in agony. Were we under attack? Was this a robbery? How far did this pain spread?

The shrieks coming from Blue and the pregnant woman lessened in intensity as we got closer to the entrance. I glanced over at the cash area and everyone was on the ground in pain. That meant it probably wasn't a robbery.

Near the store's entrance were two people on the sidewalk huddled over in distress. Further out, there were cars coming into the lot and people walking around like normal. I moved away from the building.

"Stella, put me down," said Blue.

The woman had also stopped screaming and was shivering in fear in my arms. I lightly tossed Blue and she leapt out of my arm and landed nimbly on her feet. Normally, that spry maneuver would have people taking a closer look at the old man illusion, but nobody seemed to have noticed. Blue stepped closer to me and helped the woman from my arms.

The pregnant lady blanched as she looked at my hideous form, but she still managed to stammer a thank you. Her eyes widened as I changed back to my human from.

"You're welcome," I said. "Are you okay?"

She nodded and asked, "What happened? I've never felt pain like that."

"Don't know," I said. "Did the pain lessen as we got farther away from the lumber aisle?"

The lady shuddered. "Not at first, but once we got closer to the entrance it did. It hurt, but not quite as much." Blue nodded in confirmation.

"Okay, so there is something in the building that is causing this."

Blue nodded at that and asked, "A device or an Enhanced?"

"Not sure, but I need to get the people out of there; pain like that can be fatal."

I watched in horror as a Good Samaritan ran towards the two people lying on the ground in front of the building. He got within twenty feet and then screamed and went down.

"We need to keep people back." I turned to the pregnant lady and asked, "I'm sorry, I didn't get your name?"

"Debbie. Debbie Waterford."

"Okay, Debbie, can I get you to stop people from running towards the building?" She nodded and moved closer to the building.

"Blue, call the police and request SWAT and an EIRT team. Then get as close as you can to the building and see if you can walk around its perimeter. Try and figure out where the center of this disturbance is."

Blue bobbed her head and pulled out her phone. I changed back and lumbered over to the Good Samaritan. I picked him up and moved back away from the pain zone to where Debbie was standing. I put him down and he too blanched at the sight of my form.

Debbie put her hand on his arm to steady him and said, "It's okay, she's a friend. Can you help me keep people away from the building?"

The man nodded and the two of them started intercepting anyone heading towards the building. I spotted Blue in her old man disguise, staggering a bit as she edged around the outside of the pain field. I felt bad that she had to keep subjecting herself to the pain to find the edges of the field.

I turned and proceeded towards the two people down on the sidewalk. They joined Debbie and the man in keeping people back.

As I approached the store, wails of agony echoed and it seemed more like I was heading into a medieval dungeon than a big box hardware store. For the next ten minutes, I dashed in and out of the store pulling more and more people out. I'd just pulled the last of the cashiers out when I spotted Blue waving at me.

The crowd stepped back as I approached. The wail of distant sirens was getting louder with every passing second. I changed back once I was sure I was out of the zone.

"The pain area isn't perfectly centered in the building," said Blue. "The epicenter is about thirty feet to the left of the center of the store, closer to the back."

A police cruiser screamed into the parking lot and drove directly towards the front of the store. I yelled and waved at the officer to stop but he kept going, not hearing me over the noise of the siren or seeing me wave at him. He slowed down as he got closer to the entrance and then he hit the edge of the zone. The tires squealed as the cruiser sped up and crashed hard into a display of riding mowers outside the front of the store.

I sighed and changed back. I ran over to the wrecked police cruiser and was relieved to hear screams coming from within the car; at least he was still alive. I grabbed the door and pulled it clean off the side of the car. The wailing officer didn't even notice me. I tried to reach in and release his seatbelt, but my large fingers weren't suited for such a delicate task. In frustration, I grabbed the top and bottom seatbelt mounts and yanked them out. I pulled the officer from the cruiser and carried him out of the zone.

I put him down and he instantly put his hand on his weapon as he got his first look at me. I changed back and said, "Easy there, Officer, you are in no danger." He blinked a couple of times in confusion. "Can you get on the radio and tell the other officers not to approach the building like you did?"

He glanced over to his disfigured patrol car and nodded. He unclipped his walkie-talkie and I left him to it.

I changed back and returned to the store. This time I didn't pull people out immediately. Instead I move to the center of the store. I walked thirty feet to the left and turned up the aisle. There were only two people here: a mother and her daughter. Both were on the ground screaming, though the volume was less, as if they'd screamed themselves raw.

I searched around them for any odd devices but couldn't see anything. I focused on the girl who looked like she just started puberty, and I wondered if she was the cause. Enhanced Individuals came into their powers at about her age. They usually didn't have control of those powers, which would explain why she was on the floor screaming like everyone else. Her power could be something that projected pain. Unfortunately, it also caused her to feel the pain as well. She was stuck in a loop: the more pain she felt the more her power responded, trying to protect itself. The more I pondered my theory the more it made sense to me.

"Girl hurting people. SMASH GIRL!" snarled Hyde.

It briefly took control of our form and made a fist, but I regained control before it turned her into jam.

If she was the one causing this, then I couldn't move her. I scooped up the mom and headed out. I found another employee on my way out and grabbed her too.

Once we were outside and out of the zone, the mom said, "Let me down, my baby girl is still back there!"

I put the Home Depot employee down first and then the mom just in front of the line of police tape that had been put up to keep people back. She immediately ran back towards the store before I could catch her. I turned and followed. She hit the pain zone again and went down screaming. I picked her up again and pulled her out.

This time when I put her down, she said, "Please, my daughter Emma is still in there. Help her please!"

I changed back and asked, "Ma'am, are you or your husband Enhanced?"

She blinked once in confusion and said, "My husband Dan is. What does that have to do with anything?"

"What is your name?" I asked.

"Mary Turner."

"Okay, Mary. I'm Stella. I will help Emma, but I need to ask you a couple of questions first, okay?" She nodded, and I asked, "What is your husband's power?"

"He's an empath. He can sense other people's feelings."

"Has your daughter recently hit puberty?" I asked.

She frowned and said, "Yes, but what does … oh my god! You think Emma is causing this?"

"You were both at the very center of the pain zone…"

"But shouldn't she be an empath too?"

I shrugged and said, "Super class powers are unpredictable. If she is the cause, then once SWAT or EIRT arrives I will get a power-blocking collar and that should stop all of this."

The police officer I'd rescued earlier said, "ETA on SWAT is seven minutes." He turned to Mary and guided her back behind the line.

I changed forms yet again and went back in the store to rescue more people. The store was eerily quiet now. The people left were either silently screaming or had blacked out from the pain. Emma was in the former category, which was a shame as I was pretty sure if she blacked out this would be over by now.

SWAT rolled into the lot as I came out of the store. I'd lost track of how many times I'd been in and out now.

To my surprise, when the SWAT team poured out of the van, they didn't point their weapons at me. Even better, one of them handed me a power-blocking collar. I carefully took it from the officer and went to save Emma.

I crouched down by her trembling form and attempted to put it on her. My large, misshaped hands weren't suited for this task. It took me a minute, but I managed to fasten it around her neck. The second the collar snapped shut her eyes flew open. She saw me and panicked. I prayed that she really was the cause and changed back to my human form. I sighed in relief as the wave of pain didn't hit me.

"What happened? Why am I wearing this collar?" Her voice was raw.

The girl was a mess: her bare arms were bloody where she had been clawing at herself, her eyes were bloodshot, and her face was covered in tears and snot. The front of her pink shorts was wet; I assumed she must have lost control of her bladder while in the throes of agony. To top everything off, she was about to learn that she was the one that had caused all of this.

I was about to answer her questions when I heard someone shout from the front entrance, "Police, please remain where you are. We are here to assist you."

I sighed and turned to Emma and said, "Hi, Emma, my name is Stella. Your mom sent me to help you."

Emma glanced around like a frightened animal and asked, "Is my mom okay?"

I nodded and said, "She is fine. She is outside the store and once the police get to us, we will go find her." The tenseness in her body lessened at that and I continued, "You just came into your power. The collar is a power-blocking device that prevents you from using your power for the time being."

The fear in her face returned, "No … I caused all of this? My power is causing pain? Am I in trouble?"

I smiled at the last part and said, "You aren't in trouble. This was an accident. It seems that you have the power to cause pain, but your power is new so there may be other things you can do as well." I wondered what triggered it. Usually when a kid came into their powers it was due to a strong emotion triggering it. I asked, "Can you remember what happened before all of this started?"

Emma lowered her eyes to the floor and said, "We were having a fight. I didn't want to be at the stupid Home Depot. I wanted to go phone shopping at the mall instead. Mom was being a bitch and I got really mad."

Anger certainly was a strong emotion. I was about to ask her another question when a SWAT officer in tactical gear approached. Emma tensed at the sight of him. The officer approached slowly and said, "Are you both alright?"

We nodded, and he stopped a few feet from us and added, "Emma, your mom is outside and is worried about you, how about we go see her now?"

Emma was unsteady as she got to her feet. I stepped closer to her, but she managed to stay on her feet without my help.

As we headed for the entrance, I realized that this officer was the same one who handed me the power-blocking collar earlier. The stripes on his sleeve indicated that he was the sergeant, the one in charge of the team. Other officers were helping people out of the store. A few of the victims were bloody and injured. One man had a nasty gash on his forehead.

Outside the store a large crowd head had formed behind the police tape, and now there were multiple ambulances parked out front as well. Mary ran over and hugged her daughter. Blue joined us as well.

The sergeant said, "Mrs. Turner, why don't you take Emma over to one of the ambulances to get her checked out and have those cuts on her arms tended to?"

Mary nodded and led Emma away. Once they were gone, the sergeant turned to us and said, "I'm Sergeant Shay. Thank you for your help today."

I introduced myself and Blue and mentioned that we worked together with the former Hamilton Hurricane as bounty hunters. The sergeant smiled at that and I asked, "What will happen to Emma now?"

"She'll get checked out by the EMS crew and then after we get a statement from her and her mom, they will probably be sent home. But I'm guessing you meant longer term?" I nodded, and he said, "There is a program to help Enhanced Individuals who struggle with their powers. She will be assigned a social worker who will check in on her from time to time to make sure she is doing okay. They will also provide her with less obvious power-blocking devices than that collar, probably something like a pair of discreet-looking bracelets."

I was pleased at that. The collar wasn't exactly subtle and would be noticed by her schoolmates. If the bracelets were silver or gold-plated, or one of them was made to look like a watch, then nobody would be the wiser about her condition.

"Will they train her to use her powers?" I asked.

The sergeant frowned and shook his head, "No. The program is more for ensuring that the Enhanced isn't a threat to others or themselves. If she wishes to learn to use her powers, she will have to find help outside the system for that. Truthfully, they will probably recommend that she continues wearing the power-blocking devices and not try to use her power."

I wasn't shocked by his answer. The government would see the power blockers as a solution. In some ways I couldn't blame them for that. Emma's power was dangerous, and a lot of people suffered today. Worse, as she got older, her powers would get stronger. The Home Depot was roughly the size of a city block—how large of an area would Emma be able to affect as that power got stronger?

"Can I get a statement from you about what happened?" he asked.

Blue and I spent the next ten minutes answering his questions. "Don't take this the wrong way, but you are much nicer than the Hurricane made you out to be."

Sergeant Shay had a confused look on his face for a moment and then laughed, "I think he was talking about Sergeant Murdock. Murdock is rougher around the edges than I am. As I'm the more senior officer,

I end up on more dayshifts than he does, so the Hurricane probably bumps into him more often than me."

"You're right. Murdock was the name he'd used when he was venting."

We said our goodbyes to Sergeant Shay, and I asked Blue for one of our business cards. Blue carried everything, as the dress I wore didn't have any pockets. I could wear something else, but as it would be destroyed when I turned into Hyde, it didn't seem worth the extra effort and expense.

I led us over to Mary and Emma. The paramedics were just finishing treating Emma's arms. Emma had also wiped her face and was looking much better than she had. She still had an aura of fear and nervousness around her though.

Mary thanked us for helping her and her daughter. I smiled and said, "Here is my business card. Blue and I are bounty hunters that work with the former Hamilton Hurricane. As my Hyde form doesn't feel pain, I feel that I'm in a unique position of being one of the only people that can work with Emma. If she wishes to learn how to control her powers sometime down the road, my team and I will work with her to figure out how to do that."

Mary frowned at that and said, "I'm not sure that is a good idea. You might not feel the pain, but her power reaches a wide area. How can you make sure that no one will accidently be caught up in it?"

I smiled and said, "Blue here can travel to anywhere in the world via the shadows and take people with her."

Mary's look of confusion grew. "Her?"

Blue's old man form smiled, and she tapped the bracelet on her wrist. Mary and Emma's eyes widened at seeing Blue's normal appearance. Blue hit the button again and the harmless-looking elderly man reappeared.

"We get fewer stares when Blue goes out in disguise," I said, and both mom and daughter smiled at that. "So with Blue's travelling abilities, we can easily find some out-of-the-way place that hasn't got anyone around for miles." Mary looked relieved at that and I added, "I'm not pushing you or Emma to make a decision now. Just keep my card and think about it. If Emma is happy wearing a power blocker and pretending that she is a regular human, then that's fine too. But if she wants to explore what her power is and how to control it, we'll help her with that."

Emma's expression when I finished was more curious than anything. Mary seemed unsure.

"We'll discuss this and get back to you," said Mary. "It's been a crazy day and I think we both could use some time to let all of this settle in. Thank you again for your help and for your offer."

We said our goodbyes and left them to it. We found a shadow beside a nearby parked van and used it to travel to another Home Depot, as this one was closed for the day. We still had shopping to do and only a couple of hours before dinner to do it.

A Pain in the Neck

Wednesday, May 30

In her rush for breakfast, Liv blew by me, knocking the plate of food I was carrying from my hand. I barely managed to call on my Air power and used it to save my dinner, which hovered mere inches from the floor. I glared at Liv as I leaned over to pick up the plate. Her back was to me, so my gesture was in vain. I sighed and joined everyone at the table.

I was excited about a surprise I had for the team but was going to wait until after dinner to reveal it. I learned that I wasn't the only one to have an eventful day as we listened to Stella and Blue talk about the young Enhanced that came into her power at the hardware store this afternoon.

"How bad was the pain?" asked Bree between mouthfuls.

Blue's tail went still, and in a serious voice she said, "Usually with my warrior discipline I can ignore pain, but this was like nothing I'd ever felt before. The pain was so overwhelming that I couldn't think or move."

Blue had been through a lot in her life and if she found the pain to be that crippling then I was grateful that I hadn't been there.

This girl, Emma, was an interesting case. I wondered if Stella was being too optimistic about being able to train her. Since Emma experienced the same pain as she projected, her having any sort of control of it would be a challenge. It was possible that with time and training, Emma might be able to project the power externally without experiencing it herself. If she could control it, she would be a powerful Enhanced.

Another thought hit me, and I asked, "Why were you two at Home Depot in the first place?"

Stella glanced at Blue and said, "We were shopping for supplies for a new project Blue and I are working on."

"What's the project?"

Stella was quiet for a moment and said, "It is something to help the team work better together."

"A mute button for Liv?" I asked with a smile.

Liv, drinking her glass of blood, flipped me the bird in response.

"No," said Stella, grinning back.

I wanted to pry to figure out what the mysterious project was, but I knew from experience that Stella wouldn't budge. She always kept her projects under wraps until they were done. I was surprised that she even gave us that first clue, but something to help the team work better together could have a million different meanings, so she really hadn't revealed much.

The moment dinner wrapped up, I said, "I have a surprise for Olivia and Blue."

I went upstairs to get the new toys and returned to the kitchen. All eyes were on me as I held up the large white bag with the stylized gold 'G' on it. The bag and the items inside were from Grundy's. Grundy's was the supply shop for law enforcement and heroes in good standing. They had wizards, tech gurus, and Mad Scientists on staff. They carried costumes, armor, weapons, magic charms and potions, high-tech gear, tracking devices, surveillance equipment, and just about anything you could think of for hunting monsters.

Since I was a retired hero, I didn't have clearance to shop there until last week when my application was approved. I was granted restricted clearance, which meant I was only allowed to buy defensive gear. All their nifty offensive weapons and spells were off-limits.

I sat back down and lifted the first box out of the bag. The box too was white with a large golden 'G' on it. The tag on this one read, 'Zack' so I put it aside. The next box was for Blue and the last one was for Liv. I handed them their gifts.

Liv was quicker than Blue and had her box open first. She frowned as she pulled out the futuristic wraparound eyeglasses and said, "You do know that my vampire vision is perfect, right?"

"They're not eyeglasses," I said. "Put them on and say, *Activate*."

Liv did as I asked, and her eyebrows lifted in surprise as the glasses came to life. "Whoa, this is cool, but I have GPS on my phone ..."

I put mine on and said "*Activate*."

"These aren't just for GPS. They are Grundy's latest model of communicators. These replaced the earpiece models that were loaned to us by GRC13 when we worked with them hunting the demon. They have a range up to five miles. This way, if we split up, we can stay in contact with each other. They also have a find feature on them. If you say, *Find Zack*, an arrow will display and point in my direction, and it will show how far away I am."

Olivia tried it out. "Neat, the arrow is pointing right at you. You are six feet away."

"They're also self-tinting. You can adjust at the tint level, and the glasses will automatically adjust the darkness to that level depending on how bright it is around you. They will protect you from being blinded by a flashbang or an intense light."

Blue had hers on and activated them.

I continued, "They are also fully Internet enabled; you have full access to Google Maps and IP calling. If you say *Call* and then whatever emergency service you want, it will automatically call for you. If you want to talk to both Blue and I just say, *Open Mike*." My unit chimed in response to the command and opened the microphone, so I added, "*Close Mike*," to turn it off. "If you just want to talk to me or Blue, say, *Channel Zack or Channel Blue*." My glasses chimed again so I closed the channel to break the connection I'd established with Blue's communicator.

I showed them both how to use the GPS to get directions. I was about to show off the next feature when Stella asked, "How much did these glasses cost?"

"Mine were $20,000 and Blue and Liv's were $16,000."

"Why were yours more money?" asked Bree.

"Lower your arms and I will show you."

Bree looked puzzled at my request, but she uncrossed her arms and lowered them to her sides.

"Mine have built-in Xray vision so I can now tell if someone is carrying a concealed weapon." I paused and lowered my gaze to Bree's ample chest and added with a grin, "Or in your case a pair of weapons."

Bree's arms came immediately back up and she covered her chest. Stella groaned beside me and Liv laughed.

My Werepanther companion lifted her chin defiantly and said, "We are not paying for your perv feature out of company funds; that extra $4,000 is coming out of your pocket!"

I laughed and shook my head, "They don't have Xray vision. I'm just messing with you. Mine have night vision built in. As Blue and Liv can see perfectly in the dark, I didn't bother springing for that option for them."

Bree rolled her eyes but seemed to relax. She laughed and said, "You gave Liv a pair of $16,000 glasses—twenty bucks says that she breaks them in less than a week."

Liv smacked her friend and said, "I won't."

"Yeah," I said, "I won't be taking that bet, but I have it covered. All three sets come with a 'no questions asked' ten-year warranty. As long as you can give them a chunk of the original glasses, they will replace them with a new pair at no cost. Also, you can use the Grundy's app to track them down if you ever lose your glasses."

Bree got serious and said, "I thought after Stella and Blue bought Blue's holographic old-man disguise, all large purchases were supposed to be discussed first?"

"Yeah, um," I said, "We sort of discussed it ..." All five of them look at me and I added, "After we worked with GRC13, we all decided that the communicators were something we needed, right?" I got nods from all of them and continued, "Well, at the time, I didn't have clearance to shop at Grundy's. My clearance was approved last week, and I wanted to surprise you all. Okay, these models were more money, but I think the extra features are worth it."

By their crossed arms and frowns, Stella and Bree weren't buying my argument, so I said, "I haven't pointed out the best feature. The glasses have built-in cameras and facial recognition. They are synced with the UN bounty website, so if anyone with a bounty on them comes into range, the glasses will alert the user."

Stella perked up at that and said, "Even if that feature is only used once, and we catch someone we weren't even hunting, that will probably pay for the glasses."

Bree looked thoughtful as she considered Stella's point.

Sensing that the mood in the room had changed in my favor, I asked, "Shall we vote if these purchases should be covered by company funds?"

We held the vote and it was unanimously approved. I'd figured they would be, which was why I bought them in the first place. "While I was at Grundy's there was another thing that I wanted to get, but I wanted to run it by you guys first."

Everyone at the table looked at me with expressions running from curiosity to disbelief but I pushed on, "Grundy's also makes a custom set of armor that I wanted for myself. As I'm the squishiest member of this team, I thought some more protection would be nice. It is a suit of lightweight modern armor that is bullet, claw, and fang resistant. It's high-necked to prevent vampires from taking a bite. The suit they had on display also had built-in Tasers on each arm, but I'm restricted from buying anything with offensive weaponry. I argued that I'd wanted the Tasers for use on myself for when my power ran low. They are looking into whether internally mounted Tasers would still be considered offensive weaponry by the government; they will get back to me when they find out."

"How much?" asked Stella.

I squirmed a little at that and said, "As the armor is custom made for the individual, the price varies between $80,000 and $120,000."

Liv gasped, Bree groaned, and Stella's eyes went wide at the numbers. Blue's expression didn't change.

"That is more than my truck cost," said Bree.

To my surprise Blue came to my defense, "A good set of armor is priceless. Zack does have a point that he is the most vulnerable of the group. I have armor and Stella's Hyde form is almost impenetrable. Olivia's speed and vampire healing are her armor and you in your Were form can heal almost instantly. The things we hunt are inherently dangerous. I would hate to think of us losing Zack because we didn't want to pay for his protection."

The room went quiet at that. After a few moments, Stella said, "How about we hold off on the vote until Grundy's can confirm they can add the Tasers internally, as the armor would be much more useful with that feature?"

This was a better outcome than I had hoped for and we agreed to wait for now. The armor was a lot of money, but we were making good coin and could afford this. Hell, the zombie bounty from the other night should cover the cost.

I decided to focus on our latest purchase and said, "How about Blue transports us to the training hangar in the lab and we test out these new glasses in some team drills."

Stella's head shot up at that. A look of concern flashed across her face for a moment before she regained her composure. "You mentioned the glasses have a five-mile range?" I nodded, and she continued, "Then wouldn't it make more sense to go somewhere where we have more space to test that range?"

"That does seem to be more logical," added Blue.

I got the feeling that both were trying to keep us away from the lab and the hangar and figured it must be related to whatever secret project they were working on. While I was curious about what they were up to, Stella did have a good point that somewhere with more room would be a better testing area.

A few minutes later Blue opened a shadow portal and we headed out for team training with our new toys.

***

The next afternoon I was just finishing putting my 1/72nd scale P-51 Mustang model plane together when Stella and Blue showed up in the basement looking for me.

"Zack, I just got off the phone with Sarah, there have been two fatal vampire attacks in downtown Hamilton," said Stella.

Sarah was the enforcer for the English vampire court. Canada was part of the English vampire court's territory, so I wasn't surprised she knew about something happening in our neck of the woods. Most police forces contacted the vampire courts after a vampire attack as a courtesy. The courts, in turn, usually sent a representative or two to help deal with the rogue vampire. That last part twigged something for me, and I asked, "I'm guessing Sarah's call wasn't just for our information—does she want us to deal with this?"

Stella nodded. I wasn't terribly upset that this had been dumped on us. There would be a bounty for taking down this rogue and when anything like this happened in my city, I usually would go after the offender anyways. The other bonus was if we were the court's representatives in this matter, then local police would cooperate with us and we'd have full access to their case files.

"When did the attacks happen, and why is this the first we are hearing about it?" I asked.

Stella shrugged and said, "Both bodies were found this morning. The first was found around 4:30 a.m. A prostitute was drained of her blood and left in a dumpster in an alley. She was found by a homeless guy. As the body wasn't completely drained, Hamilton police suspect that the vampire was disturbed or startled just after it started feeding and fled.

"The second body was found shortly after nine this morning when staff of a discount store did a garbage run. The corpse was inside the dumpster behind their store. The coroner's preliminary examination puts the time of death at least twenty-four hours prior to the body being found."

The time of death meant that there had been two attacks in two nights. "Any details on the second victim?"

"The victim was a known drug user and had a record of multiple possession charges and a number of minor misdemeanors like petty theft."

A hooker and a junkie; it was typical vampire behavior to pick off the weak and marginalized. A couple of sparks dripped from my hands and I forced my temper back down and brought my power under control. It didn't matter what they did for a living or what addictions they had, both were human beings and they didn't deserve to die like that.

"Let's move up to the office and discuss this in more detail, okay?" I asked.

They left me, and I did a quick clean-up before I joined them upstairs. I entered our office and saw Stella on the computer with Blue leaning over her shoulder.

"Sorry," said Stella, "I was just checking the UN bounty site to see if there was a bounty posted for the rogue vampire. Nothing yet."

It either hadn't been posted yet or wasn't going to be. Even if there wasn't an official bounty, there were set rates for things like this. A rogue vampire who had killed someone would be an automatic $25,000 US bounty and it would go up the same amount for each victim, so we were looking at a $50,000 US bounty for this job.

The vampire was either young, insane, or very old. Ever since the vampires and other monsters were outed during World War II, the vampire courts banned killing humans, or at least publicly killing them. Vampires didn't need to kill to survive. Usually they would just use their mind control powers to enthrall their victim, take enough blood to deal with the bloodlust, and the victim would be sent on their way. Other than experiencing a little lightheadedness, the victim would be totally unaware they'd been a snack. It was a job of the sire to teach their offspring how to feed without killing a victim.

Of the three, I was betting this was a young vampire that had no master teaching it. Vampires occasionally went insane and stopped following the rules of the courts. That was rare, and those vampires were quickly put down by the vampire courts. The last and most remote possibility was this was an old unsworn vampire who still believed in the old ways. Unsworn vampires weren't members of the courts and were considered free vampires. Free vampires still had to follow the court rules when operating in their lands, however. Hamilton was English court territory so a free vampire killing here risked the wrath of the English court. There were places on Earth that weren't part of court lands and usually older free vampires would hunt there instead.

"What is our first step?" asked Stella, pulling me from my thoughts.

I scratched my chin and said, "First, I'll make a call to Hamilton police and get what information they have. I'd like to mark on the map where the two attacks happened. There have been two attacks in two nights, which means there will probably be another this evening. We will go out on patrol tonight and hopefully catch this vampire before we end up with another body."

***

I'd been flying around the downtown core for hours and there had been no sign of our rogue vampire. It was coming up on midnight and yet it was still warm and muggy. I was sweating in places I didn't even know I could.

"*Possible contact,*" said Blue over the communicator.

I checked Blue's position on the heads-up display on my new glasses. She and Stella were about a block north and east of Gore Park, and I changed my heading to their direction. I was pleased with the new toys. The night vision built into mine was decent but not amazing; I could see better with them, but the green tint on everything took some getting used to.

"*Never mind; just a human in a dark coat,*" said Blue.

"*Roger that,*" I said but kept heading in their direction anyways.

It struck me as odd that someone would be wearing a coat in this heat, and I wanted a look for myself. Liv and Bree must have thought the same thing, as I saw they were moving east on the display.

I found Blue and Stella and hovered in the air above them. I spotted the guy in the black trench coat and used the magnification feature on the glasses to take a better look. He was a younger guy in his early twenties, and by his bloodshot eyes, he was seriously stoned at this moment. He fumbled with the key to the back entrance of a three-story apartment and then disappeared inside the building. I turned off the magnification and swayed almost drunkenly in the air. That change in depth perception was a tad disorienting. I made a mental note not to use it when flying.

Blue and Stella waved up at me and I waved back. Blue was using her holographic old man disguise, so the two of them looked like an elderly gentleman and his ten-year-old granddaughter out for a walk. The fact that they were out at midnight might have raised a few eyebrows, however. Though not as many as a Blue's true form or Stella's alter ego would have. Stella's huge hulking Hyde persona certainly would have done more than raise a few eyebrows.

I turned back towards Gore Park and my heart rate picked up as I caught a glimpse of a bloodred aura, outlined in black, just as it disappeared into an alley. Part of my power was the ability to see auras around other Enhanced Individuals. The auras gave me clues about what their powers were and how strong they were. This particular aura meant the Enhanced was a vampire. At less than an inch wide, the aura told me that this was a young vamp. If this was our rogue vampire, then I'd guessed right about it being a young master-less one.

"Heads-up, guys. Just spotted a vampire slip into an alleyway off Catharine between King and King William. Going to check it out; back me up."

"Roger," said Blue.

"Okeydokey," replied Liv.

I increased my speed and reached the alley in seconds. I instantly spotted the vampire about midway down the alley. I cursed to myself as he was hunched over and feeding on what looked like a homeless person.

I needed him to lift his mouth off his victim. "Hey, Fangface! Hobo season doesn't start until next week. I'm going to need to see your hunting license!"

The vamp raised his head to me with a puzzled expression on his face. His fangs were fully extended, and blood dripped down his lips and chin.

Now that he wasn't touching the victim, I shot a powerful stream of lightning at him. I'd used lightning just to mess up his vampire speed and immediately followed up with a blast of air to lift him off the ground. I raised him about twenty feet in the air and held him suspended there.

I cursed as I got a look at the homeless guy's neck. No blood was flowing from the wound, which meant I was too late. I frowned at that as the vampire had barely entered the alley ten seconds ago; draining the victim should have taken longer.

Bree's Toyota 4-Runner screeched to a stop at the far end of the alley, pulling me from my thoughts. Her hybrid Werepanther form leapt out with Liv and Alteea right on her tail.

I was just about to activate the calling feature on the glasses to call the cops when something jumped me from behind. Arms wrapped around me like steel bands. The vampire I had suspended in the air dropped as I lost concentration, but Bree was on him before he even touched the ground.

I started calling on my powers to fry whatever was grabbing me when fangs ripped into my neck.

Oh shit—there were two of them, I thought as the world started spinning around me.

There was a familiar angry grunt behind me, and the vampire was suddenly pulled off me, taking a good chunk of my neck with him. The vampire's shriek of protest ended abruptly a moment later when either Stella or Blue finished it off.

"Zack!" cried Olivia and I felt her grab me as I fell to me knees.

My vision started to fade as the blood loss kicked in. Liv placed her hand on my neck like a vise to put pressure on the wound, but I knew it was too late. I'd been wounded before, but this time was different; it was bad, really bad.

I tried to speak but nothing came out and the last of my strength gave out. A radiant silver light appeared off in the distance and I lost consciousness.

***

I blinked open my eyes. I saw tie-dye and beads around me. If this was Heaven, then God seriously loved the seventies. The familiar tingling sensation in my neck erased any doubts that I was at Marion's place. She'd healed me often enough that I instantly recognized her handiwork. Oddly though, my neck also itched, which wasn't a usual side effect of Marion's work.

As I reached up to feel my neck, Blue said, "Good, you're awake. I'll get Marion."

There was sunlight coming in the windows. I wondered what the time was and how long I'd been out. I fished out my phone and my eyes widened as the screen read 2:00 p.m. We'd been in the alley slightly after midnight, so I'd been out for close to fourteen hours.

Marion appeared and looked down at me. She was wearing a bright-colored bathrobe and glasses. The glasses always magnified her grey eyes. I was taken aback at how tired and old she looked at this moment. It wasn't from just waking up, she looked drained. Her wrinkles seemed deeper and more pronounced and there were dark circles under her eyes.

"You're alive, that's a good sign. How do you feel?" she asked with a frown.

I shrugged and said, "Not bad considering, but my power levels seem lower than normal."

"Not surprising, we had to pump a couple of pints of normal blood into you last night, so you aren't running on pure Elemental juice."

I thought back to the attack and asked, "How much blood did I lose?"

Marion shook her head. "You're lucky to be alive. It took every ounce of healing power I had to fix the damage. We needed two bags of human blood that Blue got for you to make up for the blood you lost. And as much as I hate to admit it, all of that wouldn't have been worth a damn if not for your vampire girl ..."

"Huh?" I asked, wondering what Olivia had to do with saving me.

"She forced you to drink her blood. Vampire blood has healing qualities, but she was playing a dangerous game. Has she fed from you before?"

"Yes."

"How many times?"

I thought back to the different times she'd fed off me. It happened once when she was wounded badly taking on the demon, and another time I let her feed from me to keep the peace after Bree and I had sex when Bree was in the throes of the heat. It happened again when we had sex before our final confrontation with the Acolytes and the other night in the graveyard. "Four times."

"I was afraid of that," said Marion. "If a human and Vampire exchange blood three times, the human will be bound to the Vampire as their human servant. If you drink her blood two more times, then this will happen to you."

I knew about this from my studies, but it hadn't been a big concern to me as I'd never planned on drinking her blood. There were benefits to being a human servant, like slower aging, enhanced strength, and healing abilities. The downside was the vampire had total control over the servant. I loved Liv but the idea of losing my freewill didn't appeal to me. The other issue was that the bonding didn't always work. There had been cases were the human servant craved blood, went insane, or even died. I also worried that the process could cause me to lose my Elemental powers. There were no vampire mages or vampire elementals—thank goodness. The idea of someone with vampire strength and speed having elemental powers on top of that was truly frightening.

Another thought rocked me; did Liv do this to heal me or bring me across? I knew I'd been badly wounded last night, and if Marion was correct, if it wasn't for Liv giving me some of her blood, I would have bled out and died. If I had died, there was a small chance her giving me that blood could have brought me back as a vampire. I needed to have a chat with her as she didn't have the right to decide to bring me back. "Well, thankfully it worked out and I can't change what happened now. Thanks for the help, Marion; we'll get out of your hair now and let you get some rest."

Marion nodded and in a serious tone said, "Try not to get hurt in the next twenty-four hours; I don't have much juice left in me to fix you ..."

I slowly got up from the couch and Blue hovered nearby like a nervous mother hen, but I managed to stand under my own power. Considering all that happened, I didn't feel too bad. Physically, I wasn't far off from being normal. My powers though felt like they were down by about half.

"Home?" asked Blue.

I shook my head and the room spun a little, "Lab first; Elf needs food badly," I joked. Blue looked at me confused and I added, "Old video game line, never mind."

I grabbed a burger and fries from the Food-O-Tron in the lab and Blue opened another portal. We stepped out of the shadows in the living room and I carried my food to the kitchen with Blue hovering anxiously nearby. Stella was already at the table, drinking tea with her typical British keep calm demeanor, but a closer look showed the real story: she was tired and worried. The worried part disappeared when she saw us.

"Zack!" she said. "You're okay!"

I nodded and took a seat beside her. A moment later she punched my arm hard. Harder than her childlike body should have been able to.

"Ouch!" I said, rubbing my arm. "What was that for?"

"For scaring me to death. You're supposed to be the experienced and cautious one and it didn't occur to you that there might be two of them? Or to wait until we were all there before engaging?"

"Yeah, I screwed up. But the vampire had only just ducked into the alleyway and I hoped to save the victim ..."

Stella's grim expression softened, "Unfortunately, the one that was feeding wasn't the one you saw. That one hid behind a dumpster at the mouth of the alley. The victim was probably already dead before you even got there."

I was starving and started in on my burger when Stella started talking. The amazing taste of the burger instantly faded when she confirmed the victim didn't make it. At least there wouldn't be a fourth one. I swallowed and asked, "Have you been to bed yet?"

Stella shook her head and said, "Everyone left with you to Marion's, so I stayed behind to deal with the police. I only got home just before noon."

"Who finished off the vampire that attacked me, and is the other one in custody?" I asked and wolfed down another mouthful of burger.

"No, I pulled off the one that was attacking you and Blue beheaded it with her sword. Bree, in her rage, tore the one that had been feeding into pieces."

I frowned at that. Vampires took a lot to kill, you had to behead them, stake them, or burn them to make sure, so I asked, "Are you sure the second one is dead?"

Stella laughed, "Bree ripped its head, arms, and legs off and tore out its heart and ate it; there is no way it is still alive—or undead rather."

My eyes widened at that. Damn, that girl could get seriously pissed off. Tearing its head off certainly would finish it and if that didn't do it, eating its heart would.

"There is one piece of good news about there being two vampires though," said Stella.

I had a mouthful of fries, so I just raised a questioning eyebrow at her.

She gave me a small smile and said, "The bounty is doubled. Also, I filled the claim as soon as I got home."

She had a point. It also darkly dawned on me that the third victim also bumped the bounty up. Even if we'd saved him, the price of the bounty would have gone up. Attempted murder counted for the same as actual murder. "Don't get too excited about the larger bounty; Marion promised me a substantial bill for her services last night."

Stella shrugged at that, and after finishing her tea said, "I'm going to bed now. One last thing, we voted without you and approved that armor you wanted. You might want to order it before we change our minds."

I smiled at that. Too bad I didn't have it last night, as it would have saved me a lot of pain and the team a lot of worry.

I called Grundy's right after finishing my food and told them I wanted the armor. They said they still hadn't heard back from the government on whether internal Tasers would be classed as offensive weapons or not. They did, however, add that they could start making the armor and would build in for room for internal Tasers. That sounded good to me and I told them to go ahead with it.

Once I hung up, I decided to follow Marion's advice and laid down for a short rest. Sleep didn't come easy. Alone in the dark, I had visions of that vampire ripping out a large chunk of my neck. I had no doubt that had been a mortal wound. If Liv had been a second later applying pressure to my neck, or if we didn't have Blue to get me to Marion in seconds, or Liv hadn't shared her blood with me, I would have been joining my deceased mother in Valhalla.

Not even considering that there might have been two of them was almost a fatal mistake on my part. I couldn't change the past; the best I could do was learn from it, move on, and not be dumb enough to make the same mistake going forward … sigh.

A Night out on the Town

Friday, June 1

Bree

"C'mon, it's Friday night, let's go out dancing," said Olivia as she paced impatiently back and forth in front of me.

I ignored her and had another donut. I really didn't want to go out. I was comfortable on the couch with my snacks and it had been a long week. The full moon was this week, so I'd been out all night with the Barrie pack. Last night we hunted vampires for hours and afterward sat around Marion's place hoping Zack would pull through from what could have been fatal wounds. I'd also had indigestion all day from eating that vampire heart. I sensed my beast smugly laughing about that in the back of my mind.

I still couldn't believe what we'd done to that vampire. I was also a little embarrassed about it; at seeing Zack hurt, I'd lost control and the beast took over and attacked the vampire. Once the vampire was dealt with, I managed to regain control, and no one was any wiser but me. It bothered me that I'd lost control of the beast like that. Thankfully, it just attacked a vampire that had already killed three people, but that could have just as easily been an innocent person.

I was pulled from my doubts when I spotted Alteea readying herself to dive-bomb my precious box of donuts. I just managed to pull the box away before she would have taken one.

"Liv," I said loudly. "Do we have any chocolate in the house? I'm in the mood for pixie fondue."

I smiled as Alteea engaged her glamor and disappeared. My nose tracked her as she flew behind Liv to hide.

Liv glared at me and said, "I wish you'd stop threatening to make her a meal item. You have a whole box of donuts; surely you can part with one?"

Without meaning to I growled at Liv. "Sorry. Also, she wouldn't be a meal item, as you put it—a delicious snack at best."

Liv rolled her eyes at me and said, "Whatever. The Velvet Rope is all over my Snapchat; everyone is talking about it. I don't want to be the only person who hasn't gone there."

It was my turn to roll my eyes. She'd been talking about this stupid club for days, and that was a bad sign for my plan of spending the night on this comfy couch. Usually, my bestie was easily distracted, but this wasn't one of those times. When she did manage to focus and wanted something bad enough, she wouldn't let it go.

"We got those hot little dresses and shoes last week; don't you want to show them off?" asked Liv.

I was starting to suspect Liv had been planning this for longer than a few days. I hadn't wanted to go shopping last week either, and I certainly didn't need the cocktail dress and four-inch heels that she'd somehow convinced me to buy. It was almost like she'd made me do that so I didn't have the 'I don't have anything to wear,' excuse. I groaned as I realized this was all connected.

"You should see the pictures of the hot guys at this place," said Liv as she thumbed through her phone. "You've been grumpy lately and I think you aren't getting it enough …"

I threw a couch cushion at her, which she nimbly dodged without even glancing up from her phone. There was a surprised squeak as Alteea took the brunt of the cushion intended for Liv.

"My baby!" cried Liv as she lifted the cushion, revealing a dazed pixie.

"I'm fine, Mistress," said Alteea as she shook out her wings.

She fluttered her wings and took off, as if to prove she was okay, but the erratic path of her flight instantly ended that hope. Alteea landed awkwardly and said, "Well, maybe I could use a little nap …"

Liv scooped her up gently and glared at me.

"Sorry," I said as they left the room.

I felt terrible for pelting the pixie with the cushion and was glad she was alright. I sighed. Liv was angry and I realized that the only thing that would make her happy would be for us to go to that damn club. I scarfed down the rest of my donuts and made a pretty good dent in the bag of chips as well before she returned.

"Is she alright?" I asked.

Liv sharply bobbed her head and said, "I think so. She is resting in her dollhouse now."

I picked up the remains of my snacks and said, "Let's go dancing." My best friend's demeanor instantly changed to one of excitement and I added, "But I'm driving!"

She nodded and darted off to the basement again. I dumped the garbage in the kitchen, and she was already back holding up her little black dress and heels. She was practically bouncing with excitement and I knew this was going to be a long night.

We got to the club in Mississauga a good hour and half later. The Velvet Rope's parking lot was packed so we had to drive around for a bit to find parking. We found a spot out front of an old warehouse about three blocks away. I locked the car. Even from where we were, I could hear the steady thump of the bass. I sighed and pulled a pair of earplugs from my purse. I put them in, and they helped mute the sound a bit, but I could still hear it thanks to my sensitive Were hearing.

It was a clear and warm night, not bad weather for a three-block walk, but in these heels, I wasn't looking forward to it.

The building wasn't any more impressive from the front than the back. The place looked like a converted warehouse, but they had installed large windows into the front of it. I wasn't sure why they'd bothered; they'd blacked out all of them. The only two clues that this was a dance club were the music coming from it and the large neon silver Velvet Rope sign above the entrance. The one thing the club did have going for it was its size, the place was massive. I didn't even want to guess how many people were crammed in there at the moment. Even with its large capacity there was a lineup out front that had to be a block long.

I headed towards the end of the line, but Liv yanked me in a different direction. She led us directly to the front door. I blushed a bit as the muscular doorman checked us both out for a tad longer than was needed just to do his job. Liv stopped in front of him and said, "We are VIPs. Let us in."

"You are VIPs; I'll let you in," said the doorman in a monotone voice.

I knew Liv had just mind-rolled him with her powers and shook my head at her. She smiled innocently at me and shrugged. The crowd grumbled unhappily as the doorman pulled back the rope for us.

The flashing lights and the wall of sound hit me as we entered the place. It was packed, loud and the scents of perfume, sweat, booze, and a million others were staggering. The beast growled and began unhappily pacing back and forth in my mind.

Liv pulled me deeper into the club. As we squeezed through the mass of tightly packed bodies, my beast went dead still a couple of times, as if sensing a threat, but in the chaos and confusion, it was impossible to narrow down what had triggered it.

Liv stopped in the middle of the dance floor by two of the most amazing looking guys I'd ever seen. I caught a group of women giving us the evil eye as we started dancing with the two hunks. The blond guy I was dancing with leaned in and said, "Evan."

I smiled and said, "Bree." He shifted closer to me and I followed his lead.

I had to hand it to Liv, not only did she find two stunning guys, but they could also dance. Before becoming a Were, there was no way I could have matched Evan's moves, but now it was almost effortless to keep up with him.

To my surprise, even my beast seemed to be enjoying itself as we lost ourselves in the music. I almost stumbled as my beast took control for a moment, leaning in while we danced and taking a long sniff of his neck, but I managed to quickly recover control.

I silently scolded my beast but had to admit whatever cologne Evan was wearing smelled amazing. By its demeanor, I could tell my beast approved of him. I blushed as an image popped into my mind of the beast making thrusting motions, contentedly purring all the while. I ignored it and just lost myself in the music and Evan.

I don't know how long we'd been out there dancing, but by the end, we'd worn out Evan and his dark-haired friend. I had also worked up a light sweat and when Evan suggested we grab a table and talk to take a break, I was only too grateful.

The four of us dodged writhing bodies as we made our way off the dance floor. Just as we reached the sitting area, Liv nimbly stepped aside of a drunken guy. I wasn't so lucky. He bumped into me and spilled his beer down the front of my dress. I cringed as the ice-cold liquid soaked through.

"Sorry," he slurred.

Evan grabbed him and was about to start something when I said, "Let him go. It's not worth it. Liv and I will go to the bathroom. We'll get cleaned up and meet you back here, okay?"

Evan paused. He nodded and pushed the drunken idiot away.

"We'll order some drinks. What would you like?" he asked.

"Whatever they have on draft is fine."

He nodded in approval at my choice. Liv just said she'd have the same. I smiled to myself at that, as I knew Liv had no intention of drinking that beer and she'd just slip it to me instead.

We left the men and went to find a bathroom. The one nearby had a line up, so we looked for another one. As we headed to the back of the club, my beast perked up a few times as if sensing a challenge or a threat, but with the crowd of people, I couldn't figure out whom or what was catching its attention. I made a mental note to look into it more once I'd gotten cleaned up.

We found another bathroom, and this one didn't have a line. The bathroom wasn't anything special, but it was spacious and clean. There were six stalls and four sinks. A mirror was hung above the sinks that ran the full length of the wall. A couple of girls about our age were checking their makeup in the mirror when we entered.

"—he's hot and he's going to be doctor when he is done school," said a blonde as we walked by.

"Damn, Melanie, you lucked out," the brunette replied.

I grabbed a couple paper towels and started cleaning myself up.

"Your guy seems into you," said Liv with a grin.

"At least I wasn't making out on the dance floor with mine." I shook my head at her in disapproval; she and Zack were an item. To be fair, she had made it quite clear to him that they weren't exclusive, so technically she wasn't doing anything wrong. That arrangement might work for her, but it wasn't something I'd be comfortable doing. One partner at a time was more than enough for me.

"Hey, I was hungry. Jorge made a nice snack; he's a tasty little jalapeno," said Liv with some real heat in her tone.

I laughed and said, "You're terrible. Did you really do that in the middle of everyone?"

"Just a small nibble; I'm sure no one, including Jorge, even noticed."

The music got louder again as the door opened. The girls beside us instantly stopped talking and bolted for the exit. That was odd, but I went back to dabbing the beer from my outfit.

I caught the scents of the new arrivals and my beast immediately sat up and growled. All four of the women who'd just walked in were

Weres. I glanced up and saw they were blocking the door. Worse, they were the group that gave us the evil eye when we started dancing with Evan and Jorge.

I raised my gaze in challenge and went dead still. Out of the corner of my eye, I caught Liv watching me with concern. All four Weres met my gaze but the three trailing behind the tall Hispanic girl almost instantly lowered their eyes to the floor in submission. The tall girl had thick, curled dark hair, which, at another time, I would have been envious of. Her brown eyes glowed slightly as her beast rose to the surface in response to the challenge that mine posed.

I was about to change my hand into a claw to demonstrate my power levels, as most Weres couldn't do a partial transformation like that, when she lowered her gaze. I smiled to myself at winning but sensed by their body language this confrontation wasn't over. I could tell from her scent that the tall dark-haired girl was a Wererat, and I guessed she was also the leader of the group. The redheaded girl to her immediate left and the blonde on the end were also Wererats. The heavier brunette on her right was a Werebear. The redhead caught my attention as she was scratching her arm nonstop and twitching as if she were on something or going through withdrawal.

"Chica, you're in Mississauga pack territory and you ain't pack," said the dark-haired leader.

Liv shifted to my right to back me up. My beast was pacing anxiously in my head; it wanted to fight. Part of me also wanted a put these bitches in their place. It was obvious by their demeanors that they thought they were hot shit and owned this place. They were bullies and I hated bullies. I forced my growing anger back down and centered myself again. Starting a fight in here was a bad idea. There were thousands of innocent people out there and if any of us changed, this could get real bloody fast.

Through gritted teeth I said, "We didn't know. We don't want any trouble. We'll leave."

"What?" said Liv, but I shook my head at her and she went quiet.

The leader's confidence grew at me backing down and she said, "Too late for that, honey. You come here to my club, waving those fake titties around and bringing that Trampire with you and you steal our men ..." She cracked her knuckles theatrically and added, "You owe us and you're going to pay."

"I'll show you a Trampire—" said Liv and she started forward, but I put my arm out to block her way.

I made one last attempt to settle this peacefully and said, "I don't want to hurt you … just let us walk out of here, and we won't bother you again."

The leader laughed and looked at the blonde and gave her a small nod. The thin blonde reached out and flipped the bolt lock on the door. The sound of the lock slamming home echoed loudly, even above the muted sound of the music.

The Werebear started to convulse as she began to change forms. That showed an incredible lack of control and worried me. Werebears were stupid strong. If she changed and got out of this bathroom, the carnage would be bad.

"Liv!" I shouted.

"On it," she replied, and before I could even blink, she blurred forward and crashed hard into the Werebear. The two of them flew into the farthest stall and there was a loud bang as they hit its side.

"Brittany, Sophie, take her," said the leader.

The blonde and the twitchy redhead stepped towards me. I needed to end this quickly and not give any of them the chance to change. Even in their human forms, they had great healing abilities like I did and were much faster and stronger than normal humans.

I knew they were expecting me to back up since there were two of them and only one of me, so I went at them instead. I lunged at Twitchy on the right and the redhead froze for a moment which allowed me to deliver a hard kick to the blonde on my right. She went airborne and crashed down into one of the unoccupied stalls.

Twitchy recovered and threw a punch at me. I caught it before it connected and used her momentum to pull her forward. She became unbalanced, and as I yanked her past me with my left hand, I reached out and grabbed the back of her head with my right hand. I redirected her and drove her face into the sink beside me. The noise of the sink shattering was like a gunshot. I winced, as that had to hurt. Twitchy went limp and lay unmoving on the floor.

I grinned to myself. All that hand-to-hand training I'd been doing with Blue finally paid off. I'd purposely gone for the shot to the head, as that was the only way to mess up Were healing—scramble the brain, scramble the healing.

My grin disappeared as I took a hard kick to the midsection from the leader as she finally joined the fight. I skidded back from the impact and cursed the heels I was wearing as I nearly went down. I'd just regained my balance when she followed up with a hard right to my jaw. The impact caused me to bite my tongue and I tasted blood.

The leader stepped closer to deliver another shot, and I scrambled back to get some room between us. The blow missed, but as I stepped back a bit more my back brushed against the wall; I was out of room.

The sound of fabric being torn echoed in the small room, and Liv yelled, "You bitch! I loved that dress!"

At least Liv was still in this fight. The leader stepped forward and began raining down blows at me. I managed to block most of them, but a couple got through. She pulled back to throw a roundhouse punch at me, and I went on the offensive. I hit her in the face with a quick jab that broke her nose. That stunned her, and I followed up with a combo to her midsection and blow to her jaw. She staggered back, trying to put some distance between us. She tripped over Twitchy, who was still passed out cold on the floor, and went down in a heap.

I was about to pounce on her and finish her off when I heard the distinct sound of bones cracking and muscles tearing. Someone was changing. I caught the blonde out of the corner of my eye in the stall, trembling hard at the effort of her change.

What is it with these chicks; a couple of punches and they start trying to change? No wonder Sean, my Alpha for the Barrie pack, wasn't impressed with the Mississauga pack leadership; they have no discipline. Going full Were in a packed club was insane.

I dove into the stall and grabbed a handful of long blonde hair and used it to drive her face into the tank of the toilet. I blanched as her head went through the cover and the entire tank itself, causing a bit more damage than I had intended. It worked, though; Blondie was out cold, and I'd stopped her from changing.

There was a loud crash behind me and the hiss of spraying water as the leader ripped a sink out of the wall and threw it at me. I barely managed to duck. The trajectory of the porcelain missile was so close that it brushed through the top of my hair before exploding into shrapnel on the back wall of the stall.

Another loud crack filled the bathroom as she tore another sink out of the wall and tossed it at me again. This time she threw it lower, so I had to duck to the side in the confines of the stall. I cursed as it slammed off my outer hip before impacting the wall behind me.

I was a sitting duck in the stall and needed to get out of there, but the heels and the growing pool of water on the floor were making it treacherous to move. The Wererat leader was going for the remaining sink. I scrambled forward only to slip and slide on the floor, and I barely made any progress.

In a blur of motion, Liv drove the Wererat's face into the mirror. A fresh web of cracks appeared in the mirror where she'd hit. Liv yanked the Wererat's head back by her long, dark hair. The impact had busted the girl's nose again and it bled freely. Liv slammed the dark-haired girl's head hard into the mirror again and more cracks spread out from the impact. The Wererat blindly lashed out and got lucky with a hit that sent Liv reeling back.

The Wererat leader turned towards Liv. She must have sensed me closing in on her and she turned right into my incoming fist. I popped her hard right between the eyes. She was completely dazed for a moment but that was all I needed. I grabbed her by the throat and pulled her towards me before reversing and driving her head into the mirror with all my might. This time the mirror completely shattered, and chunks and shards of glass rained over the soaked tiled floor. The Wererat's eyes rolled up in her head and I let her drop to the floor. She ended up lying beside and slightly over Twitchy.

I shook my head at Liv and laughed. Her green cocktail dress had been ripped open from her right shoulder almost to her waist, exposing the fact that she clearly wasn't wearing a bra.

Liv ignored me and checked out the blonde I'd knocked out in the stall.

"If I didn't know any better, I'd think Zack trained you to fight and not Blue …"

Liv shook her head at the sight of the blonde Wererat lying in the pool of gathering water and then asked, "Why's that?"

"Because the last two fights you've been in, you've ended up topless."

"Yeah, at least he isn't here to see it this time," said Liv as she started eyeing the two on the floor beside us.

To my surprise, Liv reached down and lifted the remains of her dress up and took it completely off, leaving her naked other than her four-inch heels.

She handed it to me. "Hold this," she said before crouching down and unzipping the back of the dark-haired Wererat's silver dress.

"What are you doing?" I asked.

"Someone owes me a dress. The stupid Werebear who ripped mine is way too chunky. Blondie's lying in toilet water, so she's out. The redhead is probably the right size, but by the way she was scratching herself earlier, she is either on something or has fleas, so that leaves this one," said Liv.

I really wasn't sure about this, but her own dress was torn too badly for her to go back out into the club, so this was probably our only option.

"Don't just stand there; help me lift her up so I can get this off of her."

I put Liv's dress down on the edge of the remaining sink that was attached to the wall and helped her.

Less than a minute later, we had the dress off. I felt a little bad about leaving the girl naked, other than her shoes, but it was either Liv or her, and she'd started all of this.

Liv slipped the dress on and found a chunk of the mirror that was still intact to check herself out.

"Little big, but not too bad," she said as she adjusted one of the shoulders.

I looked around the bathroom and shook my head at the wrecked state it was now in. There was a good half-inch of water on the floor. Water was still spraying out everywhere. A set of feet belonging to the Werebear Liv had taken down stuck out from under the far stall.

"The Werebear still alive?" I asked in concern.

"Yeah, I just drained her until she passed out; she'll be fine. Werebear blood is good stuff. I feel super strong now. Next time Blue has Dmitri by, maybe I'll ask him for a nibble or two ..."

Dmitri oversaw one of the two GRC13 teams. GRC13 were Canada's most elite Anti-Enhanced individual response teams and were part of the RCMP. Blue and he were dating. Only Liv would think about asking a federal cop if she could snack on him.

"I think Blue might not approve of that—do not piss her off," I warned.

Liv shrugged and said, "Yeah, you're probably right. Oh well. Shall we return to our dates?"

I looked at her like she had lost her freaking mind. We were both soaked to the skin, looking like drowned rats, and once we unlocked the door, this whole scene would be discovered, and this place would be swarming in cops shortly after that.

"Yeah, no. We need to get the hell out of here before—" I paused and made hand gestures at the bodies and carnage we were standing in, "—someone finds all of this."

Liv sighed and said, "Okay, let's go home then. I need to check on Alteea anyway …"

We unlocked the door and opened it to find a small line out front. The first couple of ladies in line looked at us in shock.

"A pipe burst in there … I wouldn't go in. I'm going to find the manager to report this!" said Liv as we pushed our way through.

Liv made a beeline for the front of the club and dragged me along behind her. Out of the corner of my eye, I swore I saw a Native girl in a dated beaded dress. I turned to get a better look, but she was gone. Liv kept pulling me along and I almost ran over someone, so I stopped searching the crowd for her and focused on getting out of the club.

Five minutes later, we were safely in my truck and heading towards home.

"Sorry about tonight," said Liv.

I laughed and said, "Are you kidding? The night turned out better than I imagined. We got to dance with some hot men, listen to really great music, put some bullies in their place, and you got a new dress."

Liv rolled her eyes at the last part and asked, "You're not just saying that?" I shook my head and she grinned and said, "That's awesome because there is a new club in Brampton that everyone is raving about. We can go next Friday … I'll need to get a new dress though. Maybe you can come with Alteea and me and help pick it out."

I only half listened to Liv as she went over the details of all the things we needed to do before going clubbing again. The night certainly didn't turn out how I'd planned, but I really did have a good time. I smiled as I felt my beast, curled up contently in my mind, give a soft growl of approval to that before returning to sleep.

Midnight Swim

Saturday, June 2

Early Saturday afternoon, I received a call from Donny Elwood. Donny retired from the Hamilton police about ten years ago and moved with his wife out to Turkey Point. He'd spent thirty years on the force, the last twenty of those years as a detective. We worked together many times in my early years as the Hamilton Hurricane. Before this call, I hadn't heard from him in at least five or six years.

After we got caught up, he got down to the reason for his call.

"A local teen named Chad McBride went missing last night. His mom is worried because he didn't come home and isn't answering his phone. His mom, Dorothy, works as a waitress in town and she mentioned it to me when me and the missus were having breakfast at the diner this morning. Chad is eighteen and a bit of a troublemaker but is a nice enough kid. Normally, I wouldn't be concerned, figuring he probably hooked up with a girl and will show up soon enough, but there is something odd about this that isn't sitting right with me."

Donny had been a heck of a detective during his time and his instincts were usually dead on.

"His friends said he left the bonfire on the beach where they were all partying at just after one in the morning to go take a leak and never returned. Last night, I got up at about that time to use the bathroom myself and I swore I could hear a faint song coming from outside in the direction of the lake. The snippets I was getting were like nothing I've ever heard before. I was so taken by it, that it was almost like I blacked out. After the song ended, I figured I was just having a senior's moment and went back to bed. Now I'm not so sure. The teens were only a hundred yards up the beach from my house."

I frowned at that and asked, "Can you tell me more about the song?"

"The lyrics weren't in English, but on some level, I felt I understood everything I was hearing. I only speak English, so I don't understand how that is possible but that is the best way I can describe it."

There were creatures that used sound or music as a weapon. Banshees were the first thing that popped into my mind. Only they used music to create fear and paralyze their victims. There were also some Fae creatures that used music to lure or incapacitate, but those were rare.

"Look, Hurricane, I know what I'm saying sounds crazy, but my gut is telling me that something isn't right here."

I laughed and said, "Your gut is usually right. There might be something strange going on here; I'll look into it with my team and let you know what we find out."

We ended the call and I texted Blue and Stella to let them know we had a case. They were both at the lab in London working on their secret project.

Ten minutes later, the three of us were at the kitchen table and I went over what Donny had said.

"Sounds like a Siren," said Stella. My eyes widened in surprise as she said it. "What? Don't look so shocked. Greek mythology was a large part of my early education."

"Sorry, the surprise wasn't that you knew what a Siren was, just that a Siren fits for this case. Creatures created by the Greek gods aren't exactly common in Canada. While a Siren does match the clues we have, I'm puzzled about what one would be doing in Lake Erie."

Creatures from Greek mythology like Sirens, minotaurs, and medusae existed but were rare. They also tended to be in and around the Mediterranean and not over here. It did fit though. Banshees and the fae creatures I'd been thinking of usually liked wooded environments. Chad was on a beach and not near woods, so a water-based creature was likely.

Stella shrugged and said, "Who knows, maybe it was banished from its home or it likes to explore new places. If it is a Siren, the more important question is—do they have bounties on them or are they a protected species?"

Some Greek mythological creatures were protected, meaning it was illegal to hunt them. Minotaurs were one of those. They had an island sanctuary off the coast of Greece and were protected by international law.

Blue started typing into the laptop and said with a smile, "They're not protected. There is a standard bounty of $250,000 for each one."

I whistled at the number; a quarter-million bounty was nothing to sneeze at. If anything, the large bounty number made me nervous. A rogue vampire who'd killed one victim was a standard bounty of $25,000; this was ten times that amount. How powerful were these things? It could be just because they were water-based, which would make hunting them tricky. We'd have to lure it close to shore and then nail it hard and fast before it fled out to deeper waters.

I expressed my concerns to Stella and Blue. Stella simply said, "Looks like we have some research to do."

***

The three of us, which became four when Bree got up midafternoon, spent the entire afternoon researching Sirens. Their song was their main weapon, which they used to hypnotize men and lure them to their doom. They would drown their victims and then eat them. The song only affected men, which meant 80 percent of our team was immune. Unfortunately, that meant I was the one member of the team that was susceptible.

Sirens were immortal but could be killed. Beheading them was known to work. We came up with a few ideas on how to deal with this one. Blue's first suggestion was to use me as bait and then when it was close to shore, we'd toss grenades at it to stun it and then pull it from the water to finish it off. We still had grenades left over from when we took on the master of the French vampire court.

I'd nixed that plan for two reasons: one, having grenades explode around the sleepy town of Turkey Point would have us answering a lot of unwanted questions from law enforcement. Two, I wasn't sure how effective the grenades would be against a Siren. If we missed, it would simply swim out to deeper waters.

Our second idea was for me to zap it with a lightning strike to stun it and then we could pull it ashore and take it down. I ruled that one out too. Sirens were magical creatures created by the Greek gods and they could be immune to Elemental attacks. If I hit it and it was immune, it would flee, and we wouldn't get another shot at it.

The ideas got crazier from there. Which brought us to our final plan.

***

"So, your big plan is to have Stella in her Hyde form throw me at the Siren and then I'm supposed to beat it down and drag its body to shore so Blue can behead it with her sword?" asked Liv with wide eyes at dinner.

We all nodded, and I crossed my fingers that she'd go for this plan. I cringed a bit as she said the plan out loud, as it did sound just a tad insane.

Liv broke out into a huge grin and said, "Looks like I'm going swimming tonight. I must be psychic because just last week I bought a new bikini. It's purple and the top has padding that makes my boobs look bigger."

Crazy vampire for the win! I laughed to myself that she didn't flinch at the thought of taking on an immortal creature in its own environment, and that her biggest concern was how her boobs looked in her new swimsuit.

Bree smiled. "Hey, maybe for a change you might get through a fight with your top intact."

Liv rolled her eyes and said, "That has only happened twice!"

"Twice?" I asked. "I only remember the battle with the Zombies. When was the second one?"

Bree squirmed in her seat, but Liv perked up and said, "Last night, Bree and I went dancing at a club in Mississauga—"

Bree broke in anxiously and said, "Ixnay on the Ereway."

Liv waved off Bree and told us all about their adventure last night while we ate dinner. I was horrified that five Weres and a vampire had a brawl in a ladies' room at a packed nightclub; if it had spilled out of there, the carnage would have been unimaginable. Blue was pleased that her training had paid dividends and that the two of them took down double their number without sustaining any serious injuries. Stella was more practical and said they had no choice once the door to the bathroom was locked and they were just defending themselves.

I was also a little jealous but fought that down. Liv had made it quite clear that she wanted to keep our relationship casual. I wanted it to be more than that, but I was willing to give her time. "I guess Stella has a point, you were only defending yourselves. I do have one important question though."

"What's that?" asked Bree.

"Did you get some pictures? It seems someone—" I paused and glared at Stella, "—deleted my last set of topless 'Olivia in battle' pictures."

Stella said, "You made her do all the work with the zombies, and then you took pictures of the poor girl when she was in a vulnerable state, of course I deleted those pictures. Where is your sense of decency?"

All eyes turned to me. Stella and Bree were glaring at me now. Blue just kept eating her dinner but her tail was swishing around, which meant she was amused by all of this. Alteea had a puzzled look on her face like she was trying to figure it all out, and Liv just had a small, playful grin on her face.

"Hey, I didn't take those pictures for me; I did it for the company," I said.

Stella and Bree's stern expressions changed to ones of confusion and Bree asked, "How do topless pictures of my best friend help our company?"

I smiled and said, "As this company's founding and only member of the Social Committee, I have been collecting pictures of our adventures for my PowerPoint slideshow for this year's company Christmas party. A fun montage of all the *breast*, err, I mean, *best* moments we've shared together as a team."

The whole table groaned, and I was pelted by food and cutlery shortly after that. I swear no one appreciated the effort I went through to keep up morale around this place.

***

That night I ended up walking along the sandy beaches of Turkey Point as bait. The team was fifty feet further inland, shadowing me. I'd hoped that I would be able to spot an aura in the water and then would call in the team to launch Olivia at the Siren. I was wearing earplugs to protect me from the Siren's song, but this also meant I couldn't hear anything through our communicators.

It was a warm night again, but there was a lovely breeze coming in off the lake, which made it bearable.

Every thirty minutes or so, I'd stop, take out one of the earplugs, and check in with the team. We'd been at it for three hours and my legs were killing me from the nonstop walking on the sand. I stopped to check in again and took out my earplug and said, "It's past two now and nothing. Maybe we were wrong about our Siren theory."

Liv's voice replied, "Maybe it's our bait. Last night it went after a hot eighteen-year-old. After having prime rib, maybe offering rump roast just doesn't cut it."

I heard the rest of the team laughing in the background at Olivia's shot at me and said, "Har-har. I'll have you know I'm like a fine wine; I just get better with age …"

Liv groaned at that but then I caught the first notes of the most wonderful song. I turned towards the sound and caught my breath. Rising out of the water was the most beautiful woman I'd ever seen. She had long, lush curly red locks which cascaded down her pale neck and draped teasingly over her ample bare chest.

I faintly heard my name being called but the song deepened, and tears of joy began streaming from my eyes unabatedly. The dream woman was calling to me and more and more of her stunning form was exposed as she rose higher out of the water.

Her sparkling green eyes twinkled with playful mischief in the moonlight. She slowly licked her upper lip and cocked her finger at me, beckoning me to her.

I took a step towards her, and in an instant, the illusion was shattered by a crazy purple-bathing-suit clad vampire shouting "Cowabunga!" as she came flying out of the sky and landed on my dream woman in a large splash.

Not a second later, my neck snapped back as I was pounced on from behind. I went down hard and got a mouthful of sand for my troubles. The song for the ages ceased and reality snapped back into focus for me. There was a large, warm Werepanther sitting on my back that leaned down and gave my cheek a playful lick. At least I hoped it was playful and not a quick taste before she took a huge bite out of me.

A pair of black combat boots and blue-skinned legs appeared before me and a few seconds later all sounds deadened as an earplug was stuffed into my ear, replacing the one I'd taken out earlier.

"I'm good, now get off of me!" I half yelled due to the earplugs.

Bree slowly got off me and it was nice to breathe again without having a 300-plus pound Werepanther on my back. I flipped over onto my back and Blue looked down at me with a look of half pity and half disapproval. Her gaze didn't linger though, and she turned and faced out towards the water.

I remembered that Olivia was currently battling for her life against an immortal creature from Greek mythology and quickly got up. I picked up my goggles, which had fallen off when Bree tackled me, and put them back on. The world lit up with a familiar green tint to it as the night vison from the glasses kicked in.

I looked out to the water but there was no sign of Olivia. I did see Alteea's small rainbow aura hovering anxiously over the water and figured that must be where Olivia went down.

The rest of the team was around me now, searching for some sign of our vampire teammate.

"Get back from the beach. I have an idea," I said as I used my powers to lift me into the air.

They scrambled further inland and I headed for Alteea. I reached her in seconds, and just under the water I could see a familiar red and black aura locked together with a solid grey one.

"Alteea, I got this, go join the others!" I yelled.

She paused only for a moment and then fluttered her wings. She flew directly for Bree and the others. I slowly hovered backwards, going farther out over the lake while keeping my eyes locked on Liv and the Siren.

Out of the corner of my eye there was a silver flash down the beach but I didn't dare look away for fear of losing sight of Liv's aura under the water. I figured it was probably someone taking pictures. By the amount of noise we'd made, I was surprised the beach wasn't lined with curious onlookers.

I called my Air power to me and started building up a large charge. I willed it to build faster. Once I had pulled in about half of my reserves, I held out my hands towards the water just in front of Liv and the Siren and released a huge gust of hurricane-strength wind. A large wave grew, sweeping up the combatants and driving them towards shore. The wave crested a good twenty feet high and then crashed against the beach.

The two auras were still locked together when the wave vomited them up on shore. The Siren's grey aura seemed smaller than before and I hoped that was a good sign. I flew toward them, reaching the shore in seconds.

Liv was draped over the creature's back with her mouth firmly locked on the Siren's neck, draining her. The Siren barely moved. I smiled at the sight of Liv's bare bottom exposed in the moonlight. At least this time she didn't lose her top. I pulled out my iPhone and snapped a couple of pictures for posterity.

Less amusing was the multitude of healed or healing claw marks covering her body; the Siren had put up a hell of a fight, which explained what happened to Liv's bathing suit bottoms.

The rest of the team ran over, and Liv bounced up off the creature's back and not even a second later, a flaming sword descended and cleanly sliced off its head. Blue sheathed her sword as I landed with the group.

Bree's Werepanther form growled and sprinted away from us. I thought that was odd until the stench hit me. I gagged on the smell of rotten fish that was coming from the Siren's corpse and barely managed to remain standing. It was like the smell of three-day old shrimp shells left in the green compost bin in August.

Liv blurred off, chasing Bree after she let out a loud snort of disapproval at the smell. Alteea flew after Liv. Blue quickly moved back a good ten feet, but Stella in her Hyde form just stood beside me like nothing was wrong. I figured her Hyde form must have no sense of smell.

If the stench wasn't bad enough, it had to be one of the ugliest looking things I'd ever seen. It was hard to believe this was the same creature that I'd seen as a redheaded goddess rising from the surf. The creature was a mix of human, bird, and fish. It had a large bird-like beak and tiny black eyes. Its legs were bird-like as well. It had gills on its neck and a mix of scales and dark feathers covering its body. The claws on its thin, boney hands were nasty looking too.

I was about to join Blue when I realized we'd need pictures of the Siren for our bounty claim. I gritted my teeth and tried not to breathe in while I snapped a few quick shots. We joined Blue who was standing upwind. Even there, I could swear the odor permeated through everything, but at least it was bearable.

I eyed the small crowd that was gathering down the beach from us. Thankfully, either due to Blue's and Stella's imposing forms or from the stench, the people were staying well back from us. The group of people reminded me that I needed to call the authorities in to secure the area.

I called the Ontario Provincial Police (OPP) and EIRT. EIRT was needed as this involved an Enhanced Individual and they would also be the ones to issue the federal bounty claim number. The OPP would be here in ten minutes, but it was going to be at least an hour before the nearest EIRT team or agent got here.

Liv yelled for Blue and I spotted her and Bree hiding behind a sign further up the beach. Blue headed over and a few moments later she opened a shadow portal. I spied Bree's fully naked human form and Liv's half-naked one and Alteea's small nude form disappear into the shadows a moment after that. I laughed to myself as I thought that it was a good thing I didn't have Blue's powers. I knew she sent them home; if it was me, I'd have been tempted to have the portal open at a frat party or something equally amusing, like a tenth-grade science fair.

My attention was pulled away as Stella said, "My goodness that is a pungent aroma!"

I turned, and Stella was back in her usual ten-year-old looking human form.

"I'm going to guess that your Hyde form has little to no sense of smell?"

Stella nodded and said, "You are correct. Normally that is a small weakness of that form, but for tonight, it might be an advantage."

Blue joined us and confirmed that she had sent Liv, Bree and Alteea home. I nodded and sat down on the sand. Between my sore neck from being tackled, my aching legs from walking the beach for three hours, using half my power up with that wind blast, and it being 2:30 a.m., not to mention the fact that I had nearly died a couple of days ago, I was wiped. I sighed contently as I sat down in the sand.

"Your lack of stamina is disappointing; I will have to do better in your training," said Blue with an evil grin on her face.

"Hey, my stamina is fine; it has just been a long night."

A black and white OPP cruiser pulled up at the edge of the sand between us and the crowd of onlookers. Its lights were flashing but the officer had turned off the sound due to the late hour.

"Stella, Blue, go deal with the nice officer, okay?" I said as a shifted back and lay down in the sand.

Stella clucked her tongue at me in disapproval but turned and headed towards the cop. Blue hit a button on her wrist and her holographic old man disguise instantly covered her alien looking form.

I had an hour at least until EIRT arrived and the real work began. The OPP officer was really just here to keep curious spectators away and secure the scene until EIRT got here. I closed my eyes and decided a short nap would be good.

I smiled as I heard the officer say, "Isn't it a bit late for you to be out, young lady?" This was followed by a yelp of surprise from the same officer. I assumed that Stella changed into her Hyde form to dispel the whole little girl illusion.

I must have drifted off after that. Stella kicked me and said, "Zack, EIRT is here, get up!"

I groaned as the stench of dead Siren hit me when I sat up. I yawned and got to my feet and fished my hero and bounty IDs from my wallet. I'd expected them to send an EIRT team, but it was only one agent. She was a mage and by her aura not a terribly powerful one. It was mainly red, which meant Fire magic was her specialty, with a small amount of yellow (Air) and brown (Earth) and the barest sliver of blue (Water).

I blinked as there were now five OPP officers on scene and yellow police tape had been erected to keep people back. There were now only a couple of onlookers. I assumed the overwhelming smell and the late hour were the reasons for the small crowd.

The EIRT agent was talking to one of the OPP officers and he pointed in our direction. She nodded and headed over to us.

As she approached, I looked her over. Average height and build, her suit though was nicer than what most EIRT agents wore. She looked like she was in her late twenties, but as she was a mage, she was probably over forty and it wouldn't have surprised me if it was closer to fifty, as mages age slower than normal humans. She had a plain but pretty face with her smile, though as she got closer her expression changed to a sourer one and she coughed twice as the smell hit her.

"Oh my! What is that smell?"

"That is the lovely aroma of dead Siren," I said as I held out my IDs to her.

She looked them over and said, "Mr. Stevens, I'm Agent Danvers of EIRT."

"Please, call me Zack. These are my teammates Blue and Stella."

Agent Danvers nodded and then her gaze paused on Stella and she said, "I was going to ask why you have a child out at this time, but if office gossip is correct, your other form is a Hyde?" Stella bobbed her head in agreement and Agent Danvers continued, "When I got the call that there was a dead Siren at Turkey Point, I honestly thought dispatch was pulling my leg. Since it isn't every day that we have a creature of legend show up like this, why don't you start at the beginning?"

She pulled out a pad of paper and I went over everything from my call from Donny to now. At the end of it, Agent Danvers asked if I could e-mail her the pictures I'd taken for her report and I pulled out my phone and did just that.

"If you'll give me a few minutes, I'm going to return to my car, and I will e-mail you the bounty claim number shortly."

She left, and I found the photos on my phone and sent them to her.

Ten minutes later, my phone chimed and there was an e-mail from Agent Danvers with the federal bounty claim number, as promised. She returned to us a few minutes after that and said we were free to go. I was overjoyed to hear that and was already picturing my bed and getting a good long rest.

Blue opened a shadow portal and we went home. Not a second after we exited the shadows, Liv blurred up to us and said, "Oh-good-you're-home." She turned to Blue and added, "Let's-go-out-training-now." I blinked as she continued talking a mile a minute and wondered what the hell had gotten into Liv.

I spotted Bree on the couch looking distressed and while Liv was busy with Blue, I slipped over to her.

"Did Liv take some Meth or something?" I asked softly.

Bree shook her head and said, "She had been like this since we came home. It is like a hummingbird on crack. I think it is a side effect from drinking from an immortal sea creature."

That made sense. Vampires feeding off Enhanced Individuals usually got more power than if they'd just fed from a normal human.

"Anyone up for a foot race to Montreal?" asked Liv before blurring away. She returned less than ten seconds later in a full jogging outfit, "So, any takers?"

"Hard pass; I'm beat and going to bed," I said.

Bree rolled her eyes at this and I headed for the exit. Stella and Blue were hot on my heels and we left Bree to deal with hyper-vampire until sunrise. I smiled as Bree softly begged, "Please don't leave me ..."

A Fowl Adventure!

Sunday, June 3

I was awakened shortly after eleven the next morning by my iPhone buzzing insistently on the nightstand. I fumbled for it and answered it without looking at the caller.

"Hurricane." I groaned at hearing both 'Hurricane' and Rob's voice. If he was calling me 'Hurricane,' it meant official police business. It looked like my chance at a nice lazy Sunday was quickly disappearing.

"… We have another incident that we could use your team's help with."

"What's going on?" I asked as I sat up in bed and tried to focus with my sleep-addled brain.

"We're at Dundas Valley Golf Course and we have four dead bodies on the ninth hole. We can't get near them as the creatures are still feeding from them."

The mention of four fatalities instantly jolted me awake. This was serious. "What type of creatures and how many of them?"

"We don't know what they are, but they look like a cross between a dinosaur and turkey. There are close to forty of them fighting over the remains."

Holy shit! I thought, as Rob had just described rapkeys.

Rapkeys were a fae creation and were a real problem in the fae world. Legend had it that a Gnomish farmer who bred prized turkeys had gotten upset at them being poached by wild animals, so he used a spell to modify them. The spell made them a mix between raptor and turkey. They had a raptor's head, including the long snout with a mouthful of razor-sharp teeth, raptor arms and legs with their claws, but the main body was turkey, including the wings. Thankfully, like turkeys, the wings didn't allow them to fly. Shortly after casting the spell that same farmer became their first victim as the creatures also had a raptor's appetite. The worst part was this wasn't the first time the farmer had magically tinkered with his flock. His first spell increased their urge to mate and shortened their gestation time. So, these things were man-eaters that bred like rabbits. Twice a year, the fae called the Wild Hunt to reduce the rapkeys numbers, so they didn't overrun the kingdom.

If these things got loose, the environmental damage they could do was unimaginable. These things could eat just about anything and spread like wildfire.

"SWAT is here, and we have sniper teams set up, but we're concerned that if we fire on them, they could scatter and get away."

The other issue with rapkeys was that they had a raptor's cunning, and if the cops did start shooting, they might flee and hide.

"Don't do anything, we'll be there shortly," I said and ended the call.

I hurriedly got dressed and went down the hall and banged on Bree's door. "Bree, wake up, we have a case."

"I don't want to go to school—" was the sleepy sounding reply from the other side of the door.

I banged on the door again and said, "Get up, this is an emergency!"

"Alright, alright, I'm up."

I ran downstairs and found Stella and Blue quickly cleaning up the remains of their breakfast. They must have heard me yelling upstairs.

"What is going on?" asked Stella.

"Rob called. They have four bodies in Dundas and the creatures are still onsite. We need to get there ASAP."

Bree came down the stairs wearing grey sweats with her short blonde hair sticking up in all directions. She brushed past us and headed for the fridge.

"No time for food, Bree, we need to go now," I said as I slipped on my goggles and powered them up.

She growled and said, "There is always time for breakfast ..."

"You can eat when we get there; all-you-can-eat turkey," I said with a smile.

She perked up at that. I brought them up to speed on what we were dealing with.

"Anything special needed to kill them?" asked Blue as she adjusted her communication glasses.

"No, cut their heads off, cut them in half, shoot them, strangle them, fry them, anything will work. Any other questions?" They shook they heads, and I added, "Bree, change into your hybrid form and then we are out of here."

Bree started stripping out of her clothes and I turned away to protect her modesty. I cringed at the sounds of muscles tearing and bones snapping filling the kitchen as Bree morphed into her Were form.

Twenty seconds later, an angry growl shook the house once she had finished changing. Blue opened a shadow portal in the living room. We stepped out into a muggy hot day surrounded by nervous cops. More weapons than I was comfortable with were suddenly pointed at us, but thankfully, no one fired, and when we were recognized, the guns were quickly lowered.

Rob and Dave Shay came over. I was happy to see Dave as that meant I didn't have to deal with Murdock's ugly mug this morning. I turned at the multiple distinct gobble sounds coming from out on the golf course. How rapkeys still made that sound was a mystery considering they had raptor-like heads and tongues and necks, but it wasn't something I gave much thought to.

I spotted the two sniper teams set up on the black roof of the clubhouse and felt sorry for them. The poor bastards must be roasting up there.

We quickly hashed out a plan. Stella in her Hyde form would lead with Bree and Blue trailing behind her. They would go directly at them. I'd go airborne and use my powers to pick off any that tried to get away. The snipers were cleared, once we had engaged them, to shoot any stragglers on the left or right sides that were better than fifteen feet away from any us of. I made sure that the snipers were using standard rounds and not silver. That wouldn't help if they hit Blue or me, but Bree couldn't be killed by a non-silver round.

Bree growled as if to say, 'I'm hungry, can we get going?' and I nodded and said, "Let's do this."

Stella changed in the blink of an eye and her small, diminutive form was replaced by her ugly monstrous Hyde form. She lumbered over to the ninth hole and Blue and Bree followed her down the fairway. I used my Air power to lift myself into the air and followed my team.

The rapkeys were in such a feeding frenzy over the four deceased golfers that they didn't even notice our approach until Stella brought her fist down and turned one of them into paste. A chorus of angry gobbles erupted and the whole flock turned as one and charged.

Two rapkeys on the edges of the group exploded like overripe watermelons as the sniper rounds slammed home. The echo of the loud shots followed a moment later.

I smiled as Bree bounded forward and snatched one up, snapped its neck, and stuffed the main part of the body into her feline mouth and chomped down. At least she was finally getting her breakfast. Stella was getting swarmed but even their razor-sharp jaws and claws couldn't penetrate her tough hide. She stomped and pounded on them and was soon surrounded by a cloud of gore and feathers.

Out of the three of them, I'd been most concerned about Blue. Stella's Hyde form could shrug off any attack the rapkeys could throw at her and Bree's remarkable Were healing powers could also instantly repair any damage she sustained. One glance at the whirling dance of death Blue was putting on right now eased my worries. Blue's sword was engulfed in flames and she was almost a blur as she sliced and flambéed rapkeys.

The snipers caused another couple of rapkeys to disintegrate in a cloud of feathers and gore. I had no idea what caliber round they were using but it was akin to taking out squirrels with a shotgun.

The once-immaculate ninth green had been transformed into a slaughterhouse floor and I pitied the poor groundkeeper who'd have to clean up this mess. Although rapkey blood could be considered fertilizer.

The three of them and the snipers were going through the flock of rapkeys like lightning through a graphite golf club. Once about three quarters of the pack was down, a lone gobble sounded. The tone was different than the earlier aggressive sounding ones; this one was almost more of a questioning one. It was answered by a few soft gobbles, and almost as one, they turned and ran.

Bree pounced on one of the fleeing ones, another squawked out a painful noise as Blue tossed a dagger into its fleeing back, and Stella lumbered after them but was too slow. The snipers picked off two more. This left five of them fleeing as a group, led by the one who sounded the retreat. I flew after them and caught up to them in seconds. I launched a wide strike of lightning and it engulfed the group. A cloud of blackened feathers filled the air and all five of the semi-chard corpses dropped like lead balloons.

Bree's Werepanther form showed up seconds later. She picked up one of the now-barbequed birds, sniffed it, and then growled in approval before sinking her fangs into it. She tore off a huge chunk and gulped it down.

I left her to it and looked around to make sure none of the rapkeys escaped. I flew further out and did a large circle around the ninth hole. I slowed down as I heard a faint *gobble gobble* in the wind. I sighed as I realized I must have missed one. I turned in the direction I thought it was coming from which took me deeper out on to the course. The Dundas Valley Golf Course was made up of several hills and valleys. I crested the tallest hill on the course and groaned at the sight before me in the valley. The entire fairway was a sea of black-and-white feathered rapkeys. In the center of it was a glowing portal, and with every passing second more of the deadly birds were pouring out of it. That wasn't good.

I got on the communicator and contacted Blue, *"We have a problem. There are hundreds more just east of my position in the valley below me. There is an open portal, and more are coming through. We need to close that portal."*

While I had been talking to Blue, I pulled out my phone and snapped a few pictures of the terrain and what we were facing.

"Roger, we are on our way," said Blue.

"Stay where you are, I'm coming back to you guys. We need to figure out how we are going to play this."

I turned and headed back. As I flew over Bree, I used my powers to lift her into the air and pulled her along with me. She let out a surprised muffled growl at this but didn't stop chowing down on her prize.

I used the glasses to call Rob's cell. He answered and congratulated us on taking down the threat.

"Yeah, I wish that was the case. There are hundreds more in a valley deeper into the course. There is a hill that will make a good sniper position. Move them and as many officers as you can to form a firing line. Also, get out as many patrol cars as you have and have them do laps around the outside roads of the course. We can't let any get away."

He cursed and said, *"Understood, we'll be there shortly."*

I landed just outside of the carnage on the ninth green right beside a discarded bag of golf clubs. Blue and Stella, now back in her human form, joined me.

"What is the plan?" asked Stella with concern.

I ignored her for a moment and righted the bag of clubs. I fished through the bag and asked, "For taking down an interdimensional portal, is that a five, seven, or a nine iron?"

I got two blank looks and a growl of disapproval. I missed Liv not being here; she would have found that funny. I sighed and pulled a five iron from the bag and hoped it wasn't too much club for the job. I spotted Rob, Dave Shay, and about another ten officers heading our way. The two sniper teams were just behind the main group.

Once they got there, I pulled out my phone and showed Dave and Rob the pictures I'd taken, and said, "I'm going to send Stella in her Hyde form and Bree down the hill to engage them," I paused and looked at the two of them and added, "You two need to make as much noise as possible to pull the rapkeys to you and away from the portal. I'll fly with Blue around the valley and land on the opposite side. Blue, you'll need to creep closer. I will fly over the portal and hit it and any stragglers with lightning. If the lightning doesn't take down the portal, you need to get close and hit it with your sword. Blue gave me a confused look, so I added, "The portal to fae is magical in nature, and so is your sword. Portals are tricky to create and maintain. I'm hoping that the magic in your sword will be enough to disrupt it."

Dave asked, "What do you want us to do?"

"The top of the hill is a good place for the sniper teams. You can put a line of officers in front of the snipers in case the rapkeys get by Stella and Bree."

Dave frowned and looked at my phone and said, "I agree about where you want the snipers but placing people in front of them is a bad idea. We'll set up further along the hill line. That way if the rapkeys charge the sniper teams, we can catch them in crossfire and reduce the chances of someone being hit by friendly fire."

I smiled and said, "That's why you have the sergeant stripes and not me. Lastly, once the portal is down, we need to make sure that we kill every one of these things. If a pair of them escapes and start breeding … well let's just say it would be a very bad thing for everyone. Did you get the cruisers to start patrolling the perimeter of the course, Rob?"

He nodded and said, "That is why this force here is so small. The bulk of the department is out driving around to make sure none of these things get out."

"Good. Alright, people, we have a plan, let's get to it."

Stella changed back into her Hyde form and we all headed deeper into the course. I was soaked in sweat already from earlier and in this heat, it was only going to get worse.

We reached the top of the hill and there were a few rumbles of surprise as everyone got a look at the mass of rapkeys in the valley.

Once the sniper teams were set up and the other officers were in position farther along the ridgeline, I lifted Blue and me into the air. We flew just over the treetops along the side of the valley.

A huge roar echoed around the valley as Bree announced her presence. Every rapkey in the valley lifted their snouts in response and turned in unison towards Bree and Stella. Bree began bounding down the hill with Stella's Hyde form lumbering along behind her.

A chorus of angry sounding gobbles shook the valley, and then en masse, they charged. The huge wave of marauding rapkeys looked like a miniature army from up here. The sight inspired my humor and in my best mock-Scottish accent, I yelled, "You may take our drumsticks, but you will never take our FREEDOM!"

Blue looked over at me blankly and I just shook my head and said, "We really have to get you watching more movies so you will understand these pop culture references."

"I'm sure it was quite amusing," said Blue in an almost monotone voice.

I sighed. My funniest line of the year and nothing. At least the plan was working. The only rapkeys around the portal were the ones that had just come through. I put Blue down in the nearest group of trees to the portal at the far end of the valley.

Once she was on the ground, she gave me a mock salute and I turned back to the portal. I gathered up my power as I flew and touched down just in front of the portal. It brightened slightly and a surprised rapkey popped out just in front me. It had just enough time to let out a quick *gobble* before I hit it and everything around me with a blast of chain lightning. The air around me filled with charred feathers and dying squawks as it tore into them.

Every rapkey for a good fifty feet around me was toasted and charred, but the portal was still there. It glowed again and another rapkey popped out. I didn't have time to use my powers, so I just made a two-handed swing with the five iron. I yelled out 'fore!' just as the club contacted the side of the rapkey's head. Its beady black eyes rolled up inside its head and it dropped to the green, either dead or out cold.

A loud squawk of surprise sounded behind me and I turned to see two perfect halves of a rapkey make a final twitch before going still. Blue was standing there looking smug with her flaming sword in her hands.

"Thanks," I stammered, realizing how close I'd come to becoming rapkey dinner.

The portal glowed again, and I stepped back from it and said, "Incoming!"

Blue stepped closer and not even a second after the latest rapkey came through, she'd beheaded it. A fountain of blood squirted out from it and sprayed us both. I wiped my eyes clean and said, "How about you use that sword sooner than later on the portal?"

Blue made a massive two hand swing at the portal. The portal dimmed and then rapidly started getting much brighter.

"Oh, shit!" I said. "Run!"

We turned and had taken maybe five steps when a massive *whoomp* sound went off behind us as the portal exploded. Barely a split second later, the concussion from the blast arrived. I was launched into the air like I'd been hit by Thor's almighty hammer. We were both tossed like ragdolls and I lost sight of Blue as I blacked out for a moment.

I came to as I hit the first of many branches on the way down before hitting the leaf, dirt, and moss-covered ground hard enough to knock every ounce of air out of my lungs.

Some days it is really not worth getting out of bed. I groaned in pain as every part of my body hurt. I wiggled my fingers and toes and was relieved all of them seemed to be working. It took me another few seconds to confirm that nothing was broken. I had cuts and scrapes all over and I was sure I'd have some nasty bruises tomorrow, but I'd call it a win considering.

I sat up as I remembered about Blue. I staggered to my feet and called on my Air power to lift me into the air. It wasn't one of my most graceful takeoffs, but I didn't crash.

Echoes of booming gunshots reverberated throughout the valley. I glanced down the fairway and saw Bree and Stella were both slaughtering rapkeys like it was Jurassic Thanksgiving. The snipers were picking off the ones along the edges. I was pleased to see that the rapkeys were still focused on Bree and Stella and not running for the hills.

I flew in widening circles, anxiously looking for Blue. I exhaled in relief when I spotted her shaking sand out of her scale mail on the adjacent fairway. I smiled at the perfect imprint of Blue in the sand trap, including her tail.

I landed nearby and asked, "Are you okay?"

She nodded and said, "You failed to mention anything about the portal exploding ..."

I shrugged and said, "We'll know now for next time. You up for taking down some more rapkeys?"

Blue gave me a sharp-tooth-filled smile and I lifted us both into the air.

As we approached the valley, Blue said, "Put me down at their rear. It will be a classic pincer movement that should break them."

The green where the portal had been was now nothing but a thirty-foot crater. Between that one and the ninth green that we turned into the floor of a Heinz ketchup factory, I was willing to bet the groundskeeper would quit his job or at least be demanding a large raise.

I put Blue down as requested, and she drew and ignited her sword and plowed into the back of them. Blue was right: the rapkeys were so focused on Stella and Bree, they didn't even notice Blue until she was five-deep into them. I tensed as some of the flock turned their attention on Blue. She pushed on forward towards the rest of our team, carving up any rapkey that got within arm's length.

Out of the corner of my eye, I spotted a silver glow moving through the trees a couple hundred yards away. I wanted to go check it out but couldn't leave Blue exposed. I zapped a couple of the more aggressive ones that were trying to attack her from behind, but she made it to Bree and Stella without an issue. Now that she was relatively safe, I tore off to investigate the silver glow I'd seen.

I landed just in front of the trees where I'd seen the glowing light and moved closer to take a better look. Other than finding a couple of lost golf balls, I didn't find anything out of the ordinary in the small wooded area. I knew I'd seen something here but whatever it had been was gone. I was tempted to expand my search, but the distant chorus of gobbles reminded me that I needed to deal with the rapkey threat first.

As I flew back, I wondered if the silver glow had been from an aura. My stomach tightened as the only things that had silver auras were members of the God-class of Enhanced Individuals. I had one rule when it came to the God-class and that was to avoid them at all costs. The idea that a god, demi-god, or an avatar of the gods was lurking around didn't sit well with me. It bothered me more when I realized that this wasn't the first time that I'd seen a flash of silver in recent days.

I reached my team, who were still neck deep in fae fowl and put my thoughts to the side as I lashed out with another blast of lightning.

It took another twenty minutes, but we whittled their numbers down to the point that one of the rapkeys let out a familiar questioning *gobble* and the remaining rapkeys fled in all directions. I hit the comms and said, *"Blue, send Stella and Bree after the ones going west, you go after the ones heading east and I'll deal with the ones to the south, okay?"*

The ones heading north would run into the snipers and the officers, so that direction was covered too. I flew south and started tossing lightning at the group fleeing below me. I hit the last one just at the edge of the course before the road and let out a long breath of relief. I was running on the last of my reserves at that point but turned and headed north to make sure Dave and Rob were okay. The fairway thirty feet in front of the snipers' position on the hill was covered in blood and feathers. Dave's plan about catching the rapkeys in crossfire had worked as intended.

Even better, Bobby Knight and his EIRT team had arrived and were mixed in with the group. My power sputtered out just as I was touching down beside them. Thankfully, I still managed to land with my dignity intact. One of the SWAT officers tossed me an ice-cold bottle of water. I uncapped it and drained it in one long pull.

"Thanks," I said after I'd finished and in a louder voice said, "Someone here seriously needs to taze me—I'm running on empty."

Bobby laughed and pulled his weapon. Seconds later, the two barbs dug into my chest but then the sweet, sweet juice started to flow, and I stopped caring about the minor pain. I drained it dry, yanked the barbs out and said, "Thanks, I *really* needed that."

My communicator went active with Blue's voice, "*Zack, I got most of them but the group I'm chasing split in two. I went after the larger of the two groups but the three are heading southeast.*"

"Roger that, I'm on my way," I said.

Bobby cocked a questioning eyebrow at me, and I explained what was happening.

"Relax, we can handle it. You're wiped; take a break," he said when I finished.

"Huh? You realize if a pair gets away how bad that would be, right?"

He nodded and waved the mage on his team over. The mage came over and was holding an electronic tablet.

"Show Hurricane the tracking spell map you have," said Bobby.

The mage turned the tablet towards me, and I studied it. There were twelve dots on the screen on a map of the area. Three were heading southeast, five southwest, and four to the west of us. The five dots turned into three and the four to the west turned into three. The five were the ones Blue was chasing and she must have taken out two. The four to the west, which had also gone to three, were the ones Bree and Stella were chasing. I had no worries about the ones to the west: Bree's enhanced sense of smell would track those ones down.

"As you can see, we've got this," said Bobby as two golf carts came up with EIRT officers driving them. Bobby got in the first one and the mage got in the second and they headed out after the three strays.

I was only too grateful that they had this; even with the Taser boost, my power levels were low, and I was wiped. I spied the cooler the officer had tossed me a water from earlier and after grabbing another one from it, found a nice shady spot under a tree and sat down.

Thirty minutes later it was all over except for the paperwork. Blue opened a portal for Bree so she could go home and change back to human without having to expose her naked form to everyone here. The three of us stayed to get pictures for the bounty claim. I'd never hunted rapkeys before and was pleased to find out they were worth a bounty of $500 US each.

"One hundred and seventy thousand dollars," said Stella not a second after Bobby gave us the estimate on how many rapkeys we'd taken down.

A few minutes later, Bobby e-mailed me the federal bounty claim number. He thanked us for our help and said we were free to go. Blue opened a portal and we headed home. I stepped out of the shadows into our air-conditioned living room and almost moaned in pleasure at how good the cool air felt. I wanted a quick shower to get the rapkey blood and entrails off me and then I was going for a short nap before dinner.

I stopped dead at the sight of Bree's human form sound asleep on the couch with a blanket covering her. She was lightly snoring.

I turned to Blue and Stella and said with a smile, "I guess turkey really does make you sleepy …"

<u>Ogre Anniversary</u>

Monday, June 4

I had just finished my morning coffee when a special alert came across the screen of the local news I was watching. My eyes widened at the still picture of an ogre rampaging through Gore Park in the downtown core.

I felt a sense of déjà vu at the picture. A ghost pain in my arm came flooding back at the memory of the last time I fought an ogre in Gore Park back during my hero days. It must have been ten summers ago now. That fight wasn't fun, and I'd been lucky to walk away with only a broken arm.

I unmuted the TV. "*...details are still coming in, but we have report of a giant creature attacking people in Gore Park. Hamilton SWAT are on scene and EIRT is expected to arrive shortly. We are advising everyone to avoid the downtown area. If you are downtown, take shelter immediately and do not approach the creature. We'll go live to our reporter on scene after this break ...*"

I got up and ran for Bree's closed bedroom door and banged on it, "Get up, we have an ogre to deal with."

"Go away!" answered a sleepy sounding Bree. I pounded on her door again. "Okay, okay, I'm up."

I listened and heard her get out of bed and she said, "I swear I need to get my own place one of these days ..."

Satisfied she was moving, I bolted for downstairs. Stella and Blue weren't in the kitchen, but I spotted a note on the counter—*At the lab, text or call if you need us.*

I swore under my breath at the note, whipped out my iPhone, and dialed Stella. I cursed as it kept ringing and went to voicemail. I left her a message about what was going on and to meet us in Gore Park as soon as they could.

Just as I hung up, Bree, wearing her grey sweats, walked by me and headed for the fridge.

"We don't have time for you to eat."

"There is always time for breakfast. Besides, I'm making it to go. If Blue isn't here, then you'll have to fly us down, so I can eat on the way."

She pulled out a pizza box from the fridge and opened it. My eyes widen as she rolled the entire pizza up into a giant wrap. She looked up at me and said, "Well, what are you waiting for, let's get going. You can brief me on how to fight an ogre on the way."

Once we were outside, I wrapped my arm around her waist and used my Air power to lift us into the sky. I turned towards downtown and started briefing Bree while she stuffed her face with breakfast pizza. "The ogre is trying to put the 'gore' back into Gore Park. We need to distract it until Blue and Stella or EIRT arrive. We are looking at ten- to twelve-feet of mean that weighs close to a ton. It is a fae creature but thankfully ogres rarely can do magic. They are exceptionally strong and tough and can move faster than you'd expect for their size. My lightning isn't enough to put one down. It can hurt it, but it will mostly just annoy it. It's too heavy for me to lift high enough to do any real damage. Its skin is thick, and your claws or fangs will probably only be able to scratch it."

Bree swallowed and said, "Great, then how do we stop it?"

"We don't. As I said earlier, we just need to keep it distracted until the cavalry shows up ..."

She shook her head in resignation and took another huge mouthful of pizza. I couldn't blame her for not being excited about this plan. This was going to be like trying to take down a grizzly bear with a paintball gun.

The last time I did this, I was lucky to have walked away with only a broken arm. I didn't take the ogre down that time either; I just kept it busy until EIRT showed up and finished it off. It took two full teams to do it.

As we got closer to downtown, I could see all the traffic beneath us backed up, all the cars at a standstill. I spotted cruisers with their lights going, blocking all the routes into the core. That congestion would make it even harder for EIRT to reach us, and I suspected that we'd be on our own for at least thirty minutes.

I cursed under my breath as Gore Park came into view and I spotted the ogre—make that ogress—which was even worse. Female ogres were a bigger and meaner version of their male counterparts. This one looked to be at least fifteen feet tall and I didn't even want to speculate on how much this monster weighed.

"Holy shit!" said Bree as the ogress picked up an abandoned Prius and tossed it at the SWAT sniper team on the roof of a three-story building.

There was a huge crash as the compact car impacted the roof of the building. Thankfully her aim was off, and she missed the sniper team by a good twenty feet.

I flew over the chaos and put Bree down on the roof of one of the three-story buildings opposite the sniper team. I figured being up here would give her some privacy to change and jumping down from there in her Were form wouldn't be a big deal. "Remember, we just need to keep it distracted, so only use diversion tactics. Do not try and fight this thing, understood?"

She stuffed the last of the pizza in her mouth and nodded. I left her to it and went to go play with the ogress.

A loud shot echoed in the air and the ogress roared. The sniper team was still taking potshots at it. They were using high caliber rounds, but the beast's sheer size made it seem like they were using a BB gun. The bullets were penetrating but didn't seem to be doing any serious damage.

The ogress reached down and picked up the fallen bronze statue of Queen Victoria. She readied herself to throw it at the sniper team, so I released a large charge of electricity at the statue. The ogress roared as the volts traveled through the statue and zapped her hand. She dropped the statue like it was on fire and her beady black eyes darted around looking for what caused her pain. She spotted me flying above her and roared at me. I tossed another bolt of lightning at her. She grunted as it hit home.

She snatched up a Canada Post mailbox and threw it at me. I dodged it but was forced to fly after it, worrying where it might come down. I caught it with my Air power and flew back towards the ogress.

Another gunshot boomed, and the ogress turned her attention back to the sniper team again. I dove in towards her and dropped the mailbox like a Stuka dive-bomber before pulling back up. I smiled as my 'bomb' smacked into her head with a satisfying *clang*.

Any human that took a steel mailbox to the head at the speed I just delivered it would have been dead; the ogress just gave her head a shake and bellowed up at me in anger. It snatched up an abandoned red electric mobility scooter and wound up to throw it at me. I quickly pushed the air under me to gain more altitude.

I dodged the scooter, but it pulled my attention from the ogress as I flew after it to ensure it didn't land on anyone; this was a mistake. A second later, something solid and heavy clipped my shoulder and the back of my head. I saw stars and dropped like a stone as my concentration on flying was disrupted.

As I spun towards the ground, for a brief second, I swore I saw what looked like an ancient Native man smoking a pipe with a huge silver aura around him. I managed to regain control a split second before I would have hit the ground. I rubbed my head as I shot straight up to gain some altitude. I searched for the aura I'd thought I'd seen, but I had either been hallucinating or he'd left.

My attention was pulled to Bree who dove off the roof in her standing Werepanther form and landed on the ogress's back. Bree growled in triumph and the ogress roared with anger as Bree raked her back with the claws of her feet like a kitten with a catnip toy.

The ogress tried reaching behind herself to pull Bree off, but Bree nimbly avoided the grasping hands while continuing to shred the ogress's exposed back. Thin streams of green blood began dripping from the wounds Bree was inflicting. The ogress went wild with rage and tried a different tack. She ran backwards towards one of the buildings.

Bree leapt off and sprinted away moments before she became the gooey filling in an ogress and building sandwich. The sound of shattered glass filled the air as the ogress crashed backwards into a store front. The fae giant extracted herself with a roar and pulled a traffic light out of the ground before chasing after Bree.

The ogress swung her improvised club at Bree. The traffic light put a two-foot crater in the tarmac where Bree had been only a second before. Bree sprinted between the abandoned cars with the ogress hot on her heels. It pulled back for another swing and I zapped the steel pole with a blast of lightning. The ogress yelped and dropped the metal traffic light.

It stopped and roared up at me. The ogress flinched as another shot from the sniper team hit her in the upper arm. It lost interest in me and bellowed at the SWAT team on the roof. It bent over and tore up a huge chunk of sidewalk to throw at them, but Bree came charging back and jumped on its back again.

The next fifteen minutes were one continuous game of tag between the ogress, Bree, me, and the sniper team, all of us continuing to annoy it in an attempt to keep it confined to Gore Park. The problem was the ogress was showing no sign of slowing down. Bree seemed to be okay too but between flying, shooting lightning, and using my Air power to redirect the large projectiles the ogress tossed, my own reserves were quickly running out.

Another five minutes of this and I'd be out.

As luck would have it, about four minutes later, I smiled as Stella's ugly Hyde mug grunted out a challenge and lumbered in towards the ogress. I spotted Blue on the opposite side of the street creeping closer to the ogress as well.

Thank Odin, I thought and landed on the building the sniper team was perched upon.

Stella landed a vicious punch to the ogress's kidney area, which was about as high as she could reach on the massive creature. The ogress's eyes widened at the blow and it let out a surprised *oomph* at the impact. It turned faster than anything that size had a right to and delivered a powerful kick at Stella. Seeing a six-hundred-plus-pound Hyde fly through the air like a football being kicked for a field goal was a sight I never thought I'd see. She crashed through the window of the bingo parlor and was gone from view.

Before I could even worry about Stella, Blue dashed in behind the ogress with her sword ignited.

My heart leapt into my throat. Bree with her healing abilities and Stella's Hyde being almost impervious to damage were okay to deal with this monster, but if it that thing even landed a glancing blow, Blue would be killed. I flew down to the ground and called the last of my Air power to me to lift her out of the way if needed.

Blue swung through and hamstringed both of the ogress's ankles. It roared out in pain and tried to take a step but ended up toppling forward. I swear I felt the impact of the ogress hitting the ground through the soles of my feet.

Blue nimbly jumped up on the dazed ogress's meaty thigh and almost danced up its back. She leapt up into the air and came down with her sword leading the way. The flaming blade drove itself deep into the ogress's brain stem. Blue buried the blade to its hilt. The ogress gave out one final shudder and went still.

Blue, her tail making happy circles behind her, reached down and pulled out her blade. She extinguished the flames and casually sheathed it behind her back.

A loud grunt of challenge came from the bingo parlor and an angry Hyde came charging out looking for blood. It made it about three steps and its large bloodshot eye widened at the sight of the downed ogress and her friend perched triumphantly on its head. It made another grunt which sounded more like a 'huh?' and stood there opened mouthed.

Stella wasn't the only one standing there speechless. The entire core was silent until a wave of cheers and claps erupted from the officers and emergency personnel around the outside areas of the core. Blue made a deep bow of acknowledgement and then nimbly hopped off the ogress's head to join Stella.

I groaned, as I knew Blue would use this victory as an opportunity to point out the benefits of rigorous training. I suddenly knew I would be looking at a lot of forced marches with weighted packs in my future.

***

I yawned again, and Marion said, "Am I keeping you up?"

"Sorry, long day. Draining my powers always wears me out."

Drained was almost an understatement. After the battle, I'd so little left in the tank, I needed Blue to open a portal to Marion's because I didn't have enough juice left to fly to her place. It had been a profitable afternoon; turns out that the standard bounty on an ogress was $180,000 US. I had the claim receipt burning a hole in my pocket and would file it once I got home.

She nodded, and my shoulder tingled as she used her powers to heal it. Thankfully she'd already dealt with the bump on the back of my head from where the ogress clipped me. The headache I'd developed from that was blissfully fading away with every passing second.

Marion stepped back and gave me a once over and said, "Test out that shoulder and see how it feels."

I got up and rotated my arm a few times. "Feels great, thanks."

"You won't be thanking me when you get the bill for this and that neck injury you got last week," replied Marion with a stern disapproving gaze.

"You're worth every penny."

She shook her head at me, but a smile began to creep into her firm expression. I fished my phone out of my pocket and called Blue to get a lift home. I thanked Marion again for her healing and she gave me one last lecture about being more careful out there as I headed out the door.

The moment I got home, I went upstairs to check the records from my old hero days. My jaw hit the floor when I found the date of my first ogre encounter. It was exactly ten years ago to the day. I wondered why an ogre was getting dropped into the middle of Gore Park every ten years. I sighed and realized that it could just be a fae noble or mage doing it for the laughs. The fae were an odd and mysterious bunch and something like that would be typical for them.

I e-mailed Bobby at EIRT about my finding and suggested that he put it on their calendar for ten years from now. Maybe the next time, they could have the core closed off and a whole taskforce waiting for the ogre. That way I could sit at home and watch it on the news. I'd truly had my fill of ogres for this lifetime …

Where is the Earth-shattering KABOOM?

Tuesday, June 5

I'd barely poured myself a cup of coffee when Stella and Blue pounced on me, announcing they might have a case for us.

"Something on the UN bounty site?" I asked.

Stella's dark twin braids flew back and forth as she shook her head. "No. This was something we saw during the local morning news."

She made a 'follow me' gesture and disappeared to the living room. I followed them and noticed the TV was on but paused. I took a seat on the couch with them and sipped my coffee, trying to get my sleep-addled brain functioning.

Stella hit play on the remote.

A video of a bank with a ton of police cars and officers around it came up.

The newscaster's voice filled the room. "*Last night, this Canada Trust location in north Burlington was robbed ...*"

Burlington was our neighboring city to the north of us. The camera view changed, and I whistled as the back of the bank was shown. There was a large blackened hole with debris scattered all around it. The hole was big enough to drive an SUV through.

"*... Police aren't commenting on the ongoing investigation, but residents in the area mentioned that a large explosion rocked the quiet neighborhood in the early hours of the morning. Police are asking anyone who witnessed or has information about this robbery to please contact them.*"

Stella paused the TV as the scene cut back to two familiar perky morning show hosts.

"Well?" asked Stella.

I shrugged as I couldn't see how this was a case for us. It was a little disconcerting that thieves were using explosives to commit bank robberies, but it was still a police matter and had nothing to do with us. I said as much to Stella.

Stella, without a word, picked up the remote and went back to near the beginning of the story and hit pause again. She got up and pointed to the far left area of the screen. Parked by a police cruiser was a black SUV with flashing lights in the grille. That SUV was an EIRT response vehicle. "Okay, EIRT being there means that Enhanced Individuals were possibly involved, but there was nothing new posted on the UN bounty site?"

"No. Not yet anyways."

"This is pretty thin. I mean we don't even know what we are dealing with here. There are a plenty of Enhanceds that could do that type of damage ..."

Blue shook her head. "By the charring around the area and the fact that residents heard an explosion, it is either a Fire Elemental or a super that has extreme heat or explosive abilities."

I pondered that. Blue was right that a Tank or something that was extremely strong wouldn't have left charring on the brick, but there was a flaw in her argument. "That is assuming that whoever robbed the bank used their powers to do it. They still could have used actual explosives to blow the hole. In which case, we are back to just about every Enhanced Individual out there as a suspect ..."

Both of them instantly looked crestfallen. I felt bad for dashing their hopes. I had to admit, it would be a nice change of pace to do a case on our own terms rather than react to emergencies the way we had been lately. "That said, it couldn't hurt to do some research. I'll text Bobby and see if he is willing to share any details about the robbery. We work under the assumption that it was someone with Fire or Explosive abilities and do some research. Maybe there has been a smaller unexplained incident that might give us a clue about who is behind this ..."

"We'll look into that now," said Stella with a grin. "We'll also keep checking the UN bounty site, in case they do put up a bounty on this."

And with that they both left to go upstairs to the office to do research. I got out my phone and texted Bobby. Hopefully he was working today and willing to share.

***

A couple of hours later, we were just about to give up on this case as we hadn't found anything related online and there hadn't been a bounty posted to the UN site either when Bobby texted me back.

Two male Enhanced Individuals of similar heights and builds were caught on the bank's CCTV. We suspect Super class as both used a power involving explosions to destroy the back wall of the bank's vault. Bounty to be posted shortly with more details.

I thanked him via text, and we spent the next twenty minutes refreshing the bounty listings on the UN website until it appeared.

There was a grainy picture attached to the bounty of two men in black costumes with masks on and what looked like an orange and red logo on their chests. The problem was the logo was half blocked by their arms and the picture quality was so bad that it was hard to make out much detail.

It was estimated that they were about six feet tall and weighed 185 pounds, but we had no information about their ages. They had left the scene in a stolen white van and a plate number was listed. There were the usual warnings about them being dangerous and to use caution when dealing with them. The bounty was set at $25,000 for each of them.

We didn't learn much more from that, but it was enough to motivate us to do some more research. I sent an e-mail out to my street contacts with the van's details and plate number and a message to contact me if spotted.

An hour later, we hadn't found anything and decided to call it a day. Blue and Stella left via the shadows to go work on their mysterious project they'd been working on. I decided to retire to the basement and spend the remainder of the afternoon working on my 1/72nd scale model P-51 Mustang fighter.

By six that evening, Bree was up looking for food and Blue and Stella were back too. I joined them in the kitchen and suggested that Bree have a quick snack and that we wait for Liv and Alteea to get up and join us for dinner. I wanted to have takeout Chinese food to celebrate the banner week we'd had as well as the new case. The ladies all seemed pleased with this.

The sun didn't set until almost nine and we ordered the food once Liv and Alteea joined us. The Chinese place was busy, and our order wasn't ready until close to ten. I was flying home with a crap-ton of food when I spotted two identical orange auras getting out of a white van behind the back of my local TD bank branch. The auras had a thin ring of yellow, orange, and red around the outside, which was a combination I'd never seen before.

I grinned as the expression, 'I'd rather be lucky than good' came to mind. I turned towards the bank. I pulled out my iPhone, kicking myself for not wearing my communication glasses.

I called Stella's phone and just as she answered, a loud, deep boom reverberated out from the area behind the bank. The shrill alarm of the bank pierced the quiet night just after that.

Stella answered, and I told her that the TD bank on Rymal road was being robbed by our two bounty targets and to get everyone out here. I had to repeat myself due to the noise of the alarm, but Stella said they would be there shortly.

As I approached the bank, I was more nervous about the Chinese food I was carrying than taking on two Super class Enhanced Individuals. I shuddered to think what Bree might do to me if something happened to the food. I landed on the front area of the roof of the bank and carefully placed the food against a metal vent. With that important task dealt with, I flew towards the back of the bank to deal with the robbers.

There was a huge six-foot-wide hole in the wall. By the thickness of the wall and the built-in reinforcement, I figured this was probably the back wall of the vault. By how quickly they got through that wall, they were more dangerous than I first thought. I thickened the air around me as a precaution and waited for them to exit the bank.

Less than a minute later, two guys in matching black Spandex costumes came out of the bank, each carrying a large full sack each, high fiving each other. The mystery logo turned out to be a large mushroom cloud on the center of their uniforms.

The high fives made them seem like rookies, so I decided to try and settle this verbally, "I know banking hours are a pain to deal with, but you just need to be more diligent with your schedules …" Both of them stopped dead and looked up at me. I pointed at the logo and said, "Who are you supposed to be, the Mushroom Men?"

They answered in unison, "We are the Brothers of Boom!"

The acronym BOB popped into my head and I was about to quip, "You should have gone with Brothers of Outstanding Booms instead," when the brother demonstrated their powers. Loud, deafening explosions went off all around me, tossing me about like a pinball.

Thickening the air around me earlier probably saved my life, but I still got pummeled by the concussion of the blasts.

I was deaf and half blind from the nonstop explosions going on around me. Worse, I didn't know if I was oriented up or down. As I spun, a flash of silver went by, which I hoped was the moon, and then a patch of blackness. I prayed that was the night sky and poured on some speed under me.

I hoped they had limited range on their powers and that I wasn't about to impact the ground and break my neck.

The explosions continued but they were beneath me now. I breathed a sigh of relief. I looked around and figured I was about sixty feet up and a good twenty feet above the explosions.

The familiar auras of my teammates appeared at the back of the bank lot. Before I could blink, Olivia had blurred up and sunk her fangs into the neck of one of the twins. He cried out. A large bang sounded, and Liv went airborne as he used his explosive power to toss her off. She flew back and crashed through a wooden fence that separated the bank from one of its residential neighbors.

Oddly enough, the fence concerned me more than the explosion, as a wooden fence post to the heart would kill Olivia. Thankfully, I watched her climb to her feet.

Stella in her Hyde form lumbered towards them with Bree in her hybrid form following on her heels. Blue hung back like she was assessing the two opponents and where she could best strike at them. I spotted Alteea's aura hovering a good twenty feet above Blue. Wisely, Alteea had engaged her glamour so she was invisible. I also knew that she would be filming the entire thing on her iPhone, so we'd have evidence for the bounty claim and for the authorities once they arrived.

The other brother directed a massive explosion just in front of Stella. Stella's huge form was lifted off her feet and tossed back. She collided with Bree and they went down in a heap of limbs and fur.

It was time to stop messing around. I flipped myself over in the air and dove towards the ground at top speed. Once I got close enough, I lashed out with my lightning. One of the brothers spotted me and dove to the side but his brother took a full blast to the head and chest. He screamed and twitched violently for a moment and then collapsed to the ground in a heap.

"Todd!" cried the other brother and he extended his hand in my direction.

I was already pulling up and poured on the speed to put some distance between us. There was a wall of explosions behind me that boomed continuously like the best fireworks show ever made.

I banked around and watched a clay planter impact and shatter off the back of his head. His eyes rolled up behind his mask and he went down. Liv appeared beside him with a smug look on her face. I landed beside her and she said, "I owe those people a new sunflower plant ..."

Sirens were closing in on our position, which meant I didn't have to call the cops. My team gathered around me and everyone seemed to be in one piece. Bree was looking around and growling angrily. I realized she was hungry.

"Liv, jump up on the roof and grab the Chinese food," I said. Liv leapt up the single story easily and was gone from sight.

I leaned down and checked both brothers and was relieved to feel that they both had a pulse.

I stood back and was greeted by Liv weighed down with bags of food in her arms. Bree perked up at seeing Liv too.

"Blue, take everyone home and I'll deal with the cops. Eat dinner and I'll have some leftovers when I'm done here. Alteea, send the video to my phone."

Stella was back in her human form and said, "Nonsense, we'll wait until you get home." Bree growled at that. Stella shushed her and said, "We'll stop by the lab and get you a snack, okay?"

Bree's furry head bobbed in agreement and Blue opened a portal.

The last of my teammates disappeared into the shadows just as the first cruiser came screaming into the parking lot. I sighed and pulled out my wallet and held up my hero ID.

***

Two hours later, I was at home and finally able to have dinner. I had a bounty claim ticket from EIRT in my pocket for the two brothers worth $50,000 US. The claim would probably be higher as tonight's attempted robbery would be added to the assessment as well.

Even at $50,000, it gave us another reason to celebrate our windfall of bounties this week. The whole team was gathered around the table happily eating and talking. Well, Liv and Alteea were the ones doing most of the talking since they were only drinking blood and not eating like the rest of us were.

I got up to get another beer when Liv said, "What annoys me the most about tonight is I finally got to sample some sweet Super class blood for the first time ever, and instead of chocolate, I get the Pop Rocks version. One small sip and BOOM! I end up flying through a fence …"

We laughed at this. I spied a plastic bag on the counter and decided to have some fun.

"That might have been a good thing …" I said as I picked up the bag.

Liv turned in her seat and frowned at me, "Why's that?"

My lower body was blocked by the countertop between us, so I slowly twisted the bag closed and said, "When feeding off Enhanceds, you get side effects. Remember the dark elf and how drunk you got of it? Or the Siren and how hyper you were?"

"Yeah, so what?" said Liv.

"Well, what if you gained that explosive power? Anything you touch might go bang! Even with that small sip you took, I'd be careful what you touch."

Liv rolled her eyes and said, "Whatever, I barely got a taste, so I doubt there will be any side effects."

She turned her back to me and reached for her glass of blood. The moment she touched it *BANG*, I popped the plastic bag in my hand.

Liv pulled her hand back like it was on fire. Alteea screeched, flew into the air, and went invisible. Bree jumped in her seat, as did Stella. Blue didn't react, other than giving me a big grin of pointy teeth.

"Bloody Hell, Zack!" admonished Stella as she saw me laughing.

Bree picked up a chicken ball from her plate to toss at me before she realized she was going to waste her precious food and popped it into her mouth instead.

I burst out laughing and laughed even harder when Liv said, "That wasn't funny!"

The table slowly erupted in laughter. At the end, I wiped the tears in my eyes, grabbed another beer, and enjoyed dinner with my team.

Demoness of the Woods

Wednesday, June 6

Olivia

I was wondering if Zack was right and that blood I'd sampled tonight was having some sort of side effect, as I felt unbelievably restless. With every passing second, the craving to get out of the house grew. I didn't know where I wanted to go, just out. The trouble was I could tell by Bree's posture that she didn't want to go anywhere; she was quite content sitting on the couch with her donuts watching Netflix.

I smiled to myself as Bree shifted the donuts to her other side when she sensed Alteea hovering nearby. My daring pixie was eying those sugary pastries like they were Jimmy Choo shoes at a BOGO sale. Alteea buzzed around the outside of the room to get a better angle of attack.

"Tell your little sugar thief to behave or she'll be the main ingredient in a new pixie cordon bleu recipe I found," growled Bree, wiping some powdered sugar from her mouth.

Alteea instantly disappeared behind her glamor but I knew she was in the room still as I could hear the buzzing of her wings and I caught her scent too.

"Let's go out," I suggested, ignoring her culinary threat about my tiny companion.

"It's after one in the morning, by the time we get to a club, it will be closing," argued Bree.

"No, not a club. Let's go hunting."

Bree's eyes glowed blue for a moment as her beast rose to the surface at my suggestion. "Venison?"

I nodded, and Bree almost leapt off the couch with excitement. Bree shot by me, probably to get her keys. I spied Alteea as she turned off her glamor and eyed the unguarded box of donuts.

"Did you want to come along?" I asked.

She shook her tiny head and with a grin said, "No thanks, Mistress, I think I will have a better night here."

I smiled as she made a beeline for the donuts and I left her to it.

"C'mon, Liv, sunrise is only four hours away and we have deer to catch!" called Bree from the front door.

I used my vampire speed and joined Bree, who jumped when I suddenly appeared beside her.

"Freaking vampire speed," Bree grumbled under her breath as we headed out the door.

We got in Bree's pickup and were off to the woods.

About halfway there, Bree suddenly slammed on the brakes and said, "My donuts!" and started to turn the truck around.

"Don't bother. Do you really think Alteea hasn't eaten them already?"

Bree sighed and under her breath said, "You better hope we catch a nice fat juicy deer, or it's going to be a long ride home for you ..."

We reached the woods. Bree drove the truck off the road and just inside the tree line to hide it. We got out and started stripping down. Bree dumped her sweats in the truck and immediately began to tremble as she changed. I put my sneakers and socks back on as she did this. I hunted nude, as getting blood out of clothing was a pain, but the last time we were out, I took a small tree root through my foot, and this girl wasn't making that mistake again!

By the time I finished, three hundred pounds of Werepanther was looking up at me, anxious to hunt. I nodded, and she turned and tore off deeper into the woods. I loped after her. We ran for less than a minute before Bree stopped. She sniffed the air and growled softly, and I wondered what was up. I sniffed too, trying to figure out what had her riled up but didn't catch anything odd. Her nose was better than mine, so it didn't surprise me that she scented something unusual. We stood there, dead still, and just let the woods speak to us.

I cocked my head as I faintly heard something in the distance. I turned more towards it and frowned at what sounded like chanting. "Something odd is going on. Let's check it out, but take it slow until we know what we are dealing with, okay?"

Bree bobbed her head and we started walking softly in the direction of the disturbance. As we got closer, the chanting got louder and more intense, something about it putting the hairs on the back of my neck up. Bree growled as a sign of her displeasure. I stopped as the familiar but unwelcome smell of rotten eggs hit me. Sulfur—that wasn't a good sign. Our experience hunting a demon came rushing back to me, and I clenched my fists when I thought about Stinky. Stinky was an imp we'd bought to track the demon and I really loved the little guy. He was killed by that same demon.

If these chanting assholes were summoning a demon, that wasn't happening tonight—not on my watch!

I quickly snuck up on them with Bree creeping whisper-soft behind me. I peered out from the bush we were hiding behind. There had to be twenty-five people in black robes with hoods covering their faces all chanting together. In the center of their circle, there was a large red painted star with candles on the five points. In the center of the star was an unconscious woman in a long white dress that was so sheer that she was practically nude. She was tied down with her arms and legs spread out and bound to the flat boulder she was lying on.

Standing above her was a man, no, a woman—the bald head threw me for a moment, holding a wicked-looking curved dagger.

The whole scene was so bizarre that at first, I thought they were filming a movie.

The chanting reached a frenzied pitch and the stench of sulfur thickened with every passing second. I realized I had to do something to stop this. It wasn't a movie; they were going to kill that poor woman.

Part of me wanted to rush in but there were a lot of them. Between the two of us, we should be able to take them if they were all human. I worried that they might not be or that someone would kill the woman before we could stop it.

I thought of a plan in desperation. I tapped Bree on the flank, and she followed me as I moved us fifty feet back. As a vampire, all my senses and muscles were improved and that included my vocal cords. I cleared my throat and then loudly said, "WHO DARES DISTURB MY WOODS!"

Bree made a questioning growl, but I waved her off. The chanting abruptly stopped, and a strong female voice yelled, "Who interrupts our sacred ritual?"

"IT IS I, DEMON QUEEN OLIVIUS, RULER OF THESE WOODS. FLEE NOW AND LEAVE YOUR OFFERING, AND I SHALL LET YOU LIVE!"

When I said 'Olivius,' Bree lowered her muzzle to the ground and covered her eyes with her paws. "What? I Latined it up and shit; it's fine."

"Kill her!" ordered the priestess.

"Or not," I added as the hoard of devil worshipers came crashing through the woods in our direction.

Bree instantly lifted her head and roared out in challenge.

"You play with these guys; I'm going to rescue that women tied to the altar. Try not to kill any of them, okay?"

Bree just growled and leapt towards the mass coming at us. I blurred around the group. I kicked over one of the candles, hoping that might break whatever spell they were attempting. I crashed into the priestess and she went flying and landed hard in some trees.

By the excited growls and panicked screams that were coming from the woods, I figured Bree was doing okay.

I yanked at one of the bonds holding the woman down and it snapped easily. I did the same with the rest.

Just as I freed the last one, a commanding female voice said, "Azmodeus, I am your vessel, use me to punish the defilers of your sacred ceremony!"

The area around me suddenly reeked so badly of sulfur, I almost gagged. A twig snapped, and I looked up and saw the priestess walk out from the trees. Her eyes glowed red and she had an aura of menace about her.

Her mouth opened and in a deep, male voice, she said, "You will die for this, Blood Vermin!"

Not good, I thought. I kicked around the idea of just grabbing the unconscious woman and getting the hell out of there, but I didn't know how fast this thing was and worried it might catch us. Also, if the priestess were possessed by a demon, then draining her with my fangs was probably out. Zack warned me never to drink demon blood. This wasn't a full-blown demon, just someone possessed, but I didn't want to risk that either.

I blurred forward and landed a powerful uppercut on the possessed priestess's jaw. Her head snapped back, and she flew a good ten feet back from me before crashing into a bush.

I felt pretty good about that hit, right up until she got back up, cracked her neck loudly, and charged at me.

At the last moment, I dodged to the right and avoided the punch she was aiming at me. She hit a thick tree and put her fist clean through it. The sound of the impact was like a gunshot. While her arm was embedded in the tree, I shot forward and drove my fist hard into one of her kidneys.

The demon woman didn't react to the hit and pulled her now bloody fist free from the tree. I blurred away before she could retaliate.

Another growl echoed in the woods; it was followed by a human cry of pain and I was pleased that it sounded like Bree was holding her own. Now I just had to deal with the priestess. By the way her punch went through that tree, she was obviously stronger than I was, but her charge at me earlier wasn't much faster than a normal human. I was faster. I was also naked and didn't have my sword, which was a disadvantage. Mr. Slicey would have been real handy right about now.

She charged at me again. I ducked under her swing and delivered another blow to her side. She got knocked off balance and went down in a heap, tangled up in her long black robe.

I charged in to deliver a few kicks while she was down, but she hopped to her feet in one smooth motion. I veered hard to the right and out of the range of the punch she threw at me.

The sound of tearing material filled the air and when I turned around, she was stepping out of the remains of her robes. She had satanic-themed tattoos that ran from her groin to the bottom of her neck. It wasn't a good look. I was more of a rose or butterfly tattoo type of girl.

She charged at me. At the last second, I ducked left and kicked out when she went by. I made solid contact with her right knee and I heard a satisfying crack. The demon priestess stumbled but stayed standing. Her lower leg was at an odd angle, but she just turned and limped back at me.

That blow to the knee had to have hurt, but she didn't even acknowledge it. The demon riding her must be blocking any pain.

She came at me again and I avoided a roundhouse from her right hand and landed another blow to her side. It sounded as though I'd cracked one or two of her ribs. We danced—well, I danced, she limped, around each other, and she kept taking shots at me. I'd dodge them and then hit her with a punch or kick of my own. This went on for a good minute until I landed what I thought was a knockout blow to her chin.

I got sloppy and didn't step back. She tagged me with a punch to my left side. I cried out as she broke at least one of my ribs and I flew back on my ass.

I groaned as I got back to my feet and just managed to avoid the vicious kick she'd been going for. Her foot left a three-inch divot in the ground where it impacted. What was really scary was that was using the leg with the smashed knee. I moved back out of her range and winced at the pain radiating from my side. The ribs would heal but I needed to feed to make that happen instantly.

A man in dark robes returned and said, "My dark Priestess ..." and whatever he was going to say died on his lips as he stared opened mouthed at the two of us battling it out there naked in front of him.

Snack time, I thought and blurred around back of him. My fangs sank deep into his neck and I drank deeply. My body tingled as his warm blood poured down my throat and the pain in my ribs disappeared. The she-demon roared and charged at us. I tossed his unconscious body at her and she batted my meat shield away.

I nimbly moved out of the way of her awkward charge. That feeding had changed things. My mind was clear, and my strength was back to full—it was time to end this. I ran off at top speed into the woods. I looped around the clearing and came out on the other side. She had her back to me, and her head was turning back and forth searching for me. I blurred forward and jumped on her back. I grabbed her head in both hands and twisted it hard to one side.

The sound of her neck snapping filled the air and she collapsed to the ground and I rode her down the whole way. Thick, black smoke poured out of her orifices and disappeared into the ground. I let go of her and stood up.

The forest was completely silent, and I panicked as I thought about Bree.

Out of the woods sauntered a large black cat looking pleased with itself. She turned towards me and gave a low soft growl, which was Werepanther for *'hey, what's up?'*

"I'm good, are you okay?"

Bree just nudged her large furry head against my hip in response, which I took as acknowledgement that she was fine. I smiled as I rubbed her warm head. No one besides me was allowed to do that while Bree was in her beast form.

With the scent of sulfur fading, human blood became the dominant scent. If I hadn't just fed, I would have been drooling at the smell. I wondered how many of the cultists Bree took on survived. That was a problem for later. We needed to get the authorities here, the lady on the altar looked at, medical help for any of the cultists that were still alive, and clothes and probably food for Bree. "I'm going to run back to the car and get our clothes and phones. We need to call home and the cops. Stay here and watch the girl. Don't change until I get back, okay?"

Bree gave a low growl of approval. I poured on the speed and left the clearing.

I almost collided with a coyote, which must have smelled the blood and come looking for dinner. He scampered away as fast as his legs could take him. There was something odd about that coyote. Just as he disappeared deeper into the woods, it hit me: his scent was too clean for a wild animal. It reminded me of Bree in her beast form. I wondered if it was a Werecoyote? I didn't even know there was such a thing as a Werecoyote.

The heavy scent of blood distracted me again. *Focus girl!* I thought and blurred off.

I reached the truck and got the key fob from its magnetic holder in the rear wheel well to unlock it. I grabbed our clothes, phones, and a large blanket Bree had in the back seat to keep her fur off the upholstery.

I found Bree in her Werepanther form lounging on the rock beside the unconscious would-be sacrifice. She was cleaning her paw when I appeared. I tossed the blanket over the girl to provide her some modesty that the dress didn't and put our clothes down.

Bree hopped off the rock and started changing as I put my clothes on.

"You still owe me a deer!" said Bree with a grin just as I finished getting dressed.

She took her sweats off the rock and I said, "You are probably going to have to settle for something from the Food-O-Tron instead. I'm going to call Zack."

Bree slipped on her top and frowned, "Call Stella and Blue instead, you know how grumpy he is when he gets woken in the middle of the night."

I nodded and dialed Stella instead. She answered in a sleepy voice, "Liv, it's three in the morning ..."

I apologized for waking her and told her what happened. She told me to hang on and then after a bit said, "Blue has found where you are, and we will be there shortly. I'm going to wake Zack. We will need his hero ID. The constables aren't going to be happy if Bree as a Were killed a bunch of humans, self-defense or not."

I ended the call.

Bree piped up and said, "I don't think I killed any of the cultists. I didn't bite a single one, so as not to infect them. I used my claws when I had to, but mostly I just pounced on them and banged them into trees and the ground until they went unconscious."

I smiled at her with pride. For her to control her beast like that in the heat of battle was impressive, but being impressive was one of the reasons why she was my bestie.

A few minutes later, Stella, Blue, and Zack appeared out of the shadows. Even with Zack's short hair, he had a bad case of bedhead, and by the look on his face, he was not a happy camper. He stopped in his tracks when he spotted the priestess with the broken neck.

"At least it wasn't you naked in a fight for a change …" he said with a small grin breaking through his gruff, sleep-deprived expression.

"Actually, I was naked too. Bree and I were out hunting when this happened. I only got dressed after the fight."

"Please tell me Alteea recorded the fight," said Zack with a happy eager expression suddenly on his face.

I shook my head and said, "We left her at home. She is probably passed out with a smile in an empty box of donuts right now." Bree growled at this, so I turned to Blue and said, "Can you take Bree to get some food?"

Blue nodded and opened another shadow portal but before they left Zack said, "Blue, grab some road flares and glow sticks from the house. We'll need to mark a path for the cops. Oh, and some zip ties for the cultists."

Blue nodded again and she and Bree left. Zack pulled out his phone and called EIRT and explained what happened. They were going to send a couple of teams; one for here and one to head to the hospital the cultists would be sent to, so they could test for lycanthropic infection. They were also dispatching OPP and EMS units to the scene.

I was puzzled why the OPP were going to be involved and then realized that the woods were outside of Hamilton and therefore outside of Hamilton police jurisdiction.

While we waited, Zack had me go over exactly what happened. His only criticism was that we should have called home for back-up before engaging, but he was pleased that we saved the girl and stopped whatever the cultists were trying to do with their ritual.

Blue came back with an armload of flares, glow sticks, and zip ties and we all helped mark out a trail with them. Zack waited by the flares on the road for the first units to arrive while the rest of us watched over the site. We used the zip ties to secure the cultists. A couple had started coming to but the rest were still out cold. One of them was dead from a nasty head injury. Considering Bree took on twenty-four of them, I thought only one dead wasn't bad.

Blue left again and returned with Bree just as Zack led the first OPP officer to the scene. Shortly after that, the woods were filled with officers and paramedics. EIRT showed up close to an hour later and took control of the scene. They were a team out of London that none of us had met before and were quite stern.

They had a mage on the team. He cast a spell to detect demon activity, and it came back positive. At that point, their entire attitude changed, and they were much nicer to deal with. They had Bree and I go over what happened multiple times and probably would have kept grilling me, but for once I was grateful the sun was starting to come up. Blue took me home via the shadows.

I found Alteea sound asleep in the empty box of donuts in the living room. I carefully picked her small form up and put her to bed in her dollhouse in the basement. I ducked into the cold cellar just as the sun was coming up and then death's embrace took me again.

Extreme Solutions

Wednesday, June 6

My second cup of coffee wasn't enough to stop my yawning. Cleaning up a demonic ritual all night really took it out of you. I sighed and got down to processing the backlog of paperwork that had built up in the last week since we'd been busy with all the bounties that had popped up. I filed the bounty claim on the Boom Brothers and then shifted my focus to our accounts.

The paperwork ate up my entire afternoon. I joined Stella, Blue, and Bree for an early dinner as Bree didn't want to wait for Olivia to get up and that suited me too as I was famished. After dinner, I retired to my office again. This time I took the opportunity to brush up on some of my lore reading that I'd fallen behind on.

Just after 10:30 p.m. two things happened almost simultaneously: Blue and Stella popped their heads into my office and said since nothing seemed to be happening today, they were heading to bed. Then, almost before Stella had finished speaking, my phone rang. I glanced at the screen and D. Collins showed on the display. Dave was a cop and poker buddy of Rob's.

I told Stella and Blue to hang on and answered.

"What's up, Dave?"

"Hurricane, we need you and your team's assistance. We are on the Bruce Trail near the Wentworth stairs. My partner and I just emptied every round we had into a stone giant that was crashing through the trees. The thing didn't even notice and just kept walking. SWAT's ETA is twenty minutes and EIRT's is thirty. The problem is this thing will reach the Claremont access in ten minutes tops ..."

The Bruce Trail was a green space that ran the length of the escarpment that separated downtown Hamilton from Hamilton Mountain. The Claremont Access was the main access route for traffic between downtown and the mountain. If whatever this thing was reached the Claremont, people were going to get hurt.

I told Dave we'd be there shortly and hung up.

"Another bounty?" asked Stella.

I nodded and said, "Get your gear. We have no time to waste."

I yelled down to Liv, Bree, and Alteea to do the same.

We stepped out of the shadows and onto the Bruce Trail less than two minutes after Dave's call. It was another hot muggy evening. The area was dark but at least there were some lights from the Sherman Access below that stopped it from being pitch black. The moonlight wasn't penetrating the thick leaf canopies of the trees around us.

I spotted Dave standing about twenty feet away. His back was to us and he was fixated on something farther down the trail. Dave jumped when I called his name and turned towards us.

I strained my still-adjusting eyes and looked off in the direction he'd been facing. Sure enough, there was a large rock-covered humanoid-shaped creature lumbering along. I had trouble seeing it as its coloring matched the rocks of the escarpment and it had no aura. The lack of aura puzzled me for a moment. This thing was moving and alive, so it had to be Enhanced and should have had an aura. It suddenly dawned on me what it was—a stone golem. Stone golems were constructs that were created by spells. They had limited intelligence but could follow orders. As they were magical creations, they technically weren't alive. The good news was as this thing wasn't alive, we didn't have to pull our punches. The bad news was stone golems were exceptionally strong and durable. They didn't feel pain and wouldn't stop until they'd finished whatever task they'd been ordered to do.

"Thank god you are here," said Dave. "We have units heading to block traffic on the Claremont, but it is going to be tight. They may not get it closed off in time."

"Is it just you and your partner here in the woods?" Dave nodded, and I added, "Good, you two get out of here and keep anyone else from coming down here."

"You sure?"

"Yeah, this thing is going to be hard to take down and it will be easier if we don't have to worry about anyone being caught up in fallout from the fight."

Dave and his partner made haste for the Wentworth stairs and I turned my attention to my team. I told them what we were facing and came up with a plan. Stella would change into her Hyde form and go smash this thing. The rest of us were useless, as none of us would be even able to scratch it or distract it due to its task-focused nature.

The best I might be able to do is use my Air power to bury it in some trees, dirt, and rocks but that wouldn't stop it; if I was lucky, my efforts might slow it down at best. The other problem with using a massive blast of wind to bury the golem was that, over the last decade, the mountain road accesses had been closed several times due to geological instability. I feared that my small landslide might turn out to be much larger than I wanted. There were houses all along the edge of the escarpment above us and the Sherman Access was below us. The Sherman wasn't as busy as the Claremont, but it wasn't far behind. A major rockslide could kill a lot of innocent people.

Stella changed into her Hyde form and went after the golem and the rest of us followed behind her.

A minute later, she jumped in front of it and took her best swing. The golem was pushed back a couple of feet but immediately came forward again. Stella took another swing at it and got the same result. I stood there open mouthed in shock. The sounds of Stella's hits on the thing echoed in the woods as booming thuds. There was no doubt about how hard she was hitting it, but she might as well be spitting on it for all the good it was doing.

On the third strike, the golem reacted and swatted at Stella. She took the blow and flew back a good fifty feet before crashing into a tree.

So much for that plan.

I used my Air power to lift myself into the air and flew towards the golem. I also begin building up a charge of electricity.

I ended up hovering just in front of the golem. I pointed my hands at it and released a massive blast of pure white lightning. I hit it dead center in its chest, but it kept lumbering forward like nothing had happened.

I spotted Stella's Hyde form charging in and cut off the flow of electricity since it didn't seem to be doing a damn thing. I flew back to join the others and shook my head; I'd hit that thing with enough power to fry an elephant and it didn't even notice.

I heard the impact of Stella's blow behind me but wasn't holding out much hope it would do more than slow the golem for a brief second.

Even though the golem was shuffling forward at the sluggish speed of an old lady with a walker, we were running out of time. At best, we had around five minutes before it reached the Claremont Access and then people were going to get hurt. That fear of someone getting hurt or killed was kicking in and we needed to do something. But Stella was barely an annoyance to it, my lightning was useless, and there didn't seem to be anything we could do to stop it.

As I frantically tried to think of a solution, my earlier idea of causing a landslide to bury it came back. There was a small area just before the Claremont where there were no houses on the escarpment and the Sherman Access wouldn't be beneath us. If I was going to try it, that would be the spot with the least risk. I still didn't like that plan, as there was still the chance that I could cause a much bigger landslide than I wanted.

I touched down beside my teammates and asked, "Anyone else have any ideas?"

Liv and Bree shook their heads. Alteea just shrugged. To my surprise, Blue smiled and said, "I believe I have a solution to this problem. I have been saving it for something just like this ..."

Before I could ask, Blue opened a shadow portal and disappeared.

I wondered what Blue's solution was but then got distracted as Stella crashed hard into the golem again. She once again pushed it back a few steps but that was all she managed. The golem swung at her but this time she ducked it. It immediately brought its other arm around and Stella once again went sailing away.

"Holy shit!" exclaimed Liv.

At first, I thought she was talking about the hit that Stella took, but when she added, "Where did you get that?" I turned to see what she was excited about. My stomach dropped when I laid my eyes on Blue and the freaking huge rocket launcher she had on her shoulder.

I was about to say something when out of the corner of my eye, I spotted what looked like a fox surrounded in a silver glow sprinting off in the distance. I turned to get a better look at it, but it was gone.

Blue asked with a pointy-toothed grin, "Is Stella clear?" and my attention was pulled back to them.

"Yup," said Liv.

I started to say, "I don't think this is a good—"

"FIRE IN THE HOLE!" Blue yelled.

I barely had time to thicken the air around me and watch Alteea's aura dart for the treetops like she'd stolen Bree's last donut when a loud *whoosh* filled the air. Bree and Liv dove for the ground as a plume of fire exploded from the back of the launcher and Blue was knocked on her ass.

I watched as a streak of flaming light shot towards the golem. It hit the golem dead center in its back and then I witnessed the biggest damn explosion I'd ever seen in my life. The golem disappeared in the blink of an eye.

The concussion from the blast picked up dirt, leaves, trees, and rocks, and that wave of destruction was heading our way.

"OH SHIT!" was all I managed to scream before it hit.

The Air shield I had up stopped me from getting hit by any of the debris, but the sheer force of the blast lifted me off my feet and I ended up sailing back twenty feet or so in the air before crashing back to the earth.

I lay there on the moss- and dirt-covered ground and listened as tiny bits of golem and debris rained down all around me. I wiggled my fingers and toes and was stunned that I seemed to be in one piece. My next immediate concern was my teammates.

"That was awesome!" exclaimed Liv and the sounds of her laughter followed.

A low growl of amusement came from Bree, so at least two of my teammates were alive.

"WHAT THE BLOODY HELL WAS THAT?" screamed Stella from deeper in the woods.

I updated my count to include Stella.

Liv stopped laughing long enough to say, "Please tell me you got that on video, Alteea?"

"Yes, Mistress!" replied Alteea, her voice excited.

I got to my feet and with relief spotted Blue getting her feet and dusting herself off. Her tail was doing wide, happy figure eights, so I knew she was okay and was also feeling pleased with herself.

I stomped over to her and yelled, "A rocket launcher was your solution?"

Blue shook her head and said, "Of course not. A rocket launcher wouldn't have been able to take out that golem. A Javelin Anti-Tank Missile on the other hand ..."

I stopped and just stood there dumbfounded. I tried to process 'Javelin Anti-Tank Missile,' but words failed me at that moment. I was about to tear into the insane blue alien when sirens started across the entire city. I swear it sounded like every emergency vehicle in Hamilton was heading our way.

Those closing sirens slammed home the reality of the situation. Sure, we'd stopped the golem by blowing it to pieces, but we'd also destroyed a forty-foot section of protected green space and there was a fifteen-foot-deep crater where the golem had been. I resisted searching "What is the criminal penalty for using an unauthorized anti-tank missile in Canada?" into the search engine on my phone, only because I feared that search would be used as evidence. We had only minutes before this area would be swarming with cops and we needed to act fast.

"Liv, Bree, you have one minute to search the impact site and gather up every piece of the missile you can. Go!" I ordered.

Liv blurred towards the crater and Bree dashed after her.

I turned to Blue, "When they return, take the missile debris and the launcher back to the lab and stay there until I call. Alteea, delete that video from the cloud and make sure you only have a local copy of it."

Stella arrived with a stunned look on her face and asked, "What the hell just happened?"

"No time to explain. Bree and Liv will be back in the next thirty seconds. When they do, all of you will go hide in the lab. Blue can fill you in on what happened."

Stella looked like she wanted to argue but just nodded.

I yelled, "Bree, Liv, you have fifteen seconds more to search and then get back here!"

In the end, my team just managed to disappear into the shadows with armfuls of evidence of our illegal explosive device about five seconds before Dave and his partner showed up. I crossed my fingers and prayed Liv and Bree had found every identifiable piece of that missile or we were in deep shit.

"What the hell just happened?" asked Dave.

"No idea, we were fighting with the golem and it just exploded."

"Where is the rest of your team?"

I put on my best concerned face and said, "Liv and Bree were injured in the blast. Blue and Stella took them to get blood and food, so they can heal."

"Sorry to hear that. Will they be okay?"

I nodded and said, "They should be. Vampires and Weres heal quickly, but I would like to go check on them soon."

Dave frowned and said, "I wish I could let you go, but we need to wait for EIRT to get here."

Twenty minutes later, the entire area was filled with cops, firemen, and EIRT. Luck was with me as this EIRT team was led by Bobby Knight. He knew me and might give me the benefit of the doubt. I took a deep breath and told myself that I just needed to act naturally and maybe my team and I wouldn't end up in jail by the end of this night.

I went over my exploding golem story with Bobby and the mage that was the Enhanced component of his team. Oddly enough, it was the mage that bailed me out twice.

"You said you were shooting lightning at the golem, correct?" I nodded, and he continued, "A stone golem would be an Earth-based spell, and your lighting is Air-based. Those are opposing elements. They used to tell us stories at the Academy about the danger of mixing opposing elements. I'd always figured they'd exaggerated those just to scare us but after seeing this ..."

I nodded and tried to look suitably worried.

"We did get reports of a streak of fire seen in the area just before the explosion—any thoughts on that?" asked Bobby.

I cursed silently to myself and quickly tossed out, "I was firing lightning; maybe that is what they saw ..."

Bobby shrugged and kept writing.

The two of them questioned me for the next twenty minutes and I thought we'd gotten away with it when Bobby asked, "Did your pixie get this on film?"

Shit. I thought back on the whole encounter and smiled when I realized that she'd had her glamor up the entire time. The only people that knew she had been here were me and my team. "No, she is off visiting her old swarm for the day. We kicked around the idea of filming it, but as Dave and his partner had seen the creature, we figured we'd have no issues collecting the bounty on this and didn't bother."

Bobby had an expression on his face that made me think he was going to probe deeper, so I turned to the mage and quickly said, "I didn't think a stone golem was an easy spell to cast."

The mage shook his head and said, "It's not. Earth magic is my secondary focus and I couldn't create one on my best day. Whoever created it must have Earth magic as their primary power, and they would still need to be fairly powerful to cast it.

Bobby's radio on his vest squawked and he answered it.

"Sarge, we traced the golem's path back to its origin. There is a boulder here with sacrificed animals on it; a deer, a couple of raccoons, and half a dozen rabbits."

The mage cursed and said, "Whoever did this used blood magic to boost their power. This is just what we need: another budding necromancer on our hands."

The 'another' part of his comment caught me off guard for a moment until I remembered the zombies from the other night. I wondered if these two events were related and whether this might be the same person. If it was, then they were stepping up their game. The zombies hadn't really been a big threat as they'd been trapped in the cemetery. The golem was a whole different story. If it had reached the Claremont, people would have been hurt or killed.

Bobby nodded and picked up the radio, "Hang there, Phil, we'll be right over."

The mage was already walking to the site. Bobby looked at me and asked, "You want to check this out too?"

I shook my head and said, "No. Magic isn't my forte. I'll let your overfunded multimillion-dollar agency earn its money for a change. I just want to go check on my injured teammates and make sure they are okay."

Bobby rolled his eyes at my shot at EIRT and said, "I have enough to file my report. I'll e-mail you the bounty claim number once I'm done. Call your shadow-traveler and go check on your friends. Thanks for stopping this thing; if it had gotten out of these woods, a lot of people might have been hurt."

I thanked him and called Blue. I cursed under my breath as Bobby didn't leave and just stood there adding something to his report.

A minute later, Blue popped out of the shadows and I said, "I want to check on Liv and Bree."

She frowned slightly in confusion, but immediately opened another portal and we were gone.

We came out into the lab and the whole team was sitting at one of the tables watching the video on Alteea's phone and laughing. I could swear my teammates were lunatics who escaped from an asylum and were just under my care. Blue headed over to join the rest, but I didn't follow, instead making a beeline for the Food-O-Tron.

I pushed in the code for aged brandy and waited for the machine to replicate it. The Food-O-Tron dinged, and I grabbed the glass and downed it. My eyes watered as it burned the back of my throat, but I immediately pulled the lever and made myself another. I sipped the second one as I walked over to join my teammates.

Bree wrinkled her nose and asked, "What are you drinking?"

"Brandy," I said as I sat down.

Stella frowned and said, "I don't ever recall you drinking brandy before ..."

"Yeah, well, it has been that type of night."

Blue cocked her head and said, "I am confused. You seem upset, why? We defeated a powerful foe, no one was seriously injured, and we will be collecting a bounty for our efforts. You should be happy."

I didn't respond and just rubbed my temples to soothe the headache that'd been building since a certain insane blue alien blew up half the Bruce Trail.

Thankfully, Stella came to my rescue, "I believe Zack is upset because you used a rocket launcher to blow up the golem."

"Anti-tank missile," corrected Liv with a giggle.

Stella glared at Liv. Liv just laughed even harder at that.

Blue said, "You did ask for ideas after your original plan failed. I fail to see why my solution is an issue. Our only member that had a chance of defeating the golem was unsuccessful. If the golem had reached the access, civilians would have been hurt or killed. My solution stopped that from happening."

As much as I hated to admit it, Blue was right. If Stella couldn't even dent the thing, none of us would have been able to do anything to it. Even my lightning attack had been useless.

"Yes, your solution worked, but if the authorities find out that we used an anti-tank missile, we'll all be going to jail for a long time ..."

The room went silent at that and then Bree asked, "What did you tell them?"

I relayed everything I told EIRT, and at the end, Liv laughed and said, "They actually bought your 'the golem just exploded on its own' story?"

I nodded and said, "Thankfully, I don't think that any of them are crazy enough to imagine that we used an anti-tank missile, so unless they find a piece with a serial number, we should be okay."

I took another sip of the brandy and another thought occurred to me, "Where did you get the missile?"

Blue grinned and said, "Same place I got the grenades when we took on the master of the French court. I grabbed it then and had it tucked away in my room here for a special occasion. If you recall, Sarah's advice was to hit Giselle with an anti-tank missile from a distance. The armory I took it from really has lax security considering how many wonderful toys they have there."

Sarah had been joking about the anti-tank missile, but she had said that. I processed all of what Blue had said, and asked, "What else do you have tucked away in your room here? An ICBM or an Abrams battle tank?"

Blue snorted at that and said, "Of course not. Neither of those things would fit in my room..."

Thursday, June 7

I was up just before noon and nursing a slight hangover thanks to all the brandy I had the night before. I was pleased to note that our house hadn't had the front door knocked in by a GRC13 team with an arrest warrant for us using a prohibited explosive device. Even better, there was an e-mail from Bobby with a bounty claim ticket on the golem for $50,000 US.

After getting some food and an Advil for my headache, I sat down in front of my computer and filled out the claim form for the golem on the UN bounty website. I had just finished when my phone started buzzing on the desk.

I recognized Greg's name on the display and picked up. Greg was a retired real estate developer who I had known since my early hero days.

We made small talk for a bit, during which he mentioned that his new cottage would be finished by the beginning of August. I felt instantly guilty; we'd been the reason his old one got burned down while we were hiding out in it when Liv had a contract on her head from the French vampire court.

"I'm calling because I want to know if you are familiar with the Sunnyvale housing project in Binbrook," said Greg.

Binbrook used to be a small, rural community just outside of Hamilton. It was amalgamated into the city of Hamilton around 2001. In the last decade a ton of new houses had been built there.

When I told Greg the name didn't ring any bells, he said, "It's a housing project by DiSanto's Construction; they are building over 500 new houses on a huge chunk of land they bought out there. I've known Gino DiSanto for decades and this is their biggest project to date. It's so big that they needed to raise outside capital for the project. I took a 10 percent stake in the project."

"I thought you were retired?" I asked.

Greg laughed, "I'm retired, not dead. I keep my eyes open for good investments and this was one of them. Gino is good people, and his company does solid work. The real estate boom means those houses will sell like hotcakes, and I stand to make some great money on this …"

"You're not the type to call and brag, so I'm assuming something has happened to take the shine off this gold mine?"

"Yeah, in the last week the site has been plagued by accidents and issues. They've had two electric fires, a ruptured gas line, and over twenty-five different workplace injuries. A couple of the incidents were serious enough that two workers are still in intensive care. Contractors are starting not to show up because they feel the site is cursed. The whole project is grinding to a halt. If things are delayed too long, it will bankrupt Gino and I'll be out my investment."

I felt bad for Greg, but I still didn't understand why he was calling me, "Sounds like a run of bad luck but construction sites are dangerous places and accidents happen."

"Sure, but not like this. DiSanto's is a big firm and safety is a key focus for them. They had only ten accidents all last year so twenty-five accidents in a week doesn't make any sense. I think something supernatural is happening here. I'll send you a video I have that Gino sent me. Yesterday a parked bulldozer started up on its own and drove into a house that had two guys working in it. They had to jump from the second floor and got a busted leg and ankle for their troubles."

This sounded like the plot of an episode of Scooby-Doo and not something that I'd usually look into. The problem was I owed Greg for ruining his cottage, so I said, "Send me the video. I'll give it a look over and take my team out there tonight to take a gander; maybe we can get to the bottom of this. Can you clear this with Gino?"

"Thanks, Zack, I appreciate this."

We ended the call and a couple minutes later an e-mail arrived with a video attached. I watched as the bulldozer drove itself into the house, just as Greg had said.

Maybe the site really was haunted. However, I suspected that this wouldn't end with us pulling a rubber mask off a villain who says, "Curses, I would have gotten away with it too, if it wasn't for those meddling kids …"

***

We got out to the site via the shadows just before 10 p.m. as we had to wait for Olivia to wake up and get some blood into her. It was another hot, muggy night and I already missed the air conditioning at home. The only upside to the heat was Liv was dressed in a white crop top with no bra and the cheekiest pair of cut-off shorts I'd ever seen. I loved the outfit, but it certainly wasn't helping to lower my temperature any.

We hadn't been there a minute when Bree stopped and said, "Oh my God, what is that smell?"

Liv sniffed and made a sour face. I inhaled but didn't catch anything, but my sense of smell was bad for a human and nowhere near as sensitive as my Were and vampire companions was.

Alteea suddenly went squirrelly. She let out a little scream and dove behind Liv and hid in her ponytail. She made herself invisible, but I could still see her tiny rainbow aura. I could see it trembling, which confused me for a moment until I realized that she was shaking in fear.

"What's the matter, little one?" asked Liv in soft, calming tome.

"G-g-gremlin, Mistress!" she squeaked in reply.

I looked around the darkened site. I didn't see any auras nearby but decided not to take any chances, "Blue, open a portal to home."

Blue moved back to the shadows we arrived from and made a small gesture with her hand to open a shadow portal. Alteea darted out of Liv's hair and was the first one through, the rest of us behind her.

When we emerged from the shadows in our living room, I looked around for Alteea but didn't see her anywhere. Liv stopped just as she came out of the shadows and her head twisted back and forth looking for Alteea too. She turned in the direction of one the speakers and said, "Come out little one, you are safe now."

Bree ignored us and made a beeline for the kitchen. Stella and Blue were the last through and moved off to the side with a confused look on their faces.

"Are you sure, Mistress?" asked Alteea in her normal high-pitched voice.

"Absolutely, and even if there were a gremlin here, I would drain it dry before it even got close to you."

Alteea fluttered up from behind the speaker and even had dropped her glamor. She flew over to Liv and landed on her shoulder and hugged Liv's neck.

"That's my brave pixie," said Liv with a smile.

Bree returned carrying a box of donuts, and to everyone's amazement, she held out a powdered jelly one to Alteea. I swear Alteea's green eyes widened to three time their usual size at this gesture.

She reached for it but stopped and asked, "Are you sure, Mistress Bree?"

Bree smiled and said, "I think you need this more than I do at this moment."

Alteea snatched the donut from Bree and a cloud of powdered sugar surrounded her as she dove into her treasure.

Liv beamed at her best friend but frowned when a blob of red jelly leaked onto her shoulder. A muffled "sorry, Mistress" came from behind the donut and a tiny clawed hand scooped up some of the errant filling.

"Well, thanks to Alteea, we know what has been causing the mishaps at the site. Now we just have to figure out how to deal with it."

"What is a gremlin?" asked Stella.

Stella was quite knowledgeable about many mythical creatures, but I wasn't surprised she didn't know about gremlins. World War II was the peak of gremlin activity, and Stella had been in suspended animation during that time, so it made sense she wasn't aware of them.

"When the dark fae were working with the Nazis during World War II, they created gremlins to wreak havoc with all things mechanical, especially aircraft. Unlike most fae creatures, gremlins have no issue with iron. But like most fae, they have glamor which makes them invisible to normal humans. They are about three-feet tall and look like giant naked mole rats. Their legs are more like a rabbit's than a rat. They also have rows of razor-sharp teeth and claws. They are fast buggers too, and thanks to those rabbit-like feet, they can jump extremely well."

"Okay, if iron doesn't burn them, how do you kill them?" asked Liv.

"Fire is the best way," I said, and Liv blanched at that, "But beheading them works too. Any normal fatal injury, like crushing their skulls or stabbing them in their hearts, also kills them."

Liv smiled, and her fangs showed, "Draining them?"

I nodded.

"Why was Alteea so freaked out?" asked Bree after finishing her own donut.

"Pixies are a favorite prey of gremlins. A single gremlin is no match for an entire pixie swarm, but these things are sneaky little devils. They usually go after a lone or small group of pixies. Which reminds me, even though they are only three-feet tall, don't underestimate them. They are cunning and vicious little bastards and there could be more than one of them."

Blue nodded and asked, "Their glamor makes them invisible like Alteea's does, but does it make them silent too?"

"No, why?" I asked.

"Good, because I can hunt them by sound."

Liv turned to Alteea, "Is that smell common for gremlins?"

I grinned as Alteea looked up from her donut, her face was covered in jelly and powdered sugar.

"Yes, they always stink like that."

"What did you smell?" I asked Bree as her nose was the most sensitive.

"A mix of oil, dung, and burnt plastic …"

I excused myself and disappeared upstairs to the office and found the lore book that contained gremlins. I quickly read over the section but nothing new or relevant popped out at me. It was time to gather up the troops and go deal with this thing.

***

Ten minutes later, we were back at the construction site. We geared up so Blue, Liv, and I were wearing our goggles. We decided to split into three groups. Blue and Bree in her true Werepanther form were one group and they tore off deeper into the site almost immediately. Liv and Stella in her Hyde form were another group. I was on my own and had gone airborne to get a better view. We left Alteea at home for her own safety.

I hadn't been in the air for a minute when I spotted a small rainbow aura with a black and grey outline around it perched inside one of the timber-framed houses. I'd found our gremlin. I was about to use the communicators to let everyone know where it was, but I didn't know how good its hearing was and didn't want to spook it.

I smiled as its attention seemed to be focused on Stella and Liv who were a couple hundred feet away. I'd call on my lightning and dove towards it. I let out a massive blast of lightning when I was about forty feet from it. I hit it square in the center of its chest, but the thing leapt down and sprinted off.

Great, it's immune to electricity, I thought. I was about to chase after it, but I noticed the two-by-fours I'd also hit were starting to smolder. I used my air power to starve the wood of oxygen until they stopped smoking.

There was a familiar flash of silver off in the distance and I remembered the aura I'd seen at the golf course. I turned towards it, but it was gone now. My stomach knotted up— this couldn't just be a coincidence.

A grunt of anger from Stella pulled my attention to her and Liv. I spotted the gremlin's aura darting away from them. I was about to go after it when a large slab of concrete came flying my way. I just managed to avoid it and heard Liv yell, "Stella, NO! It wasn't Zack. Look!"

Our Hyde turned and spotted the sparking electrical cable near her foot. She grunted in anger and stomped her feet. The sneaky bastard had shocked Stella and she assumed it was me.

A gleeful cackle came from another set of half-built houses across from us. Stella roared and charged towards the laughter. Liv pulled out her sword and blurred away as well. I joined the chase.

I cringed, and Stella went through one of the timber framed houses and it collapsed around her. Liv was standing over an open sewer drain cursing when I landed beside her.

"It ducked down here, but it is too narrow for me to follow," she said.

I smiled and opened the comms, *"Blue, we found the gremlin. It went into the sewers. Keep an eye on any drainpipes near you as I'm going to flush it out."*

I called on my Air power and let a massive charge build. After about ten seconds, I thrust my hands into the pipe and released a huge blast of wind. Manhole covers down the unpaved street suddenly went airborne and a scream of terror echoed through the night sky as a rainbow aura blasted out of the ground like a rocket at the end of the street.

"There it is!" I pointed.

Stella roared and lumbered after it, and Liv was off in a flash. I took to the air in pursuit. Liv made it there first, stopping just as the rainbow aura hit the ground. She swung her sword, but the gremlin nimbly jumped over it. She reversed her swing and went higher this time, but the aura ducked under it. Her third swing she chopped at it vertically. The gremlin dodged to the side and then it leapt at her. I heard fabric rip and Liv cursed as the gremlin pulled off her top and jumped away.

It was still invisible, but it waved the white crop top back and forth at Liv and cackled again. It suddenly squeaked in panic and the ruined top floated to the ground as Stella came barreling in. Stella crashed down where the gremlin had been only a second before. A cloud of dirt and rocks flew up from where Stella landed.

I'd briefly thought she'd nailed it, but I spied a rainbow aura making a beeline for cover away from her.

Liv turned, frantically looking for the gremlin, but with the noise and cloud of dirt Stella made, it hid its scent and sound, so she couldn't track it.

Stella stepped out of the crater she'd made and at the bottom of it were the remains of Liv's top. Liv looked down at it and sighed. She saw me flying toward them and yelled, "Don't say a fucking word!"

I just laughed and flew by. A deep roar filled the air, followed by the sound of wood cracking. I spotted Bree's panther form extracting itself from a shattered wall of two-by-fours and she pounced after the gremlin again. It dodged out of the way and she took out another wood-framed wall. The upper part of the house lurched and then the whole thing collapsed, burying Bree. I sighed as I spotted the gremlin's aura dart off into the night.

"Bree!" yelled Liv in a panic and she blurred up to the edge of the debris to help her friend.

A pile of timber and floorboards exploded upwards and a loud angry roar split the night as an extremely pissed off Werepanther came flying free.

Seeing that Bree was fine, I used my Air power to lift myself into the night sky and shot after the fleeing aura.

So far it was gremlin three points and Team Zack zero, but we just needed to score one solid point and this game was over. I was tired of screwing around; this fairy was going down ... *hard.*

The aura disappeared into a half-finished house. I flew over the house to make sure it wasn't sneaking out the back way. I hovered in the air just above and behind the house waiting for it to come out.

After thirty seconds, the gremlin still didn't emerge. I spotted a shovel in the backyard and gently landed beside it. I picked the shovel up and cocked it in my hand like a baseball bat and headed in through the door-less entrance. In the center of the house, there was a tarp loosely covering something big and square. I assumed it was lumber, but in the center of it, there was a three-foot-high bump.

Gotcha! I thought with a smile. I crept forward on my tiptoes, not making a sound. I tensed as I got closer, silently willing my fae friend not to move.

As soon as I got in range, I swung that shovel like I was in the World Series with a man on base and my team down one run in the bottom of the ninth. The solid metal impacted the bump with a loud *clang*.

I cursed as the vibrations of the shovel travelled up my arms and damn near shook loose all the fillings in my mouth. Whatever I'd hit was metallic and not organic, which meant I hadn't just brained a gremlin.

The hairs on the back of my neck rose and I spun around. Across the room, a nail gun rose with a rainbow aura behind it. I just managed to put the shovel head in front of my face and the handle across my groin when the little bastard stitched a line of nails up my leg and chest before a couple pinged off the shovel.

The pain of the attack followed a moment later, and I dropped to the floor with a scream. A cackle of evil glee pulled me from my agony. I watched in horror as the nail gun lowered its aim towards my prone form.

I had just started to call on my Air power to thicken the air in hopes of saving me from becoming more of a pincushion when three hundred pounds of beautiful black panther came bounding into the room looking for blood.

The nail gun clunked to the floor and a rainbow aura darted out of the room with Bree right on its heels.

"Go get 'em, Bree!" I yelled and then winced as a nail shifted and made its point in my thigh.

Liv suddenly appeared in front of me and said, "I smell yummy blood … oh shit, Zack, are you alright?"

"I now know what a floorboard feels like, so no, I'm not alright. Find Blue, I need to visit Marion now!"

A loud crash echoed nearby, followed by an angry roar and then a confused growl. I figured it was now gremlin five points and Team Zack zero.

"Hold on, I'll find Blue," said Liv and she blurred out of the room. I looked at the bleeding line of nails running down my chest and leg and debated the wisdom of pulling them out. I decided to leave them as removing them might cause me to bleed out. I really should have put a rush delivery on that damn armor I ordered.

The next couple of minutes there were a series of crashes, followed by snapping wood and other sounds of destruction and then angry grunts and growls. I sighed as it sounded like the gremlin was racking up the score on Stella and Bree. I wondered why the hell Liv was taking so long to find Blue.

The night was cut by a high-pitched squeal that stopped before it really even started. I didn't recognize the tone and wondered what happened.

I heard Liv exclaim, "Blue, you got it!"

"Of course I did. While you idiots were stomping around like elephants, I used my brains and stealth. We are really going to have to work on all your training …" Blue's voice was smug.

***

Blue opened a portal for me shortly after that and I came out just in front of Marion's door with my trusty vampire holding me upright.

I knocked, and after a good thirty seconds, a sleepy looking Marion opened the door in a tie-dye bathrobe and fuzzy pink bunny slippers.

She adjusted her glasses and looked at me, "Doing home renovations again, Zack?"

"Har, har. Less chatty-chatty, more fixy-fixy, if you don't mind."

She opened the door and we limped in behind her. Marion tossed an old looking towel on her couch and pointed.

Liv helped me over to the couch and I grimaced in pain as I sat back.

Marion left the room and came back a few moments later. She tossed a colorful Grateful Dead T-shirt to my still-topless vampire. It bothered me that in my haze of pain, I'd completely forgotten she was flashing her tatas to the world. Thankfully, my keen wit was still working, "I hope you don't care about that shirt—the way her luck has been going with tops recently, we'll be attacked by a rabid squirrel on the way home who'll take it from her and use it as a flag to rally other squirrels to his banner and take over their rightful rulership of this world ..."

Liv's head popped out the top of the shirt in time to eye-roll hard at my comment and Marion added, "Nah, I have a spare and that one has always been a little small for me," she paused and then grinned. "Besides, I feed the squirrels and have assured myself a comfortable position in the new squirrel order that is coming ..."

We both laughed at that. Or least I did until a nail shifted, and suddenly things weren't as funny.

Marion pulled a small stool closer, sat down, and started healing me. She'd numb the nerves around a nail, pull it free, and then heal the wound. Each nail she pulled out she handed to Liv, who was hovering anxiously nearby.

Seeing Liv lick each of the nails clean was really disturbing.

She shrugged and said, "Not letting tasty Elemental blood go to waste."

I rolled my eyes and winced as Marion pulled another nail out.

Thirty-minutes of fun and I was nail-free and more importantly, pain-free.

I sat up and Marion shook her head at me and said, "You are a very lucky man that none of those nails hit anything vital. Honestly, Zack, this is the third time I've healed you this week ... for Pete's sake start being more careful out there, okay?"

I nodded, and we left her so she could go back to sleep.

We called Blue for a ride, as I was too drained to fly us home.

We got home, and everyone was there but Stella. I assumed she'd gone to bed but then Blue said, "I'm going out to help Stella."

"Where is she?" I asked.

"Still at the construction site waiting for EIRT to arrive so we can collect the bounty," replied Blue who then stepped through the shadows and disappeared.

At least someone thought of the bounty. I told the girls I was heading to bed and they wished me a good night.

I had just got under the covers when my phone buzzed. I was tempted to ignore it but spotted Greg's name on the display.

"I heard from Gino that you got the gremlin that was causing all the problems. Thank you, but did you have to do so much damage?"

"What damage?" I asked.

"Four partially completed homes destroyed, a bulldozer turned over on its side, a quarter mile of sewer piping ruined, a small fire, fourteen new windows smashed and there were other damages that I can't remember at this moment, for a start."

"Yeah, not our finest hour, but at least the accidents will stop now. Did you hear that I took eleven nails to the chest and leg?"

"Oh shit, I didn't hear that part. Are you alright?"

We chatted a while longer. By the end of it, Greg seemed okay with everything and thanked me for dealing with the gremlin. He did admit that Gino figured all the damage wouldn't set the project back for more than a couple of weeks, probably less as they could continue work while the stuff we broke got fixed.

After the call, I thought about tonight's adventure. I still felt guilty about what happened to his cottage while we were hiding out there, but knowing I'd saved his investment did help ease that guilt. For now, I'd take that win.

Why Did It Have to Be Snakes?

Friday, June 8

The next morning, I found a note on the counter that said Blue and Stella were at the lab working on their mysterious project. The rest of the team was either asleep or, in Olivia's case, in a death-trance.

Having a quiet house and no emergencies to deal with made for a nice change of pace. Cup of coffee in hand, I retired to my office and filed the paperwork for the gremlin bounty claim online.

An hour later, I finished all the outstanding paperwork and was at a loose end. I was pleased with all the bounty claims we'd filed in the last week or so, but the sheer volume of work did have me a little concerned. This uptick in supernatural happenings seemed a bit odd to me.

The silver auras I'd been catching glimpses of during these encounters had me concerned that there might be something more at play than just a busy run. The silver aura meant a God-class being could be lurking behind all of this. Silver ruled out Judeo-Christian deities, as angels and prophets had pure white auras and demons and their like had black ones. The problem was that silver was a common aura for Norse, Greek, Roman, and a host of other pantheons, which left my suspect list in the thousands.

I needed to narrow it down. I perked up when I remembered the fox with the silver aura I'd briefly spotted on the Bruce Trail. At the time, I'd been more concerned about not going to jail for Blue's explosive solution to our golem problem, but now this might be the clue I needed to figure out what was going on.

I opened up my browser and started doing Google searches for deities with fox associations. If you'd asked me to name a fox-related deity, I would have been hard pressed to come up with one before my search. I quickly found out there were tons of fox references in mythology. Africa, Europe, the Middle East, East Asia, and South America all had lore about foxes. There were hundreds of pages about fox-related legends from Japanese and Chinese culture alone.

Before I knew it, the sun was down and Liv and Alteea were up. I took a break and joined them and the rest of the team downstairs for dinner. I kept my fox theory to myself and when asked about my day, just answered that I had been studying lore. I tried to get more details out of Stella and Blue about their mysterious project, but they were being just as coy about it as always.

After dinner, I retired back to the office to continue my research.

In the end, other than learning some fascinating, yet extremely obscure, facts, I didn't have a good suspect for who might be behind this uptick in activity. Most of the fox-related creatures weren't powerful enough to manipulate or cause the events we'd been involved in recently. The ones that were strong enough to do something like this were based in Japan or China, but there had been no reports that they operated outside those areas. As both those counties were halfway around the world, it seemed very unlikely these beings would be meddling in Hamilton, Ontario.

By 11:30 p.m., I'd had enough and was yawning more than I was learning anything new.

I popped into the living room to say good night to Liv, Bree, and Alteea when my phone rang.

So much for nothing happening today, I thought as I spotted Dave Collin's name on the display.

"Zack, I need your help," said Dave.

I was a bit taken aback at Dave calling me Zack. If this was official business, then he'd usually call me Hurricane. I wondered what was up.

"… I finished my shift and was heading home when I spotted light flickering from inside King's Forest. I pulled over and there was a guy in the woods wearing a brown robe sacrificing wild animals over a crude stone altar. I was going to get out to put a stop to it, but if this guy is the mage that created the stone golem …"

I didn't blame Dave for not wanting to take on a mage alone. He was calling us because it would take SWAT twenty minutes to get there, and they too would be reluctant to challenge a mage. EIRT would be at least thirty minutes before they could get there. If this guy was creating another stone golem, we were the only ones that had a chance of getting there in time to stop this. "You did the right thing. I will assemble my team and deal with it. Where are you exactly?"

Before Dave answered, Liv blurred by me and headed upstairs; I assumed to wake up Stella and Blue or to get her sword and glasses. Bree was already stripping off her clothes in preparation of having to change her form. At seeing their quick reactions, I had to admit that these constant bounties were turning our team into a well-oiled machine.

I finished getting the details from Dave, told him to hang tight and we'd be there soon, and ended the call.

Liv was back and had her sword and communication glasses on. Even better, she grabbed mine too. I could hear Blue and Stella moving around upstairs, so she had woken them as well.

Two minutes later, we were all together in the kitchen and just about ready to go, "Blue, can you find a shadow nearby but not too close? If this is the mage that created the stone golem, he may have put up wards to prevent him from being interrupted."

Blue turned off a few lights in the room and stared quietly into one of the newly created shadows. After a few seconds, she nodded and said, "There is a shadow near Dave's car that we can use."

"Perfect. Let's take this slow and steady. We will approach with Liv in the lead. Liv, if you sense the wards, stop and tell us." Liv nodded. "The rest of us will follow, but I want at least five feet between all of us, so if he does hit us with a spell, he won't be able to hit all of us. Alteea, go airborne and stay at least twenty-five feet back from the end of the group and film it. And lastly, no rocket launchers!"

"'Anti-tank missile,'" corrected Liv with a giggle.

I glared at her, and then asked the group, "Any questions?"

Everyone shook their heads and Blue opened a portal.

We came out of the shadows about twenty feet in front of Dave's parked car. I headed over to him.

"He's over there," said Dave, pointing into the woods. "I called this in and SWAT and EIRT are on their way but they'll both be at least twenty minutes, probably longer. They aren't sending any marked cruisers—we don't want to spook this guy."

I glanced over towards the forest and spotted the candlelight in the trees. A man in a hooded brown robe was putting a bloody knife down on the boulder in front of him. His aura threw me off; it was a brown ring surrounded by a green one, and it was about three inches wide. Brown and green represented Earth and Nature respectively. The EIRT mage had said to create a stone golem the perp would need

Earth and Nature to be his primary focus. But if he really was a mage, then his aura should have been large sections of brown and green with small slivers of red, yellow, and blue, as mages can access all four of the major elements. The aura was smaller than I'd been expecting too. The EIRT mage's aura was twice the size and he said he couldn't cast a stone golem spell, so if this was our guy, he'd managed to do that with half the power. The blood sacrifices might explain that, as they would have boosted his spell-casting abilities.

My eyes widened as it hit me what we were dealing with: this was a druid. Druids weren't common in urban environments and I'd never seen one before, but it fit. Druids were spellcasters but they only had Earth- and Nature-based spells. They usually also had the ability to change into an animal form as well.

There was a pile of dead animals on the boulder and what looked like a large wicker basket sitting on the crude altar. My concern grew as his hands started moving in sharp motions as he began casting his spell.

I left Dave and ran back to my team.

"He is casting, so we need to get to him before he finishes. Liv, you lead and watch for traps or wards. Let's go."

Liv turned to the forest and walked towards it. She kept her head down and was slowly moving her gaze back and forth, carefully searching the ground in front of her. Stella transformed into her Hyde form and followed Liv. I was five feet behind Liv. Blue and Bree were trailing behind me. Alteea was hanging well back of the group.

I thought about taking to the air, but the tree tops this time of year were so thick that I wouldn't be able to see through them. I did, however, thicken the air in front of me as a precaution. The woods were about a hundred feet from us, and he was about fifty feet inside of that.

As we got closer, his chanting grew louder. I hoped that was from us getting closer and not because he was getting near the end of the spell.

Just as Liv reached the edge of the forest, the druid's tone and intensity peaked and then it went dead quiet. I cursed as I realized he finished casting his spell. Deeper in the woods there was a streak of silver that shot away from behind the druid and disappeared farther into the trees. I wanted to go check that out, but we needed to deal with the druid first.

We crept closer, and I held my breath waiting for the results of his spell to manifest, but for ten long seconds nothing happened.

Just as Liv was about halfway into the woods, the wicker basket started shaking violently on the crude altar. The druid stepped back. The basket started to expand slightly outwards and looked to be straining to contain whatever was inside it.

A few more long seconds ticked by, and then suddenly the basket disintegrated and a huge scaled form appeared. I blinked as a huge freaking snake appeared and continued getting bigger with every passing second.

"Yes! My beauty! YES!" excitedly yelled the druid as the snake grew.

We all stopped moving forward and stared in horror as the snake rapidly gained more and more mass.

It stopped growing after another few seconds and then it raised its serpentine head and flared out its hood. Its forked tongue flicked out and tested the night air. The giant cobra stood about twelve feet tall and towered over the druid. The worst part was the rest of its long, coiled body meant this thing had to be at least a hundred feet long. Odin only knew how much this monster weighed.

Its eyes glowed a malevolent red, which gave it an unnatural sense of menace. It opened its mouth and hissed in anger, revealing a set of giant fangs. Liquid oozed from the fangs and the forest floor sizzled as the droplets of poison hit.

This is going to suck. I stepped around Stella and Liv and loudly said, "Dispel the snake and surrender, or we will use lethal force!"

The druid turned his hooded form towards me, surprise etched on his face. I guessed he had been so caught up in his casting that he hadn't been aware of our arrival.

That surprise changed to anger and he said, "Never! For too long humans have abused the All-Mother's gift and poisoned this planet with their presence. With this wonderful creature, I will strike back at the polluters and make them—"

Holy shit!

In the blink of an eye, the giant cobra struck and swallowed the druid whole. The guy didn't even have time to scream. I watched in horror as the snake's gullet widened and the druid's body moved down inside of it.

The snake then turned and slithered off deeper into the woods, leaving us standing there, speechless.

The speed at which it all happened had my fear bubbling to the surface. To counter that, I joked, "Snakes. Why did it have to be snakes?"

My teammates all gave me blank looks, except for Blue who with concern asked, "Are you afraid of snakes?"

I shook my head and sighed, "Really? I quote one of the greatest movies ever, and not one of you gets the reference?"

Liv perked up and said, "Are you talking about that Samuel L. Jackson movie?"

I blinked at that and stood there dumbfounded. "We are so having an Indiana Jones movie night to correct your ignorance ..."

Blue pointed at where the giant snake had been and said, "Shall we dispense with your pop culture references and deal with the large reptile that is getting away?"

I nodded. "Liv, Bree, go! We'll follow behind you."

Liv blurred off and Bree was hot on her heels.

"Stella, take point and Blue and I will be right behind you."

Stella grunted and lumbered after our two teammates. I called up Liv's position on my glasses and then ran after Stella.

As I ran through the woods, I began calling on my lightning and building up a charge. I didn't know if lightning would work against this monster, but if it did, it would probably need to be a massive blast due to its sheer size.

The idea of running through a darkened wood in the middle of the night after a man-eating snake really wasn't on my top ten good ideas list. Unlike the last time we were in a woods with the golem, at least this thing was biologically based which meant it could bleed, and if it bled, we could kill it. It shouldn't be able to hurt Stella in her Hyde form, though the way the forest floor sizzled when the poison from its fangs dripped on it did have me a touch concerned for her safety. Liv should be quick enough to avoid its strikes. Bree would probably be able to avoid them as well. Even if Bree wasn't quick enough, her healing abilities could likely deal with the poison. Blue and I were the two most vulnerable. This was why I had Stella lead. Blue, however, was capable and would stick to the shadows and not give the snake an easy target. I'd planned to use my lightning from range and if it did turn its attention to me, I was going airborne to get the hell away from it.

I kept one eye on Stella and the trail in front of us and the other on Liv's position on my glasses. She had been heading dead east and then suddenly went straight south for a short distance and stopped.

I heard her cursing deeper in the woods. Stella must have heard it too as she turned towards the noise. We found Olivia lying against some tree roots on the ground.

"You okay?" I asked.

"Yeah, yeah. It bitch-slapped me with its tail when I caught up to it."

She sprang to her feet, and the sounds of ripping cloth filled the air. A large section of her white crop top was pinned under an exposed tree root. The top, now missing its back section, slumped forward down her arms. "Not again!"

I laughed and said, "You really need to start buying those things in bulk …"

"Shut up!" Liv snarled as she tossed the remains of the wrecked top to the ground.

A triumphant growl followed by an angry hiss echoed from deeper in the dark woods. Bree was engaging the giant cobra. Liv pulled out her sword and blurred off to assist her friend. I ran after her.

I reached the fight just as Bree's black, furred form dove off the back of the pissed off snake, which had now turned to strike at her. Bree nimbly slipped between two thick trees and a loud *crack* followed as the snake's head impacted one of the trunks. The cobra reared back and shook its head, as if trying to shake off the blow.

Another loud series of *cracks* resounded, and the impacted tree split and toppled to the ground with a huge crash. A cloud of dust and dirt filled the air around it.

I briefly worried that Bree might have been hit by the tree, but thankfully I spotted her aura flittering through the distant trees.

The giant snake hissed as Olivia streaked by and cut a long bloody gash in its side. The cobra's head darted towards Liv, but it missed, and it just got a mouthful of dirt for its trouble. Liv laughed and blurred off deeper into the woods.

I raised my hands to direct a large blast of lightning at the beast, but Stella's huge form stepped in front of me. She charged and delivered a massive blow to the end of the cobra's long serpentine form. The blow lifted a large back section of the snake and pushed it ten feet in front of her but didn't seem to do any damage. The snaked hissed and that same tail section came flying back in. It smacked into Stella and she went flying off into some trees.

With Stella clear, I aimed my hand to strike again, but this time it was Bree's dark form that stopped me. She came bounding in and landed on the creature's back, about midway down its body. Her front claws dug in and she began raking the scaled back with her hind claws.

The snake hissed as long bloody gashes appeared from Bree's savage attack. It reared up to strike, but at the last moment, Bree jumped off and disappeared into the trees again.

I finally had a clear shot and raised my hands. I cursed and lowered my arms as Liv's blood-red aura came zooming in down the snake's right flank. I couldn't see what damage she'd done as she was on the other side of the cobra but by the angry hiss it made, I figured she must have done some damage.

The snake had had enough and slithered off like it was on fire.

Damn, this thing could move, especially considering it had a belly full of druid and a bunch of injuries, I thought as it vanished into the darkened woods.

Stella's Hyde form came lumbering back, looking for another go at it. She stopped just in front of me and her head looked back and forth in confusion.

"That way!" I pointed, and she nodded and stomped off after it.

I sighed and began running after her and the snake. Ahead of me, Bree roared and chased after it. Liv's topless form blew by Stella and me like we were standing still.

As I ran, I opened up the comms and said, *"Blue, you still with us?"*

"Yes, just waiting for my moment…" was her instant reply.

I glanced over my shoulder and spotted a small rainbow aura darting through the trees behind us, which meant the last of my teammates was okay too.

Liv was way out in front of us now and I tracked her progress on my glasses. A loud series of curses rang out from up ahead and I noticed her path had suddenly taken a hard right and then stopped.

I grinned and opened a channel, *"You might want to watch out for that tail …"*

"Bite me!" she replied, adding, *"Mr. Slithers is starting to piss me off. I'm not only going to make snakeskin boots out of this thing but a whole freaking wardrobe, curtains, and a set of tea cozies to boot!"*

"And maybe a sturdy top that can't be ripped off..." I joked as I continued running.

The channel closed without a reply from Liv. If she had answered, it probably would have been a curt two-word reply.

After a good five minutes of running, I was starting to worry. This thing was making good ground, and while King's Forest was big, it wasn't that big. There were a ton of houses all around the outside of this place and if the snake got out into a residential neighborhood, a lot of people were going to get hurt.

It also dawned on me that I was barely winded. Blue's constant physical team training was paying dividends; not that I would tell her that. A run like this a year ago and I'd have been puking up a lung by now.

Liv got in a couple more sword strikes in this time before getting swatted again. The good thing was that while this thing was booking it, it was leaving behind a blood trail that was easy to follow.

And then, just like that, the trees cleared, and I was running down a fairway. We'd hit King's Forest Golf Course. With no more trees above me, I smiled to myself and called on my Air power to lift me. The snake was almost at the end of the fairway, so I poured on the speed. Bree was twenty yards behind it and Stella was a good hundred yards back. I overtook both of them and raised my arms to strike.

I let out a massive blast of pure white lightning from the charge I'd been building since this fight began. The cobra stopped in its tracks when the huge jolt of electricity hit, and it started twitching harder than a junkie in withdrawal.

I laid into it for a good five seconds before I cut the juice. I'd have liked to hit it longer, but in that short time, I'd probably drained more than half my reserves.

It continued twitching, and not a second later, Bree pounced on its back again. She tore into it. Liv came streaking in, too, and opened a large gash along its left side. Blue suddenly appeared out of the trees and ran in towards the stunned snake. She nimbly leapt up onto its back and then ran up its length. The cobra had just started to lift its head when Blue jumped up and came down with her flaming sword and buried it to the hilt in its reptilian brain. Blue jerked the sword forward and cut its entire head open lengthwise.

The massive cobra gave one last shudder and collapsed onto the green. Blue jumped off and hurried further down the dead snake's length. She stopped at the lump about a third of the way down its body and ignited her sword again. She made two swift cuts: one in front of the lump and one behind. She leaned in and pushed against the section she made. In a bloody mess, she rolled it away from the body. Stella's Hyde form caught up and she immediately leaned in and grabbed the section Blue had made. She lifted one end and shook it until the druid's body fell out. Blue leaned in and put her fingers to the druid's neck, looking for a pulse. To no one's surprise, she shook her head; the druid was dead.

I used my goggles to call the Hamilton police and let them know where we were and what happened. I ended the call and had Blue portal us back to the house to grab some road flares. When Blue opened a portal, Liv's topless form blurred in first with Bree's furred body just behind her. Blue was about to step forward when Alteea flew by and said, "I'll send you the video, Master. Bye!" and disappeared after them. Blue then entered the portal.

I made another call to Dave and told him what had happened. He'd been waiting in his car in case I needed him for something. I heard him yawn and told him to get some sleep. I wished him a good night and ended the call.

Stella's crisp British accent cut the air behind me, "So, what is the bounty on a giant cobra worth?"

I looked over at our fallen foe and shrugged, "No idea, but by its size and the damage it could have caused, I'm thinking six figures at least ..."

Blue reappeared, and after we laid down flares around the snake so the authorities could find us, I sent both of them home to get some sleep.

Blue opened a portal and said, "Call me when you are done."

I shook my head and said, "I'll fly home or get someone to drive me. You and Stella get some sleep."

She nodded and they disappeared into the shadows.

Thirty minutes later, EIRT arrived on scene. I spotted Bobby Knight's large form emerge from one of the SUVs.

He walked over and joined me and Hamilton's finest. He glanced over to the cobra's head, which was currently leaking poison over the green, destroying more of it by the second, and said, "You keep ruining golf courses like this, and you are going to have trouble getting a membership anywhere …"

I laughed and said, "At least this time it was only one hole and not two. Maybe the next time, I'll only destroy a porta-potty on the back nine or something."

I was pleased to see it was the same mage from last time on Bobby's team. I told him about the altar and showed on Google Maps where it was. He thanked me and said he'd go check it out to see if it matched the one from the other night. He and two EIRT officers jumped in the second SUV and pulled out.

I spent the next hour giving Bobby and the Hamilton police my statement. I sent a copy of Alteea's video to them as well. Near the end, the mage called Bobby and confirmed the magic signature at the altar was the same one use for the stone golem. After I finished recounting what happened, Bobby wrote me up two bounty tickets: one for the druid, and one for the giant snake. Both of which would make a nice addition to our bottom line.

I said goodbye to Bobby and his team and then took to the air. I was going to head home but changed my mind and decided to do a couple of circles around King's Forest to see if I could spot that silver aura again.

Twenty minutes later, after having no luck, I turned towards home. The latest sighting of silver had convinced me that something was going on. I vowed to take another shot at more research tomorrow. This time I'd hit it from a different angle and look for odd or unexplained things that had happened locally. It was time to get to the bottom of this.

Alteea's Nutty Adventure

Saturday, June 9

Alteea

*G*reat hairy troll's balls, what's that infernal racket? I sat up in the bed and stretched out my wings. I yawned as I leaned over and hit the home button on my iPhone to check the time. The darkness of my dollhouse lit up with the brightness of the screen: 6:32 a.m.

Another series of loud clanks sounded, just like the ones that had woken me. It went silent for a few moments, and then the din started up again.

Who could be doing this? My Mistress and the beast lady went to bed when I did, so they were out. Master Zack was never up this early. The only people left were Mistresses Stella and Blue and they were too civilized to make this much noise at this hour of the morning.

Maybe the house was under attack? I fluttered up from my bed and flew out the window of my sanctuary. The basement was dark, but I flew up the stairs to the main level with no issues.

The clanking noise happened again so I followed the sound to the far wall of the house. I spied a note as I flew over the kitchen counter that said Stella and Blue were at the lab, which ruled them out. The noise stopped when I reached the far wall.

I hovered and listened for any signs of intruders. I heard the metallic sound again, just on the other side of this wall. Whatever was going on was outside. I debated waking Master Zack, but he isn't pleasant at this hour and I didn't wish to rouse his anger if this turned out to be nothing. I would investigate it first.

I zipped back to the basement and headed for my escape hatch. Living in this enclosed structure was nice as I didn't have to worry about raccoons, coyotes, or other predators looking for a pixie snack, but it also made me feel trapped. One of the first things I did when I came to live here was build an emergency exit. I opened the small hatch I'd built into the vent pipe to the outside and slipped inside. I barely had enough room to fly but managed it. At the end of the pipe was a mesh screen to stop things from getting in. I undid the small wire holding it closed and pulled it open.

I engaged my glamor and emerged out in the sunshine to what was an already hot day. I took a moment to let the sun caress my skin. I loved spending my time with Mistress Liv, but I also missed the sun and being outdoors like this.

The clanking noise happened again and reminded me of my duties to protect the house, so I flew higher to see what was going on. I rose above the house and did a slow leisurely circle, trying to find the source of the attack. There were no humans or other dangerous large creatures to be seen. I wondered if the attackers had glamor too.

I spotted a squirrel in the large walnut tree beside the house. He shook the branch he was on and a couple of undersized walnuts fell off. They hit the roof, rolled into the eaves trough, and then went down the drain spout with a series of clanks. At the bottom of the spout there was a growing collection of walnuts piling up.

This wasn't an attack, just a stupid tree-rat collecting nuts. This rodent was the reason for my sleep being interrupted. My anger grew, and I launched a huge fireball that was almost as big as I was at the black-furred devil. He squeaked in fear but nimbly leaped for the thick trunk of the tree. He skittered down the trunk at top speed, jumped onto the fence, and fled for the end of the yard. He hopped from the fence into the tree at the back of the garden and scrambled up it.

I rubbed my hands together in satisfaction at a problem solved. I dropped my glamor to show the tree-rat who had bested him and threw him a salute. He brought up his large fluffy tail and shook it at me in disapproval. Worse, he chittered angrily at me.

The nerve of him swearing at me like that. He was lucky I let him live.

"Stop swearing at me, or I will make a coat out of you!" I yelled at him.

His tail motions became more intense and his squawks of rage got louder.

I could not let this insult stand; I would teach this impudent squirrel to respect my authority!

I launched another fireball at him but missed. He didn't even flee this time and just kept up his tirade at me. I let out my fiercest pixie war cry and charged. His beady eyes widened as I flew like a rocket towards him and he fled.

Too late for that, my furry friend— the hunt was on!

He darted down the tree, hopped the fence, and tried to disappear into the woods behind the house, but I had him in my sights as I flew through the branches in hot pursuit. With each second, I was gaining on him as he frantically leapt from branch to branch, trying to avoid my wrath. I had his scent now and this battle would only end when one of us was dead.

I dove towards him with my claws and fangs leading the way. He dodged left at the very last moment and I barely pulled out of my dive in time to avoid the tree trunk.

I was gracious enough to mentally give him the first point of this match for his quick reflexes. I looped around, and by reflex, engaged my glamor when I spotted a coyote skulking through the wooded trail beneath me. My heart beat faster at memories of my old swarm members that had been lost to coyotes over the years. They were a cunning and dangerous predator.

A retreat to the safety of the house would be the logical move, but, alas, the passion of the hunt consumed me. As long as our battle stayed in the treetops, the coyote couldn't interfere.

The coyote looked up at the sound of the squirrel tearing along branches, but to my relief, he quickly lost interest and continued on his way.

I dodged over and around branches at speeds that only the bravest of pixies would dare and soon closed in again on the tree-rat. I swooped down on him like a hawk, but just before my claws could sink into his flesh, he batted his tail at me. The thick fur blinded me and knocked me off target. I overshot my lucky opponent.

He chittered at me as I flew by and he leapt for a branch that led in the opposite direction of my flight path. I grudgingly awarded him another point for his tail maneuvers—this truly was a worthy opponent.

I looped around and resumed my hunt. I closed in again, but this time stayed parallel with him before swooping in sideways and keeping a wary eye on his tail.

He squealed in despair as my claws found purchase in the flesh on his flank. He stumbled, and we tumbled along the branch until we slammed into the trunk. My head smacked against the solid bark of the walnut tree and in my daze, I lost my grip on him. The squirrel leapt away as I got to my feet. I shook my head and wings and checked myself for injuries. I was intact.

There was blood on my claws that I happily licked clean. I called the encounter a draw as I had drawn blood, but he had shaken me off and gotten away.

I took to the skies again and zoomed after my quarry. I could smell his fear now as I closed again. He leapt, darted, and dodged like he was possessed, but I stayed with him. He led me through the treetops and the chase continued.

After a good two minutes of him narrowly evading me, and me barely avoiding trees and branches, he made his final mistake. He leapt from the trees onto the roof of one our neighbors. I swooped down on him. I sank my claws deep into him and he stumbled again. I buried my fangs in his neck and drank deeply as we rolled along the rough black-tiled roof.

We slid to a stop, mere inches from the edge of the roof. He gave out a soft muted cry, and with that, the battle was over.

I made a small offering to the goddess of the woods while keeping a wary eye out for large birds of prey looking to steal my kill. I happily filled myself on his blood. With my adrenaline pumping, I knew sleep today would be long in coming. That was good as I now had hours of work ahead of me.

It was mid-morning before I was done and back in my now-quiet bed. As I lay down on my new soft, black-furred blanket, I wrapped my arm around the comforting fluffy tail and decided it was all worth it.

A Witch's Yarn

Saturday, June 9

Blue

Our new training facility was taking shape. The entire structure was modular, consisting of thirty-two cube sections. We could quickly reconfigure it from a one-story structure to a two-story or even three-story structure. It could be setup to mimic a residential house, or a commercial structure like a bank or warehouse in less than fifteen minutes.

I was still disappointed that the traps were designed to be non-lethal, but I suppose Stella had a point. The traps would sting or be messy, which would drive home the training lesson for Zack and the others. There was a small part of me that was anxious to see the results and their reactions to them.

While the structure was built, we still had to build and design the traps themselves. I could tell by Stella's expression as she frantically sketched out and revised her drawings that she was in her element. I had no doubt this was the part of the project she was most excited about.

While Stella would accept my help, I always got the impression that she was happier doing the designs herself. She was much better at this than I was, so leaving it in her capable hands seemed to be the most logical course of action.

I would, however, keep her company while she proceeded in her endeavors. I found my needlepoint and lost myself in it. I'd barely started when I realized I lacked adequate supplies to complete my current project. A trip to the local merchant would solve this.

I announced my intentions to procure more supplies to Stella and was amused that she was so engrossed in her designs that she barely acknowledged me.

I opened a portal, engaged my old man hologram ruse, and stepped through. I emerged into an empty alley behind the Sheered Sheep Wool Emporium.

This Canadian summer weather was pleasing. The warmth and humidity reminded me of the jungles near my village back on my lost home world. I shook my head and forced myself not to dwell on what was gone and focused back on the task at hand.

A cheery bell rang as I entered the shop. The shop's layout was cramped and crowded with its wares, but I always enjoyed the experience of shopping here. There were so many wonderful treasures to be found tucked away here and there. The elderly matron proprietor greeted me, and I returned her friendly greeting as protocol required.

I fought my instinct to be as efficient as possible and leisurely browsed the many items available. I had to hand it to humans that their commerce system and the vast selection of goods available were far superior to anything I had back home. We were lucky to get four merchant caravans come through a cycle and their range of wares was always limited. I did miss haggling though.

I chided myself as I glanced down at my overflowing basket for picking up more than required, but thanks to the plethora of bounties we'd taken in this past week, I could afford to splurge a little. I joined the small line and waited.

I was just about to step forward when an older lady cut in front of me. This jumping the queue was one of those human traits that displeased me. Back home, no one would dare do this for fear of giving insult and starting a duel of satisfaction.

I wasn't about to let this stand. "Excuse me, ma'am, I believe I was next in line."

The lady turned to me and said, "Do you know who I am?"

I will blame my poor manners on what followed on spending too much time with Zack; I was more direct than what was required, "Yes, someone who is rude and doesn't understand the simple concept of a queue."

The expression of concern and fear on the attendant's face was odd and she said, "Penelope, please I beg ..."

The rude lady, Penelope, held up her hand to silence the merchant and made an exaggerated gesture that I should proceed. I nodded in satisfaction and stepped forward. I completed my transaction and took my purchases with me.

When I was heading for the exit, I stepped aside to let a young woman pass through the narrow aisle. She had dark hair and tanned skin, but it was her clothes that caught my attention. The knee-length dress she was wearing was obviously handcrafted from animal hide. The beadwork that formed the shape of an elk was extraordinary. Even her moccasins were impressive with their sturdy construction and the beadwork accents. I hoped that this was a new trend on this planet; anything would be an improvement over the soulless garb Bree and Olivia usually wore.

I flashed back to my time as a young girl, working with my mother and our extended family as we all sewed our formal outfits for the God-King festival. The beadwork reminded me of my aunt's handiwork. I remembered pleading with my aunt to add some to my dress and the joy I had when she was finished with it.

The well-dressed young lady thanked me as she passed, and I gave her a smile and nod.

As I reached the door, I caught a low murmur behind me, and my body tingled for a brief moment. I looked over my shoulder, but nothing seemed out of the ordinary. I shrugged and left the store.

I ducked behind the store again. I glanced around to make sure I was alone and opened another shadow portal.

Stella was still hunched over the workbench sketching away when I returned. I waved to her and she gave me a smile and a quick wave before returning to her work. I retired to my room and unpacked my bags.

I returned to the lab and went to offer Stella a tea but all that came out was, "EE-AHH!"

Stella looked up from her work and giggled.

I opened my mouth again and the same braying donkey sound came out.

"My goodness, Blue, what has gotten into you?"

I tried to answer her but got another, "EE-AHH!" for my efforts.

Stella frowned and said, "Knock it off, Blue. This isn't funny anymore."

My mind raced as I tried to figure out what was going on. A memory of the elderly priestess from my childhood village came to me. She used to hex children with something like this when they were disrespectful to their elders. My encounter with Penelope at the Sheered Sheep came rushing back. I'd felt something odd when I left the store; she must have cast this on me.

"Blue! Blue?" called Stella.

I joined Stella at the workbench, flipped over the plan she'd been working on, and took her pencil from her. I wrote, *Cannot speak. I may have been hexed by a witch.*

Stella's eyes widened, and she asked, "What are we going to do?"

Rather than write anything down, I pulled my Keetiyatomi blade from its sheath and ignited it. The witch assaulted me, so it was time to burn the witch.

"No, we aren't burning witches!" said Stella with disapproval.

I shook my head firmly at her and waved my sword back and forth to argue my point.

"Do you know who did this?" she asked.

I nodded. I put away my sword and picked up the pencil. I wrote *Penelope, customer at Sheered Sheep.*

Stella read my note, "Do you know her last name?" I shook my head and she added, "Okay, we'll go to the store and see if we can get a last name. Once we have that, we can track her down and get this resolved."

Oh, we'd get this resolved alright—killing the witch would break this spell.

"We'll get it resolved, *peacefully*, understand?" said Stella firmly.

My short but wise companion knew me too well. For this affront to my honor, the witch deserved to die, but this wasn't home. The laws of this land didn't account for honor like they did in my old world. I also knew killing the witch would upset Stella and I didn't want that. I sighed, which also came out as a loud braying noise, and with clenched teeth, I nodded in agreement.

Stella smothered a giggled as I glared at her.

"Sorry. Let's go find that witch."

I turned on my old man disguise and opened a portal.

We waited by the entrance to the store until the last customer left. As we entered, I flipped the lock on the door and turned the sign to 'Closed.' We approached the front cash and the owner looked up. She smiled as she saw me and said, "Mr. Moon, you've returned. Did you forget something on your last trip? And who is this little angel?"

Stella's young form always seemed to garner that sort of comment.

"I'm Stella. My grandfather has been hexed and I'm hoping you can help us."

A look of concern flashed across the lady's face for a moment, but she covered it quickly. "That is awful but this is a wool shop. There's a magic shop two blocks from here, maybe they can help you."

"He was hexed by Penelope, and we would like her last name and a home address if you have it."

"I-I-I can't help you. Please leave," the lady stammered.

Her expression and body language radiated fear now.

Stella sighed and said, "I'm sorry, you were under the mistaken impression we were asking …"

Stella gave me a nod and I hit the button on my wrist to deactivate the hologram. I flashed the merchant a toothy grin and Stella transformed into her Hyde form.

The owner's eyes went wide, and she started to tremble visibly. Stella returned to her human form and added, "Your witch picked the wrong alien to mess with. Now give us a last name and we'll be on our way."

"P-p-please, she will do horrible things to me," pleaded the owner.

Stella's young face set itself in a determined look. "She isn't here now, and we are. Give us the name or sheep won't be the only thing sheered in here!"

The owner's resistance crumbled. Her shoulders slumped and she said, "Whiterose, Penelope Whiterose. I don't have her address, I swear. She lives somewhere nearby, but I don't know where. All I have is a phone number for her."

The older matron wrote the number on a piece of paper with shaking hands and handed it to Stella.

Stella gave her a nod and said, "Thank you. Do not call her and warn her or we'll be back."

I hit the button on my wrist and turned the old man disguise back on and we left the store.

From behind the Sheered Sheep, I pulled out my phone and did a search for Penelope Whiterose's address. There were two P. Whiteroses listed in Hamilton. One was on the mountain and the other was an address that was three blocks away. The closer one matched the phone number that Stella had been given. I used the shadows to spy on it. I smiled as I found the witch in her living room doing paperwork.

I opened the note app on my phone and typed, *Found her. Do we knock or portal into the house?*

"Let's call Zack and get him and Bree to come along too."

I shook my head. I'd thus far not become a target for Zack's humor and wanted to keep it that way. If he found out about my current condition, he would be unbearable.

No. Just us. If the two of us couldn't handle one old witch, then we deserved whatever happened to us.

Stella looked like she wanted to argue but just nodded and said, "Shadow portal. If we knock, she may have traps and spells guarding the door."

I approved of Stella's choice and agreed with her tactical reasoning. I opened a portal and stepped through with Stella right behind me. The witch looked up in surprise at our sudden appearance in her living room. While she was my enemy, I did approve at the tasteful décor of her humble home. It was done in what I believe was called a country theme. The pine floors and bright wallpaper gave the place a warm, homey feel.

"You!" exclaimed the witch at seeing me.

"We don't want trouble, just undo the spell you cast on Blue and we'll be on our way."

"Hush child," said the witch and made a gesture with her hand.

Stella opened her mouth to argue but no words came out. We'd tried it Stella's way, but now it was my turn. I hit the button on my bracelet and dropped my disguise. The witch's eyes widened at my true form.

I drew my sword but before I could ignite it, the witch said, "Freezium!" and gestured at us both.

I suddenly couldn't move. Stella seemed to be locked into place as well.

The witch smiled but it wasn't a comforting gesture. "You weren't what you appeared to be but no matter, you have brought me a tasty child. I haven't had one of those since the old country. I've never had alien before but I'm sure you will be delicious with a little seasoning."

She left the room. I tried everything I could to escape the hold of the spell, but nothing worked. I could sense the energy around me but any attempt to push or move against it failed.

The witch reappeared carrying a wicked and obviously well-used butcher's knife and I will admit at that moment, I regretted not heeding Stella's earlier advice about bringing Zack and Bree along too.

Spells were a matter of willpower and there was no way this old crone had more willpower than I did.

She stepped closer to Stella and licked her lips in anticipation.

I focused on the Keetiyatomi blade and willed it to ignite. The blade was magic and if I could get it to flame, I was sure it would break the spell.

The witch placed the blade against Stella's left hand and said, "I have a lovely recipe for you, little one, but I can't resist a quick taste first.

NO! I silently screamed in my head and poured my rage into the blade. I smiled as the flames danced along the metal of the blade and I was free.

"Impossible!" cried the witch as she scampered back from us.

On a hunch, I tapped Stella briefly with the blade and she cried out for a moment and then transformed into her Hyde form.

While I'd been freeing Stella, I'd heard steps retreating along the wooden floor. I turned to see the witch running up the stairs at full speed.

It was time for my original plan—burn the witch! I dashed after the hag and found the staircase to her upper floor barred with thorny vines. I slashed with my sword and the vines withered and died. I sprinted up the pine stairs with my sword in front of me for protection. Stella lumbered behind me.

A door slammed as I reached the top of the staircase. I turned down the hall towards the closed door. I heard chanting coming from the other side of the door and increased my pace. Whatever spell she was casting, I didn't want to give her time to complete it.

I cleaved the door into pieces and the chanting stopped. The witch lifted a gnarled branch and small wooden darts fired out of it. Time seemed to slow down as it always did in combat for me. I intercepted all of the darts with my Keetiyatomi blade. The darts turned to ash and were gone. I wrinkled my nose at the acrid smell and realized that the darts had been poisoned.

I kept moving forward, not giving the witch another chance to cast anything else.

"No! Please!" she cried as my flaming blade descended for her neck.

My aim was true, and I separated her head from her shoulders. The head hit the floor with a heavy thump. I remembered Zack's lecture that a witch's power was in her heart. I brought the blade in one more time and buried it deep into her chest. A blue flash briefly filled the room.

The body rapidly decayed and then turned to dust before my eyes. The immaculate country interior faded, becoming old and worn. The floral curtains in front of me disappeared, and the window behind them became boarded up and covered with graffiti. The lovely throw rug and the pine floor disappeared and were replaced by old cracked linoleum tiles that might have started life as white or cream but were now a sickly yellow color. The jars of herbs and spell components just faded away.

There was a loud crash behind me followed by an annoyed grunt. I ran from the room and spied a large hole where the staircase used to be. I looked over the now broken and bent railing and spotted Stella's Hyde form getting to its feet in the basement and angrily dusting herself off.

The once pretty house had turned into an abandoned and decaying wreck. All traces of the witch were gone.

"Stella, are you alright?" I yelled down. I smiled as I realized I could talk again.

She nodded her big, beautiful misshapen head and started to climb out of the basement. The whole house trembled at this.

"Stop! I will come down to you."

I used the shadows to transport myself to the basement. Stella changed back to her human form and said with a smile, "I thought we agreed no burning witches?"

"Technically I beheaded and stabbed her so there was no burning …"

At that moment, a door creaked open. I turned towards the noise and brought my sword up but then lowered it. Inside the old furnace room were two adult-sized skeletons lying against an ancient broken furnace. Stella gasped at the sight and said, "You should have burned her."

I nodded in full agreement. I guessed the two bodies were the house's original owners, probably killed when the witch moved in and took over.

Stella asked, "Do we call the authorities?"

I thought about it. I wasn't sure if we were legally justified in assaulting her in her home. She admitted she'd killed and eaten children before, but it would just be our word for it. Her body had turned to ash and disappeared, so we didn't even have proof she had even been here. It was just us and two dead bodies.

In the end, I shook my head and said, "No. We were never here …"

Stella gave me a surprised look at this and asked, "What about those two?"

"Five minutes ago, this was a beautiful and well-maintained house on a quiet street. If the outside matches what has happened to the inside, I'm sure the authorities will be called in shortly to investigate what happened."

Stella nodded. A mischievous grin appeared on her young face and she said, "EE-AHH!" and then laughed and added, "Okay, let's go home."

A Senior's Moment

Saturday, June 9

Zack

I found Stella and Blue's note on the counter when I got up. They would be at the lab all day and told me to call or text if they were needed. It also reminded me to file the bounty claim for the druid and the giant snake.

I guess after I made Stella and Blue file all those zombie claims last week, the least I could do was file this one. I made myself a coffee and retired to my office.

After filling the claims, it was time to get to the bottom of the silver aura mystery. I texted Bobby at EIRT and asked for any reports of odd or unexplained activity in the region for the last month. I did the same with my cop buddy Rob in case there was something at the local level.

With that done, I opened my browser and started doing searches for odd happenings in the area.

A couple of hours later, my phone buzzed on the desk. I glanced at the display and saw 'M. Smith.' I always found Marion's last name amusing and kidded her that it was an alias she used to hide from the feds due to some illegal protest she'd been a part of in the seventies.

As soon as I answered, I knew something was going on by the alarm droning non-stop in the background and asked if she was okay.

"I'm fine. I'm at Sherman Heights Retirement Village visiting Patty. We are hiding in her room from one of the other tenants who is firing lightning from his room. He keeps yelling about agents of the Kaiser and demanding that Albert, his apprentice, attend to him."

I recalled Patty was an old friend of Marion's and they used to protest together. Marion had joked that the two of them had burned so many bras together that they kept Wonderbra in business. That had been way more information than I needed.

Patty had dementia and was a resident at the retirement home on a secure floor. If the guy tossing lightning about was on the same floor, then he probably had dementia too. My first thought was that he was an Elemental like myself, but when Marion mentioned apprentice, a mage was a better fit. What didn't make sense was *how* he was tossing lightning about. Any Enhanced Individual who had something like dementia would have been fitted with a power-blocking collar for their and other people's safety. Either he'd gotten it off somehow or it had failed.

Whatever was going on, Marion was in danger and I wasn't about to let that continue happening. "Stay in Patty's room, I'm on my way."

I ended the call, grabbed my phone and my keys, and headed out. The second I stepped outside, I regretted that I wore jeans today due to the heat. I was also grateful for the first time about being outed as the Hamilton Hurricane during the fallout from the Acolyte case; not having to wear my knitted black balaclava was a bonus on a day like this.

I barely had taken off when I spotted something odd. I hovered above my house and wondered why I had a dead squirrel head mounted on my back fence. I made a mental note to ask Liv, Bree, and Alteea about it and resumed my flight.

I had never been in Sherman Heights Retirement Village. I remembered when they broke ground on it a few years back. By the size of the lot, I'd guessed it was a good-sized grocery store or a school that was going in there. As the months went by, I was stunned at the rapid progress in construction. It seemed like every time I flew over it, another floor had been built. The signs were up by that point, so I knew it was going to be a retirement home. When it was completed, it was a massive ten stories tall. The sheer size and scope of the place was impressive.

The Kaiser comment came back to me. It likely meant that the mage had been a veteran in World War I or an even earlier conflict. Mages had extended life spans and if this one was in his final years, he could be well over 200 years old. Mages got more powerful as they got older but, like humans, their strength declined once they reached a certain point. Still, a mage with that much time and experience could be a dangerous opponent, even with his dementia. I wondered if I should call Blue and Stella for backup. I guessed his primary focus was Air due to the lightning he was tossing about. Being an Air Elemental, I'd be immune to or even get a boost from any of those types of attacks.

The problem was mages usually had secondary elements, and if he was proficient in Fire or Ice then things could get dicey.

I spotted the building and could hear the alarms as I approached. There were already four police cruisers parked out front. There were also a ton of confused and scared elderly residents and staff milling around outside the building. If the police were here, I had no doubt SWAT was on its way and probably EIRT was en route too. I figured they would be my backup and decided to let Stella and Blue continue working on their secret project.

Five minutes later, I was on the secured fourth floor with a couple of cops I knew and the manager of the residence. All the doors on this hallway were closed except for the one that had the mage inside of it. The mage's name was Allister St. Clair. The manager said that Mr. St. Clair been one of the first residents when they opened. He was generally no problem but, on occasion, could be rude or brisk with staff. There was an orderly just inside the room, lying unconscious on the floor after being hit by lightning. They tried to get him out, but every time anyone approached the room, he would shoot lightning at them. My first goal was to get the injured attendant out of there so he could get medical attention. Thankfully, Marion was in the building, so if I got him out, she'd fix him up in no time.

It was also confirmed that the mage was wearing a power-blocking collar but for whatever reason it didn't seem to be working. The manager gave me the release code for it, so I could take it off. I arranged for the SWAT team to drop off a new collar once they arrived. They would knock on the wall to let me know it was ready for me. Their ETA was ten minutes.

I was tempting to wait until SWAT arrived but with the unconscious attendant needing medical attention, I didn't have the luxury of waiting. I took a deep breath and approached the room. I'd barely stepped into the room when I heard a surprisingly strong voice say, 'Shazam!' and a bright flash almost blinded me. The lightning struck the center of my chest and my teeth almost vibrated with the energy coursing through my body. I hummed with so much power that I was shocked I didn't break out in dance and start singing, "Pardon me boy, is that the Chattanooga Choo Choo?"

It took me a second to realize the mage had started talking to me, "… there you are, Albert." I looked up from patting out the smoldering four-inch hole in the center of my T-shirt at the frail old man on the bed. He looked as though the slightest breeze could knock him over. His eyes, though, had a strength to them that belied his physical appearance.

He pointed at my shirt and said with an English accent, "Sorry about that, lad. A little soap and water, and I'm sure that stain will come right out."

I almost laughed at that. I could see my chest hair through the hole; there would be no saving this T-shirt.

"What is with the dungarees, Albert? Why aren't you in your apprentice robes?" he asked, sternly pointing at my jeans.

It hit me that he thought I was his apprentice. Since he wasn't tossing more spells at me, I figured that was a good sign and didn't want to correct his mistake. I decided to play along, "Same reason you aren't, sir—a robe makes one a target for German snipers."

"Quite right, lad, quite right."

I glanced down at the unconscious attendant and the mage said, "German agent here to poison me, but I dealt with him. The Huns will have to do better than that to take down Allister St. Clair!"

"He is still alive, sir. I will remove him, so the MPs can question him. There may be more of his kind lurking about, and with luck, he might give up his comrades."

The mage rubbed his chin and said, "Good idea, my boy, but hurry back; we have work to do!"

I was going to use my Air power to lift him but stopped myself. If I suddenly displayed power that Albert didn't have that might tip him off. I hooked my hands under the attendant's arms and dragged his heavy body along the carpet. Thankfully, the trip wasn't too far. Once I had him in the hallway and out of sight of the mage, two officers came forward and took him from me.

I sighed in relief that the attendant would get help and was sure that Marion would take care of him. I took a deep breath and braced myself for another lightning strike as I headed back to the room. Just as I was about to enter the room, the door to the stairway at the end of hall opened. I almost stumbled in surprise at the sight of the ancient Native man with a huge silver aura around him. It was the same guy I'd seen in Gore Park the other day. He touched his fingers to his head in a mock salute and closed the door.

At that moment I knew whoever or whatever he was had to be the silver aura I'd been seeing. I longed to chase after him and get some answers, but Allister was already raising his hands in my direction and I had to deal with him first. Allister lowered his hands when he recognized me or Albert and didn't cast the spell.

He frowned and asked why I wasn't in my robes. That comment made me take pity on the poor man's condition. Here was a veteran, and by his aura, a powerful mage, and yet dementia had destroyed his keen mind to the point he couldn't remember what he'd said less than two minutes ago.

I repeated my excuse about German snipers and got almost the same response from him as last time.

"At least their infernal artillery is quiet today. I do hope that means the Huns aren't planning something. We have to be ready, Albert, in case they launch another poison gas attack. We'll use our spells to deal with it and keep the lads in the trenches safe." He frowned and said, "This war with its gas, trenches, tanks, airplanes, and assassins is a nasty bit of work. I almost miss the days of trying to stop Napoleon from ravaging the continent ..."

Napoleon was alive during the early 1800s and by the math in my head, that made Allister over 200 years old, probably closer to 250. I was in awe of what this man had seen during his lifetime. When he was born, monarchies would have been the most common form of government, horses the main form of transportation, and the infant and child mortality rate would be almost unimaginable today. He'd seen royal dynasties that existed for hundreds of years fall. We'd gone from the horses of his youth to putting a man on the moon. Diseases that killed family and friends during his early years had been eliminated through modern medicine.

As a mage during that time, he would have been well regarded and sought after for his services by some of the highest members of society. He very well could have met and talked with people who shaped the world in the last couple of hundred years: Churchill, Victoria, Wellington, Nelson and Odin only knew who else.

Allister began talking about his day and getting to the canteen before it was picked clean or if the break in Hun artillery meant he'd finally get a quiet moment to catch up on his spell work. His eyes gleamed as he talked about the experiments he'd been working on involving increasing the oxygen in a target area to make lightning spells set off a fireball. He lost me when he went deeper and talked about containing the oxygen density in the target area to maximize the effect.

A knock on the wall interrupted his rant and let me know that the power-blocking collar was just outside the door. This is where things got tricky. I could easily manipulate the air around him to silence him and prevent him from casting any more spells. After that, I could call in a couple of officers to hold him while we swapped the collars, but with his frail condition, I was afraid he might get hurt in the process. The man was a mage and veteran and deserved better than that.

I decided to continue with my ruse, "That was the lab boys; they have a new magic stealth collar for you."

A puzzled expression appeared on Allister's wrinkled face, "Stealth collar? What is this nonsense you speak of, boy?"

I pointed at his neck and said, "The collar hides your magic abilities, so the Huns can't find you, sir. The old one you are wearing failed, hence the Hun agent earlier."

He touched the collar on his neck and seemed surprised to find it there. He frowned and asked, "Why aren't you wearing one then?"

"My magic isn't as strong as yours, and therefore the Huns can't detect me like they can you, sir."

He nodded and said, "Well, don't dawdle. Fetch me that new collar."

I ducked out of the room and found the collar just outside the door. There was an armed tactical team with Dave Shay at the lead just down the hall. I held up my hand to indicate they should stay where they were and then gave Dave what was hopefully a reassuring thumbs up.

I braced myself as I entered the room again. Allister once again raised his hands and mumbled something softly under his breath, but no big flash of lightning followed, so I took that as a good sign. He asked about the collar in my hand and I went over my story from earlier again.

He seemed wary but waved me forward to change the collars. I found myself strangely lightheaded, which was odd as I was humming with power just a moment ago. I took a few more steps and stumbled and barely managed to stay upright. A memory of training with my mother came to me and I knew what had happened. I checked the air around me and there was no oxygen left in it.

"Good try, Hun, you look like Albert, but he never calls me 'sir,' just 'Master,' like a proper apprentice should. If you have harmed him, I will make you pay!" said Allister in a grim and determined tone.

Unlike a mage, I didn't need to speak to access my powers. I called on my Air power moments before I would have blacked out and flooded the area about me with oxygen. I sucked in a lungful of air and felt my strength returning.

Allister gasped at me in surprise as he realized I'd circumvented his spell. He raised his hands at me, but I was quicker and dampened the air around him to silence him. He said something, but no sound came out. He frowned, and to my amusement, raised two fingers to flip me the bird, British style.

"Dave!" I yelled out, "In here now!"

Not five seconds later, Dave and his team charged in the door.

I held out the collar and said, "I have silenced the air around him to prevent him from casting spells. Can you put the collar on him? Please be gentle with him, okay?"

Dave nodded, took the collar, and had two member of his team secure Allister. I was pleased to see that both officers used as little force as possible.

A minute later, the new collar was in place and I turned off the field I'd put around the mage. He was confused now and asked, "Why are their constables in my room? Where is my nurse?"

Dave smiled at him and said, "Your nurse will be here shortly, Mr. St. Clair. We had an issue on the floor and we're just making sure everyone is alright."

I didn't want to upset Allister any more than he was already, so I turned to leave in case he still thought I was a Hun agent.

"Thanks for the visit, Albert," said Allister just as I was about to leave.

I smiled and said, "You're welcome, Master. See you again soon …"

I left the room and a nurse passed by me to go check on Allister. A couple of officers came up and thanked me for my help. I excused myself and ran for the stairwell. I opened the door but the deity I spotted earlier was long gone. I used my Air powers to fly down the stairs at an almost reckless pace. I landed when I reached the main level and dashed for the exit. The moment I was outside, I took to the air to get a better view. I circled around the building, hoping to see a flash of silver or to spot my mysterious visitor but cursed as I had no luck.

At least now I had more to go on than just a silver aura. It was time to bring the team up to speed and deal with this threat.

Saturday Night's Alright for Fighting

Saturday, June 9

That night, once Liv and Alteea were up and eating breakfast, I called a team meeting.

"I have some bad news," I said, glancing around the kitchen table. "I don't think this run of bounties is natural ..." I explained about my afternoon with Allister and seeing the old Native man with the large silver aura, which made him a member of the God class of Enhanced beings. I added that I'd also seen this same being at Gore Park during the ogress battle. I covered all the encounters where I'd seen a mysterious flash of silver.

As I was filling in the team, part of me realized how thin some of my evidence was and by the looks I was getting around the table, I wasn't the only one thinking this.

The moment I finished, Bree frowned and said, "Today was a definite sighting, but you did take a nasty hit to the head during that battle with the ogress in Gore Park. The others might just have been people taking photos, or hallucinations from blood lost. You did lose a lot of blood from that vampire attack. Even the one you saw today. You said it was an old man with a large silver aura. You were at a retirement home, what if he was just visiting a loved one? This god/demi-god might have had nothing to do with the mage's collar going on the fritz."

"Yeah, but, I'm telling you this run of bounties just seems too good to be true. I have been doing this for six years and never had a week anything like this."

Bree shrugged, "You were also on your own for those six years. Some of the bounties you weren't even involved in, like Emma at the Home Depot, or the Cultists, and those added to the totals. You said before that business has peaks and valleys, maybe this is just a remarkable peak."

Heads bobbed in agreement with Bree's comments. I had to admit that Bree brought up some good points. Maybe this was just a coincidence, but my gut was telling me something else. Bree bringing up the bounties I wasn't involved in brought another line of thought to mind, "You may be right but before I let this go, I want everyone here to think long and hard about the past week. Do you recall anything that seemed odd or out of place?"

Liv put down her pint of blood and said, "After the battle with the cultists, I headed back to the truck to get our clothes and phones. On the way, I almost ran into a coyote in the woods. The encounter bothered me as the coyote didn't smell right; it was too clean, like a Were would be. I didn't know there was such a thing as a Werecoyote."

"There isn't. Whatever you saw wasn't a Werecoyote, it was something else," I said. Liv bringing up the coyote reminded me of the fox with the silver glow around it on the Bruce Trail when we took on the golem. It had been dark, and foxes were more common than coyotes around here, so I'd assumed it was a fox, but it very well could have been a coyote. It also hit me that the silver glow around it might have been an aura. At the time, I hadn't even considered the glow was an aura due to its size, but now it fit. I told everyone my thoughts.

Blue suddenly perked up and said, "At the Home Depot when Emma lost control, as I was circling the building trying to find the epicenter of the disturbance, I saw a coyote run off into the distance. At the time, I thought it was odd being in the open like that in the middle of the afternoon, but as I had more pressing matters to deal with, I forgot about it."

Alteea fluttered her wings in excitement and said, "During my great squirrel battle today, I spotted a coyote in the woods out back, Master."

"Squirrel battle?" asked Liv with a half amused and half concerned grin.

Alteea spent the next couple of minutes regaling us about her warrior prowess. At the end, I asked about the squirrel head mounted on the fence out back.

Alteea lifted her tiny head proudly and said, "That is a warning to other tree-rats not to disturb my sleep."

"Okay, so we have had four coyote sightings as well." I turned to Bree and said, "And before you start, Bree, I know coyotes aren't uncommon to the area, but I have only ever seen two in my life ... and never one with a giant silver aura around it." Bree tipped her head at me to acknowledge the point. "Anything else odd that anyone can think of?"

The entire table, except for Bree, shook their heads. I raised an eyebrow at her, and she said, "When we were at Velvet Rope, as we were leaving, I saw a Native girl in a dated beaded dress. The beads made up a design of a deer."

I didn't think much of this. Fashion trends changed all the time, so maybe Native culture was becoming the next hot thing, but then Blue asked, "Could the beadwork have been an elk?"

Bree shrugged and said, "I guess, why?"

Blue gave Stella a sideways glance and Stella gave her a nod. "Today at my favorite yarn shop, I was hexed by a witch. As I was leaving the store, I also saw a Native girl in a beautiful hand-crafted dress that had an elk done in beadwork."

I frowned at what sounded like the same girl being at both places, but also about Blue being hexed by a witch, "Why is this the first time we are hearing about you being hexed?"

Blue went quiet for a moment and then said, "The witch has been dealt with, but we weren't sure about the legality of what happened, so Stella and I decided it was best if we pretended the whole incident never happened."

"Yeah, I'm going to need more details on that ..."

Blue nodded and went over the whole encounter. I wasn't pleased that that they took matters into their hands, but as the witch had admitted to eating children and was going to eat both my teammates, Blue dispatching her was probably best for all concerned. With the witch turned to ash, and no witnesses, there wouldn't have been a bounty on this anyways. They were also correct that their being at a site with two dead bodies would have been a legal hassle.

I decided to let the matter drop and focused on the issue at hand, "So we have an ancient Native man with a huge silver aura, flashes of silver which might or might not have been me spotting that same aura, four coyote sightings and a Native girl in a unique dress at two different locations all in this past week. This seems more than coincidence. I think we need to do some research."

Bree crossed her arms and said, "So you're thinking some Native god created all these Enhanceds that we've taken on out of thin air, just to test us or something?"

I shook my head, "No, creating creatures out of thin air is more God with a capital 'G' or the work of a pantheon of gods. I suspect that this god is using its influence to nudge them in our direction. Or push us towards them."

"Huh?" said Bree.

"Let's take your cultists as an example. Let's say they were based in Toronto. This creature/god/whatever knows they are going to perform the summoning ritual. He mentally nudges the priestess to think that she needs to find a more remote spot for the ritual and plants the image of your woods in her head. He also puts an urge into one of you to go hunting, knowing that there is a good chance you will bump into the cult. Or the rapkey portal, maybe it was supposed to open in the Black Forest in Germany, but he uses his powers to mess with its location and it ends up opening in Dundas instead. Or the Siren, it might have been living in Lake Erie for years, just eating fish, but our god starts mentally urging the Siren's craving for human flesh. Does that make more sense?"

Liv got excited and said, "I thought it was the Boom Brothers' blood that was making me restless, but that night I did have an overwhelming urge to get out of the house."

The table went quiet for a few moments and Blue asked, "Let's say you are right, and this god is manipulating things towards us; is that such a bad thing? The bounties we have taken in this last week have been quite lucrative …"

It scared me sometimes at how mercenary Blue could be at times. I'd admit she had a point and that we'd made some really good money, but that didn't make up for the number of people that had been hurt or killed by these encounters. I was disappointed to see a couple of my teammates nodding in agreement with Blue.

"An eighteen-year-old lost his life thanks to that Siren, and the four golfers that were killed and the three people the rogue vampires killed in downtown Hamilton, not to mention the cultist, the witch, and the druid, though with those three, I have much less sympathy. Now those aren't our fault, but if we don't do anything about this god and more people die, that is on us." The expressions around the table became serious and remorseful but I wanted to point out one more thing before I was done, "These Enhanceds that we've been dealing with are dangerous. I was almost killed this week. I also really don't like reacting to these events. Our business model is to find a bounty on the UN website, research the target's abilities, locate it, and take it down at a time and place of our choosing. That method is the safest way and hopefully lessens the chance of any of us getting hurt or killed."

I was pleased to see nods of agreement around the table and was just about to bring us back to researching this godling when my iPhone buzzed.

My eyes widened at the name on the display; I didn't get calls from the Hamilton chief of police on a regular basis.

He got right to it, "We have a problem. The upstate New York chapter of the Moon Ghosts is spending the night at a motel on Upper James. They are currently drinking at a bar near the motel and the staff and patrons are concerned. We've put in a call to EIRT, but as the Moon Ghosts aren't breaking any laws, they aren't willing to send a team out."

I mentally groaned at this. The Moon Ghosts were a Werewolf outlaw biker gang. I immediately had two big concerns, "Do the Misfits or the Six Nations pack know they are here?"

"Not yet, but it is only a matter of time. If either of those groups does learn about the Moon Ghosts being here, it's going to get ugly fast."

The Misfits were Hamilton's own criminal biker gang. Their members included a wide range of Enhanceds such as Weres, vampires, warlocks, Elementals, and even fae. They claimed the city as theirs and would respond in force if they learned about the Moon Ghosts being here. The Six Nations pack also claimed Hamilton as part of their territory and wouldn't be amused about another group of Weres showing up.

"Why are they in town anyways?" I asked.

"When they crossed the border in Niagara, they told customs that they were heading to Windsor for a national club meeting. Windsor is currently getting dumped with a ton of rain from remnants of that hurricane that came up from the Gulf. I'm guessing they didn't want to ride in that at night and pulled in here to wait the storm out."

My earlier thoughts about the god and his supernatural nudges influencing events came flooding back. It would have been trivial for the god to delay their start. A small mechanical issue would be enough to cause the gang to stop in Hamilton instead of Windsor for the night.

"Chief, I don't mean to be disrespectful here, but I agree with EIRT that they haven't broken any laws, so I'm not sure what you want me to do?"

"I was hoping that you and your team would pay them a visit and convince them to leave. Look, I know that isn't your job, so I'm willing to authorize a $30,000 service fee if you can make them move on."

I was a bit shocked at the money. The Hamilton police department didn't usually splash around that sort of cash, but the chief was indirectly saving the city money; if the Misfits or Six Nations pack intervened, the damage would make that $30,000 seem like nothing.

I sensed the chief was a little desperate too, so I decided to have a bit of fun, "We'll do it, but for $30,000, and you'll enroll Sergeant Murdock in anger management classes."

SWAT Sergeant Murdock was always a pain in my ass, and I knew he'd hate those classes. I figured the chief wouldn't let him know it was me that did this, so I made a mental note next time I saw him to drop a large hint that I was the reason he got stuck in those classes.

The chief smothered his laugh with a sharp cough and said, "Deal."

I ended the call shortly after that. Liv and Bree had perked up during the call, and thanks to their enhanced hearing they'd heard every word. I went over the details of the call with the rest of the team. Stella and Blue grinned at the news but Alteea wasn't as impressed.

"A whole pack of beasts!" said Alteea with a shudder. Her eyes widened as she realized what she had said. She turned to Bree and quickly added, "No offence, Mistress." Bree grinned and made a wave of dismissal and Alteea pleaded, "Can I stay home?"

"Of course, you can, little one," said Liv.

Stella frowned and said, "How do you plan on getting them to leave?"

I just smiled and said, "I have a plan ..."

A chorus of groans came from my team. Bree stood up and peeled off the top she was wearing, exposing the plain white sports bra underneath. The table went quiet as everyone looked at her in surprise.

"What?" snapped Bree. "If he is coming up with the plan, then it probably involves me getting naked in front of a group of leering bikers, or topless Jell-O or mud wrestling or some other perverted thing ... I'm getting changed into my Were form here," she paused her rant and looked at me and added, "so, if that was your plan, you'll have to come up with a new one, quickly."

I covered my heart theatrically with my hand and gave her my best 'you wound me' look. Bree snorted at that and rolled her eyes.

I laughed and left the table. I headed upstairs to my office safe as I needed cash for my plan to work. It hit me that Bree had been extra confrontational this evening. From playing devil's advocate about my theory that a godling was messing with us to just now. I grinned as I pulled the money from the safe; Bree being extra aggressive worked nicely into my plan …

***

Ten minutes later, we were standing in front of Joe's Sports Bar on Upper James. I guessed the ten Harleys lined up in a row might have had something to do with the otherwise deserted parking lot. We didn't help with the empty parking lot either. A Ford pickup pulled in just after we arrived. After the driver saw Bree's snarling Werepanther form and Blue with her flaming sword out, he peeled out of there like he was on fire. It was a good thing that Stella was still in her little girl form or that poor driver might have been cleaning his underpants.

"So, what is the plan?" asked Liv.

I just smiled and said, "You'll see."

I spied one of the bikers near the window of the bar and I could see our appearance had caught his attention, but he hadn't reacted yet. For my plan to work, I needed to get them out of the bar, and I eyed the motorcycles and was tempted to mess with them in some way but dismissed that idea. Outlaw bikers were aggressive and protective about their rides, doubly so for Were bikers. The Were part of that last thought gave me an idea, so I turned to Bree and said, "Bree, I need those bikers out here. Growl loud enough to get their attention."

Bree nodded her furry head and then took a deep breath before releasing a growl that echoed impressively in the night sky.

Not twenty seconds later, the bikers poured out of the bar. They stopped about twenty feet from us and Bree locked eyes with the group. All the bikers except for the red-haired one with the long beard almost instantly lowered their eyes. The redhead easily had the largest aura of the group, which marked him as the Alpha. Bree and he locked in a silent test of wills for a long thirty seconds before he lowered his eyes with a growl.

Point for our Were-panther, I thought. The group was made up of ten men and two women and all of them, judging by their auras, were Werewolves. Seeing this group in their leathers, I thought the lack of tattoos was odd. Weres usually couldn't get tattoos. Well, they could get tattoos, but the only way to make them last involved silver needles and spells—a painful and expensive process, which made the redhead's forearm Moon Ghost tattoo that much more impressive. Anyone who was willing to sit through that wasn't someone I was going to take lightly.

The Alpha spoke first, "What do you want?"

"We have been contracted by the local police to ask you to move on …"

"We ain't going anywhere, and haven't broken any laws, *yet*."

The sheer menace he put on that 'yet' was remarkable and a bit disconcerting. "I don't blame you for not wanting to leave; riding in a downpour can't be fun. The problem is our local biker gang and local pack will find out you're here and things will get ugly …"

He cracked his knuckles and said, "Our colors don't run—if they find out we are here, we are happy to entertain them."

The group of Weres growled and laughed in agreement.

"I was afraid you were going to say something like that. So, how about a friendly wager?" I asked as I pulled the thick stack of hundreds from my pocket.

The groans from my own team at this didn't exactly boost my ego.

The Alpha, though, was instantly intrigued, "And what are the terms of the wager?"

"Three fights. You pick your three fighters and I'll even allow you to pick which three of my team they'll go against. First to win two fights takes all. We win, you leave. You win, you get the $10,000 and we leave."

The hard-looking dark haired woman on his right leaned in and said, "Easy money, boss."

The Alpha slowly looked us over. He scratched his chin through his thick beard and said, "A bit too easy … the vamp is carrying a silver sword and the blue alien chick's flaming sword has me concerned."

The woman argued, "So we don't pick them. I can take the Were-kitty. Anyone here can take the little girl and the Elemental looks soft."

I frowned at that last part, but all the Werewolf men were much bigger than I was, so I wasn't about to argue.

The Alpha eyed me and asked, "The fights to the death?"

I shook my head and said, "Friendly wager, remember? Unconscious or tap out."

He nodded and said, "I'll take your wager—on one condition. If I pick you, you can't use your Air power to fly during the fight."

It took everything I had not to smile at that. I tried to look concerned at his terms, "And if I don't agree to that?"

"Then we go back inside and enjoy our food."

I went quiet for a good five seconds. The Alpha grinned as he watched me seem to struggle with this and said, "So Elemental, do we have a deal?"

I paused for another few seconds and softly said, "Deal."

"Johnny, you're up first. You get the little girl," said the Alpha.

The biggest guy in the pack stepped forward and frowned, "Boss, I don't want to fight a little girl …"

A tough-looking blonde woman snarled and pushed the big man out of the way, "I'll do it. For $10,000, I'll kick anyone's ass."

The Alpha shrugged and said, "Okay, Jody, she's yours."

The blonde smiled. She looked at Stella and said, "Don't go anywhere. I'll be right back."

The woman turned and headed back to the bar. She was already stripping off her clothes as she ducked around the side of the building.

The bikers backed up and formed a half-circle on their side of the parking lot. We did the same thing, leaving Stella alone in the center of the newly formed ring.

Stella just stood there, calmly watching the side of the building attentively.

A minute later, an angry howl filled the night. A large silver and brown wolf came bounding out around the building. I thickened the air around me as a precaution in case it had forgotten who it was fighting.

The bikers opened their part of the circle and the Werewolf came charging in. I was a bit concerned as Stella hadn't changed into her Hyde form yet. As the Werewolf made a beeline for Stella's vulnerable, tiny human form that concern was quickly turning to panic. The

Werewolf leapt with its jaw wide open, showing off a mouthful of deadly fangs.

A split second before the Werewolf would have torn Stella apart, she changed. The Were hit the massive Hyde like a sledgehammer, but our Hyde didn't even flinch. On the impact, the wolf let out a confused yelp and crashed back to the ground in a slight daze. Before it could recover, Stella reached down and wrapped her large, misshapen hand around the center of its body and snatched it up. She lifted the panicked Were over her head and then drove the beast headfirst into the pavement.

The sound of the wolf's head impacting the tarmac was so loud that I worried Stella had killed it. She released the limp Were and it lay still on the ground. I exhaled at the sight of the Were's flanks slowly rising and falling as it breathed; it was just knocked out and not dead.

There were some angry rumbles and mutterings from the Moon Ghosts and the dark-haired woman stepped forward and said, "You tricked us! That wasn't a fair fight!"

I shrugged and said, "You didn't have to pick her. Not my fault you assumed she was a helpless little girl."

The Alpha grabbed the woman and said, "They pulled one over on us, we just need to make sure we win the next two. Get changed and use your anger to deal with the Werepanther."

The woman nodded, and to my surprise, started stripping off her clothes right there.

The Alpha said, "Johnny, grab Jody and clear the ring."

The big man stepped forward and cast a wary eye on Stella's massive form as he approached.

"Step back, Stella; it's Bree's turn now."

Stella grunted and moved back towards us. Johnny heaved the unconscious Were onto his shoulders and carried her back to the Moon Ghosts.

The dark-haired Were was naked now. My attention instantly went to the scars running across her body. She was covered in them. The only thing that could do that sort of damage to a Were was silver. Judging by the amount, I'd guess someone had tortured her with silver knives. This woman was also all muscle too, and her five-inch aura told me this wouldn't be an easy fight for Bree.

The woman threw back her head in a silent scream as her body started rapidly changing. Her fingers extended, and long sharp claws began to materialize. Dark fur rapidly sprouted across her body. Her jaw stretched and grew into a snout filled with fangs.

I watched Bree out of the corner of my eye. She silently eyed her opponent as she changed, but her whole form was tense and ready like she just wanted to get this started.

The air was split with a deep howl as the woman had now been replaced by an all-black Werewolf standing there in its hybrid form. The moment the howl ended, she leapt at Bree. The two of them came together in a mass of snarling dark fur. Claws and fangs darted in and out almost faster than I could see. They rolled across the parking lot a few feet, locked together, raking each other without mercy.

Bree kicked the snarling Were away and they both sprang to their feet. Bree had a large bloody gash on her right flank and a smaller wound on her left arm, but both were already healing. The Werewolf had wounds on her face, chest, and leg but they too were starting to heal before my eyes.

They circled each other, looking for an opening. The Werewolf snarled and Bree growled in response. The Werewolf lunged left, but it was a feint and she jerked back right. Razor-sharp talons slashed for Bree's midsection, but Bree nimbly dodged the vicious swipe. Bree countered and raked her claws down the side of the Werewolf's face leaving three bloody claw marks in her wake.

The Werewolf gave a small yelp at the blow and leapt back to put some space between them. Bree went on the offensive and closed on her. Bree swiped with her right hand but didn't connect. The Werewolf started to back away more but then suddenly changed direction and leapt at Bree. The move caught Bree off guard, and they went down with the Werewolf on top.

The Moon Ghosts cheered and got louder as the Werewolf's open hungry maw descended towards Bree's exposed neck. At the last moment, Bree jammed her furry left arm into the slobbering mouth to prevent it from latching on to her neck.

Liv cried out and started to move forward, but Blue firmly grabbed the back of Liv's shorts and held her in place. Blue whispered something firm and harsh in Olivia's ear. Liv frowned but reluctantly nodded.

The Moon Ghost's gasped as Bree struck with her right paw and tore four long gashes across the Werewolf's belly. The Werewolf tried to bite down on the arm wedged in its mouth, but the arm was too far back for its fangs to do any damage.

Bree arched suddenly with her hips and pivoted her body left and threw the Werewolf off her. She nimbly got to her feet and her opponent mirrored this move. The Werewolf snarled and charged in again. Bree kicked up with her right leg and caught the charging wolf in her stomach and knocked her back on her ass a good ten feet.

Bree charged at the downed Were, but it sprang to its feet just before Bree could pounce on it. Bree though, instead of pouncing, leapt high into the air and jumped over the Were. She twisted her body in the air and landed behind her confused opponent. Bree sprang forward and crashed down hard on to the Werewolf's back. She drove the Werewolf face down into the pavement. She slid her arm around the prone Werewolf's neck and tightened her grip.

The black Werewolf snarled and tried to buck Bree off her back, but Bree wasn't about to be denied. Bree stayed locked on the Were's back and continued choking her.

The Werewolf spent the next couple of minutes desperately trying to shake Bree before its eyes rolled up in its head and it went still.

Bree lifted her head and growled loudly in triumph. She released her chokehold and got to her feet. Liv blurred over to her and wrapped Bree's furry form into a big hug.

The Moon Ghosts were quiet, and all looked at the Alpha for direction. I could tell he wasn't happy, and I kept the Air thickened around me in case this went south. He looked over at us and Liv pulled out her sword and Blue ignited hers again as the tension rose.

After a long silence, the Alpha spat on the ground and said, "Mount up, boys, we have a long ride ahead of us ..."

A couple of the Moon Ghosts came forward and picked up the downed Werewolf. It took them a couple of minutes to lash the two unconscious Weres to their riders, but they got them in place.

A loud rumble of exhausts filled the silent night as all the Harleys roared to life. The Alpha glanced over at me and gave me a sharp nod before slowly rolling out of the lot. The rest of the Moon Ghosts followed.

We watched them turn onto Upper James and then disappear onto the highway access ramp.

As the sound of the Harleys faded into the night air, a steady clapping sounded behind us. We all turned. Standing on the roof of Joe's Sports Bar was the old wizened Native man slowly clapping his hands with a grin on his face. His silver aura radiated around him like a small star.

I called my lightning to me and started building up a massive charge. He frowned and then waggled his finger at me. I raised my hands at him to strike but then he was gone.

I sighed and released the power I'd built up, "Is that enough proof for you, Bree?"

A soft growl which meant 'whatever' echoed beside me.

The sky opened up not a second after that, instantly soaking us to the skin, which put the cherry on this night.

Late-Night Shopping

Sunday, June 10

It was still raining when I awoke. I listened excitedly for a moment, but it was just rain and no loud thunder, which meant I wouldn't be getting a nice little pick-me-up for my powers. I sighed and got out of bed.

A short while later, I found Stella and Blue at the kitchen table focused on the laptop in front of them. I made myself a coffee and joined them.

Stella said, "We've started doing research on this god. He is called the Coyote and is a Native-American trickster god. He loves to pull pranks and do things for his own amusement. There are a host of stories and legends about it. It has three forms: coyote, old man, and young girl."

After a sip of coffee, I asked, "That sounds like our god, anything on how to banish or kill it?"

Stella shook her head, "No, but we've only been doing research for less than an hour. We did find some lore on how to summon and make a deal with it. The ritual seems pretty simple, you just need to burn some herbs, birch bark, and feathers and call its name three times. For the deal, we need a puzzle to amuse it, venison to feed it, and some tobacco leaves to please it. If it approves of our gifts, it will be willing to make a deal."

I frowned at this. This thing had indirectly caused ten deaths and the idea of rewarding it didn't sit well with me. I told Stella my concerns.

"Well, we have just started research, so maybe there is a more permanent solution to be found."

After breakfast, I excused myself and headed up to my office to do my own research and make some calls. My first call was to Sean, the Alpha of the Barrie pack. He knew the Alpha of the Six Nations pack and I hoped he could make some inquiries about the Coyote in Native lore for me. He said he'd try and would get back to me. My next call was to Walter the wizard who had made the wards protecting my house and done other spells for me in the past.

We exchanged greetings and I bought him up to speed on what was going on.

"You're nuts, dude. God-class creatures aren't something you want to piss off. Taking on that demon was bad enough, but you are talking about taking on a god," he said. The line went quiet for a moment and he added, "I have nothing in my spellbook that would even remotely work for this, but I'll make some calls. I'll warn you though that a spell or device to banish or kill a god won't be cheap, if such a thing even exists."

"Understood, but see if there is something out there, and how much it will cost, okay?"

"Sure. I'll call you if I find anything." And with that he ended the call.

I knew Walter would do his best to try and find us something, but his warning about price did have me a little concerned. For the work he'd done for me in the past, he'd charged me between $10,000 and $100,000. I shuddered to think how much something he'd called expensive would be. We could be looking at hundreds of thousands or even millions. We'd made some good money since the trouble with the Coyote began, but how much were we willing to blow to get rid of this thing?

Theoretically, banishing or killing it should be bounty applicable, but we'd need to prove it was responsible for the deaths it had indirectly caused, and we'd need proof that we banished it or killed it. The bounty on taking down a god would be sizable and might even cover the cost of the spell. We could film the takedown and that would be proof, assuming of course that the Coyote showed up in the recording. It would be my luck that he couldn't be recorded, and we'd just have a video of us fighting an invisible thing, which wouldn't be enough to convince the UN bounty commission it was real. Even if we got it on film, we'd still needed to prove it was the one behind all the attacks. We only had circumstantial evidence against it. I doubted it would be enough to convince the commission. This meant I was back to square one, and if I wanted to use a spell to take this thing down, the price was coming out of our pockets.

I sighed and started researching again. I was shocked by the sheer number of stories and legends about the Coyote. This deity had a long and rich history with the Native people. Some of the stories were amusing, and I couldn't deny the Coyote had a great sense of humor. The more I read though, the more concerned I got. This wasn't a minor player and trying to take this thing down would be like trying to take on Odin himself. Walter's warnings came rushing back to me. If we did try to banish or kill it and failed, we were in deep trouble. Right now, it was only playing with us; I dreaded to think what it might do to us if we pissed it off.

I wondered what we had done that had attracted its attention in the first place. We didn't have much interaction with our local Native community. I also couldn't think of anything we'd done that might have offended the Native community in general. Maybe it was something like Blue's uniqueness of being the only of her kind on Earth, or maybe Bree's cat nature offended its Coyote aspect or something else had attracted its attention. In the end, why it picked us really didn't matter, we just needed to put a stop to it.

Just before lunch, my phone rang. I saw Sean's name on the display, and I answered it.

"I talked to Jim at Six Nations and told him what you were looking to do. After he finished laughing, his exact words were, "Tell your friend if he tries this, to undo his pants, bend over, and kiss his ass goodbye.""

Well, that wasn't encouraging, I thought

"That bad?" I asked.

"According to Jim, the Coyote has existed since the dawn of time. Many people have tried to take it down, but none have even come remotely close to succeeding. There are also no legends or lore that he is aware of that even hint the Coyote can be killed or banished. He finished the call by saying, 'Your friend would have more luck trying to take the sun out of the sky—tell him to make a deal.'"

I cursed under my breath and then thanked Sean for his time and effort and ended the call.

I hoped Walter would have better news for me.

***

Once the sun went down and Olivia was up, we all had a team meeting at the kitchen table.

"... so, other than making a deal with it, our only hope is that Walter finds someone who has a spell or device to take this thing down. The problem is Walter warned that if he did find something, it would be expensive," I said.

"How expensive?" asked Bree.

I shrugged and said, "If I had to guess, I'd say at least a few hundred thousand and maybe millions ..."

There were a few gasps around the table, and Bree asked, "How much have we made since all of this started?"

Stella typed something on her laptop and then said, "Just over a million dollars US, if all the bounty claims we've submitted are approved."

Bree nodded and said, "Look, Zack, I know you want to take this thing down, but if the spell does cost millions, that is going to wipe out every penny we've made this year. Besides, aren't you the one who keeps reminding us that we are bounty hunters, not heroes?"

Bree's comments made me realize that I'd have a hard road to travel to convince my teammates that it was worth spending whatever money was needed to take down the Coyote. Bree, out of all of them, was the biggest idealist. She would be the first to step up and offer her talents to do what was right. Stella tended to be the most practical. Blue was the most mercenary and Liv tended to be the most materialistic. If Bree was questioning the cost, then it didn't bode well for me getting the funds I might need for the spell.

I took a deep breath and said, "Look, I agree, and if the spell does end up being millions of dollars then we will need to pass on it and just go make a deal with the Coyote. I think what we need to discuss is how much we would be willing to spend ..."

I was pleased to see nods of agreement around the table and Stella said, "Since we have made just over a million since all of this started, I think that has to be the upper limit of our range."

Blue shook her head, "I think it should be less than that. We might have made a million, but we have yet to receive the bill from Marion for Zack's healing sessions. The money that Zack spent on the communication glasses should also be taken out. Finally, as Zack was almost mortally wounded and demonstrated the need for the custom armor that he has ordered from Grundy's, that too should be deducted from the total. Therefore, $800,000 US should the highest we are willing to go."

I grinned and added, "Don't forget the crap-load of tops that Liv has gone through—they also need to be added to the expenses."

Bree laughed at that. Liv had been taking a sip of her pint of blood, so she just flipped me the bird.

Liv put down her glass and said, "Hold on here, so we are going to make no money for all our hard work in the past week or so? Some of us have important expenses and have made financial promises ..."

Bree rolled her eyes, "Like what?"

"I've been eying a pair of Ferragamo shoes that I must have. I also promised Alteea that I'd get her that new Apple mini-tablet she wants."

Alteea nodded her head solemnly at that.

I did some quick math in my head and threw out what I thought was a fair number. "Shall we vote on $700,000 US being the upper limit of what we are willing to spend on a banishing spell?" I asked. Everyone nodded. "All in favor of that being the upper limit?"

I put my hand up and not even a second later everyone followed. I was about to announce that it was unanimous when my phone buzzed in my pocket. I fished it out and saw that it was Rob on the display.

"Hurricane, we need your help," said Rob, getting right to the point.

"What's up?"

"We are at Lime Ridge Mall and we have one fatality. There is a creature in the food court that is responsible. SWAT is twenty minutes out, but I doubt they will be able to do anything against this thing. EIRT is en route but their ETA is at least thirty minutes."

I checked my watch and saw that it was just coming up on 10 p.m. and with it being a Sunday, the mall had been closed for almost four hours, which at least meant there shouldn't be many people there now. The fatality concerned me, and I asked, "Officer or civilian?"

Rob paused and said, "Civilian, a mall security guard."

"Can you give me more detail on the creature?"

"I've never seen or even heard of anything like this. It is probably close to ten feet tall, but its entire body seems to be made from live mice, rats, and bugs. Just looking at this thing makes me queasy."

Rob was a steady and composed officer, but I swore I caught a hint of panic in his tone, and that had me worried. What concerned me even more was that his description of this creature matched nothing that I'd ever read about. I hated being ignorant about something I was going to fight. Knowing a creature's strengths and weaknesses was a huge part of being able to safely take it down.

"What is it doing now?"

"Raiding a Subway for food."

"Okay, keep everyone back. We will be there in five."

I ended the call. Liv had already blurred out of the room, presumably to gear up, as she'd have heard the entire conversation. Bree also was already stripping out of her clothes to change into her Were form. I relayed the gist of the call to the rest and said, "Gear up, people, we have work to do."

I headed up to my room and fetched my communication glasses. I changed from my shorts to jeans to get a bit more protection. It was too bad that body armor was still on order as that would have been really useful at this moment.

Less than two minutes later, we were all back in the kitchen.

"Okay, everyone, we have no idea what this thing is, so we are going to take things slow and steady. Alteea, stay way back from this thing and get it on video. We'll need that footage if we have any chance of making a bounty claim; I've never heard of this thing, so chances are no one else has either. It has killed one person already, so we take this thing down hard. Got it?" Everyone nodded. I turned to Blue and added, "Open a portal, but not too close to the food court. I don't want us coming in on top of whatever this is, okay?"

Blue nodded and headed to living room with all of us in tow. She used the shadows in the corner of the room to open a portal. Stella instantly changed into her Hyde form and went through first, the rest of us on her heels.

We came out in the center of the mall and surprised a couple of cops that were nearby. Thankfully they recognized us, and the one said, "Rob's that way," and pointed towards the food court.

"OH MY GOD!" exclaimed Olivia.

I immediately began calling on my power and searched for the threat.

"The new fall lineup is out!" she squealed.

I cursed under my breath at the crazy fashion-conscious vampire and released the power I'd been building up. "Focus! Creature first, shopping second, alright?"

Liv gave me a pout but nodded in agreement.

We headed towards the line of cops at the edge of the food court. I found Rob in short order, but my attention was pulled to the creature at the far end of the food court. I blinked, trying to understand what I was looking at. The thing was vaguely humanoid in shape, well, other than having four legs versus the normal two. Its entire form was a writhing mass of vermin. Its arms were elongated and reaching deep into the Subway store. Travelling up its arms was an array of cold meats, vegetables, and bread. The food was then absorbed into the head and chest areas of the creature.

It dawned on me that the creature had no aura around it and that puzzled me. This thing had to be Enhanced and, therefore, it should have an aura. If it didn't have an aura that meant this was natural, which made no sense either. How do thousands of bugs, mice, and rats suddenly develop the intelligence to work together like this naturally? Maybe it was like the stone golem, but I'd never heard of a vermin golem before.

I spotted the fast food restaurants to the left side of the Subway. Both their steel roll cages had been peeled apart like someone had a giant can opener. This creature wasn't only large but strong as well.

Rob's voice pulled me from my thoughts. "So, what is this thing?"

I was about to answer him when I spotted human remains in the center of the food court. Every piece of clothing and flesh had been stripped from the body and all that remained were the bones. In the center of the skeleton was a metallic object. I studied it from a distance and realized it was a belt buckle. On one side of the corpse was a silver nametag lying on the floor and a hand-held walkie-talkie on the other side.

"By Odin's beard!" I said as I realized that was all that was left of the mall security guard.

"Yeah, not a nice way to go," said Rob in a soft voice beside me.

I nodded firmly at that. "And to answer your question, I have no idea what that thing is. But whatever it is, it's powerful and dangerous."

"So, what is the plan?"

I shrugged and said, "We let it keep pillaging restaurants and hope that the sketchy taco place will be enough to kill it?"

"Har, har," said Rob. "Somehow I doubt even that place will be enough."

Truthfully, I had no idea how to deal with this thing. Hell, I didn't even know what it was. Judging by the dead security guard, the one thing I did know was I didn't want any normal human anywhere close to this thing. "Get everyone out. Secure all the exits from the outside. Call me once they are secured. When SWAT arrives, have them stand by as back up in case this thing tries to break out. When EIRT arrives, call me and send them in to help."

Rob eyed me critically for a moment. "You sure?"

"Yeah. This thing is made up of vermin, so I doubt your guns are going to be any use in taking it down. Go. We'll be fine." I was surprised that my voice sounded much more confident than I felt at this moment.

Rob nodded and got on the radio.

While we waited for the cops to leave, Blue asked, "What's the plan?"

"Once Rob calls me and says the exits are covered, I'm going to try and zap it with lightning. If that doesn't work, Stella can go in and try and smash this thing, and Liv and Bree will back her up. You stay in reserve. If you see an opportunity to strike, do so. Alteea, get up to the second level and film from up there; do not get anywhere close to this thing."

Blue and the rest of the team nodded. Alteea had kept her glamor up since we'd arrived but I watched her aura dart up to the next floor.

"Dark and squirmy needs a name," said Liv as she eyed the creature.

"The Verminator," I said not even a second later.

Liv gave a small nod of approval. With that important task settled, we all just stood there watching it consume Subway's inventory.

Five minutes later, Rob called and said the exits were covered.

Showtime, I thought. I called my Air power and used it to fly closer to the center of the food court. I took the precaution of thickening the air around me as a shield, in case the Verminator had some sort of ranged attack. The center of the food court by the escalators was open to the second story, so I flew a bit higher. If this went sideways, I wanted to retreat to the upper level where it hopefully couldn't reach me.

The creature ignored me and just continued feeding. I started building up a powerful charge. I prayed I could fry this thing with one good blast.

I activated the comms to Liv and Blue and said, *"Standby, I'm going to hit it with lightning. If that doesn't work, send Stella in."*

I got a *"Roger,"* in response.

I took a deep breath and raised my hands towards the Verminator. I released a pure white bolt of lightning directly at the center of its back. The lightning hit, and the creature made a chorus of buzzing noises and high-pitched squeals in response. A few dead bugs and rodents dropped to the floor when I hit it.

My eyes widened as it suddenly opened a large hole in its chest so my lightning just went through it without hitting anything else. I moved the lightning higher, but it just keep opening itself up so I couldn't hit it.

It turned towards me and its arms started rapidly growing in my direction. I tried redirecting the lightning at the arms, but they shifted quickly around it.

Shit, time to go, I thought as the arms closed on me. I dropped the lightning attack and increased the air pressure under me to get farther away.

A loud grunt from below let me know Stella had started her attack. The arms stopped coming after me and went for Stella instead.

Stella's lumbering form closed on the creature and the arms swarmed over her upper body, but she kept moving forward like it was nothing.

I realized the Verminator was trying to eat Stella like it had the security guard but her near-impenetrable skin was preventing that from happening.

Stella closed to striking distance and took a mighty swing and went clean though the thing. It had opened up the area of its mass where the punch should have hit. I cursed at that.

How do you hurt something that can reshape itself at will? I pondered. We needed something that could do damage to a wide area. I kicked around the idea of sending Blue for the grenades we had tucked away in the lab. It was tempting, but the fallout we'd get for using high explosives at a freaking mall forced me to put it on the back burner. It would also be my luck that she'd have another anti-tank missile tucked away in her room. We'd been lucky and gotten away with it on the Bruce Trail, but inside a mall with video cameras everywhere, I doubt we'd get that lucky again.

Stella kept swinging but the Verminator just kept reforming itself so none of her blows could connect. It also seemed to realize that its arms weren't doing any damage to Stella's tough form. It pulled them back, thickened them, and swung at Stella. The left arm made contact and the meaty sound of the contact rang out through the entire food court. Stella was thrown back and went through a row of six tables. The tables had been bolted to the floor, but they were knocked aside like they had been child's toys.

Seeing Stella's six-hundred-pound form tossed back like that had my guts churning. This thing was strong, and worse, we couldn't seem to even hit it.

A loud roar pulled my attention back to the fight. Bree and Liv charged in. At that moment, I'd realized I'd made a mistake in my planning. Stella's Hyde form could withstand the bites from the vermin, but Bree and Liv's forms couldn't. I yelled at them to get out of there, but I was too late.

For a brief moment, I thought they'd be okay as they both nimbly dodged the arms as they shot out at them.

"Liv, Bree, pull back!" I yelled.

In horror, I watched the arms each split into two. They spouted out in opposite directions, but in less than a second, they encircled Bree and Liv. The circles rapidly shrank, and both my teammates were engulfed by the writhing mass.

Liv screamed, and Bree let out a pain-filled squeal as their flesh was consumed. They both tried to get away but couldn't free themselves from the Verminator.

Stella was getting to her feet, but I knew she wouldn't get there in time. Blue had ignited her sword and was also charging forward, but she was even further away.

I needed to save them. I quickly lowered myself to the ground, calling on my power on the way down. I raised my hands and let loose two bolts of lightning. Both bolts slammed into Liv and Bree. I knew

I couldn't hit the Verminator but hoped that by hitting Bree and Liv that the electricity would fry whatever was touching them. I'd also lowered the power of the blasts so it was enough to fry any vermin but not enough to kill my friends.

Dead bugs, mice, and rats dropped to the floor around them. I called on my Air power and used it to lift them up and away from the creature. I hastily pulled them towards me.

Bree was already healing the horrific damage that was done to her, but Liv was in bad shape. Her crop top was gone, but this time I found no mirth in that. Her entire head and upper body looked like someone had run her up and down a giant cheese grater. She was covered in blood from the multitude of bites. I almost wept at the sight of her face; her lips, nose, and eyes were almost totally gone. She was out of her mind in pain and just kept screaming.

I pushed them together in the air and Bree wrapped her furry arms around Liv protectively and held her. Liv fought her for a moment, but then realized it was Bree holding her and clutched her friend tighter. She almost stopped screaming.

Stella had engaged the Verminator again.

Blue's voice came over my comm, *"Zack, over to your left. I have a portal to the lab open."*

I spotted Blue and redirected the girls to her and launched them through the portal. "Go with them and get some blood into Olivia." Blue nodded. Suddenly it struck me how to deal with this thing. "I need you to bring back two of the large cooler bottles of holy water, okay?"

Blue nodded and disappeared into the shadows. Stella was swinging wildly at the creature, but it kept reshaping itself so none of her blows connected. The Verminator once again hammered Stella with a powerful blow and she was sent flying back. She crashed hard into a tray stand and it was totally destroyed. Stella immediately got to her feet and headed right back at creature.

The two were in a stalemate as neither could harm the other. Stella couldn't connect with any of her powerful blows. The Verminator could hit Stella and knock her away but couldn't hit her hard enough to put her down.

I had a plan to fix that but needed Blue to return with the water.

A couple of minutes later, Blue returned with two nineteen-liter watercooler bottles. She ran over to me and put them down. I started yanking off the light blue plastic cap from the first one.

"Is the creature demonic in origin?" asked Blue as she watched me.

I shook my head as I removed the first cap.

"Then why do you need holy water?"

I smiled and said, "I just needed water. Can you get the other cap?"

Blue nodded and I used my Air power to lift the bottle into the air. I moved it until it was ten feet to the right of the creature and then lowered it to the ground. I used the air to tip it, so the open nozzle was pointed towards the creature. The water chugged out of the bottle and the puddle slowly crept towards the Verminator.

Blue had the cap off the second one, so I used my power to lift it into the air and did the same thing with this one but on the left side of the creature.

I started calling on my power and waited for my opening. Stella was back and swinging at the creature, but it easily avoided her blows.

The water now had completely spilled out and the Verminator was standing in the puddle. It lashed out and connected a massive blow that knocked Stella back a good thirty feet.

With Stella clear, I raised my hands and released a powerful bolt of lightning at the water.

The Verminator let out a loud buzz followed by a chorus of squeals as the electricity did its job. I kept up the blast and with each passing second, the creature shrank. The thing was melting like a snowman on a hot summer's day. I grinned; this thing might be able to reshape itself, but it still had to obey the laws of gravity.

Once it was down to about four feet in height, a dark thing leapt out of it and skittered away. The mass of vermin completely lost cohesion and collapsed to the floor. The critter that jumped away from the body was about six inches in size. Its body was like a crab, complete with two front pincers, but its legs were a mass of short tentacles that looked like octopus legs but worked like a centipede's legs did. This thing had an aura around it that had a solid black core, which meant demon, and the outer ring of the aura was a small, pale-green outline. The pale green meant it was telepathic or had some sort of mental abilities. I guessed that was how it was able to control the vermin. This also explained why

I didn't see an aura originally as it was hidden inside the mass of mice, rats, and bugs.

"Don't let that thing get away!" I yelled.

Blue ignited her sword and charged after it, Stella following. Tables were smashed and flew apart as Stella charged through them on her quest to catch this thing. I used my powers to lift myself into the air and went after it as well.

It had been heading towards Stella, but then stopped and skittered away from her. That was the last mistake it ever made.

Barely a second later, Blue's flaming sword descended and neatly cut the thing in two and after a brief sharp scream, it was dead. Green ichor leaked from the creature and spread over the tiled floor of the food court. As I flew over, I got a whiff of sulfur and rot and nearly gagged at the stench.

I landed about ten feet away and eyed the ugly critter, "Nice swing, Blue."

Blue nodded. She wrinkled her nose and quickly stepped away from the thing.

Alteea suddenly appeared in front of me with a worried look on her tiny face. "Master, I filmed the entire encounter and got a close up of the foul dead thing, can I go check on my Mistress?"

"Blue," I said, "can you open a portal for Alteea? She wants to see Liv."

Blue looked around and spotted a shadow. She headed towards it with Alteea right behind her.

I pulled out my phone and dialed Rob. I let him know the creature was dead and it was over. He said he'd be there shortly and hung up.

"Pungent little thing," commented Stella beside me.

She was back in her human form and I nodded in agreement and we both moved away from it.

Blue joined us, and I asked, "How was Liv?"

"She was cursing up a storm when I left her but seems to be back to normal. I would also like to check on her though."

Stella nodded in agreement and I said, "Go, I'll deal with the police and EIRT. I'll fly home when I'm done, so no need to wait up."

They wandered off and disappeared into the shadows seconds before Rob and a ton of other officers showed up. Rob whistled as he looked at the damage. A good quarter of the food court's tables had been destroyed in the fight, plus the three restaurants that had been damaged by the creature in its quest for food. It did look pretty bad, but it could have been a lot worse.

I was about to comment when I spotted a large silver aura outside of the glass ceiling of the second-floor atrium. The Coyote in his old man form smiled, gave a mock salute, and then disappeared.

"Son of a bitch," I muttered under my breath.

Rob looked up to see what I had been staring at. "What?"

"Nothing. A problem for another day."

Once EIRT was done processing the scene, I flew home and walked into the house about ten minutes later. I was surprised that Stella and Blue were still up and sitting at the kitchen table.

"How are Liv and Bree?" I asked.

"We're fine," said a somber and subdued Liv as she, Bree, and Alteea came out from the living room.

Bree nodded and added, "At least for this bounty the Coyote wasn't to blame …"

I shook my head and said, "He was. He waved at me from the glass roof above the food court after you guys left and then disappeared."

Liv cursed and said, "Tomorrow when you are talking to your wizard friend, if my $20,000 makes the difference in getting that banishment spell, it's yours." I raised an eyebrow at that, and Liv added, "Re-growing eyeballs truly sucked, and if the Coyote was responsible for that, then the bastard needs to pay. I'm glad that I don't dream in my death-trances as I'd be having nightmares about that for months …"

Let's Make a Deal

Monday, June 11

The next morning after breakfast, I rang Walter to see what he had learned about the Coyote.

"I didn't have much luck," said Walter after we exchanged hellos, "Most mages and wizards that I talked to didn't think it was possible to banish or kill a god with a spell, at least not without using dark or blood magic. I did find one mage who studies theoretical magic for the Mages council, and he believed it might be possible to create a spell to do this. The good news is if he does create the spell, he won't charge you for it, as long as he can be there when you use it so he can document the results."

I perked up at this. Free was good, and if this guy worked for the Mages council, then he was a seriously powerful mage.

Walter then crushed my hopes, "The bad news is that he is currently wrapping up an existing project and once he is done that, he will start the research on the god banishment spell. If all goes well, he may have something in a couple of years ..."

Two years. The Coyote had indirectly killed too many people in the two weeks since this had started; I dreaded to think what the body count would be in two years.

I thanked Walter for his time and ended the call. My phone rang a second later. I first thought it was Walter calling back because he'd forgotten to mention something, but the 'D. Collins' on the caller ID dispelled that notion.

"What's up, Dave?"

"Thought you'd like to know that detectives raided the apartment of James Hogan Atlee yesterday."

The name didn't mean anything to me. "I have no idea who that is."

"Sorry, that is the name of the deceased spellcaster who created the stone golem and the giant snake."

Now he had my attention, "Did they find anything interesting?"

"Oh yeah. Besides being a member of a couple fringe eco-terrorist groups and being super radical about the environment in general, they found his manifesto and diary. The diary confirms he was responsible for the stone golem, but he was also the one who raised the zombies at Hamilton Cemetery."

I smiled at that. If he was the one that raised the zombies, then he'd be re-classed as a necromancer, which meant his bounty would be doubled. I was also pleased as that meant we didn't have a budding necromancer still out there, and that should be the end of zombies in this area for the near future. It was interesting that with the stone golem he just left the altar and didn't bother cleaning up, but for the zombies he did. After thinking about it for a bit, it made sense though; necromancy was an automatic death sentence whereas the rogue golem would have only been a jail term. That difference would have caused him to be more careful about not leaving evidence.

After I hung up my call, I headed downstairs to find Stella and Blue to break the news to them.

"The larger bounty is good news. However, it looks like we have no choice but to make a deal with the Coyote," said Stella after I'd told them about my calls.

Blue's tail flicked back and forth, and she said, "What if we use the summoning ritual to ambush it?"

It was a tempting idea. We gather the tribute, make it look like we wanted to make a deal and when the Coyote arrived, we hit with everything we had. I quickly dismissed it and said, "The problem is the Coyote is a god, and we don't even know if we can kill it. If we attack it and fail, the consequences would be terrible. This thing can also appear and disappear at will, so it might disappear before we even land the first blow. Lastly, I have no idea about its powers; it could be listening to this conversation right now … I mean, is it even possible to surprise a god?"

Blue's tail went still for a moment and she nodded.

Stella piped up, "I guess we have no choice but to get the tribute and make a deal with it then."

I nodded slowly at that. I really wasn't happy about rewarding the Coyote for all the trouble it had caused, but unless a new solution miraculously appeared, we had no choice.

I felt my anger grow at being forced into making a deal and made myself take a deep breath and said, "I think it would be best if you or Blue negotiated the deal rather than me."

Stella's eyes widened at that. As leader of the group, I should be the one making the deal, but I knew myself too well. This thing had pissed me off, and I worried my temper would get the best of me during the negotiation and I'd screw it up. Stella was the most rational of us and Blue never let her emotions get the better of her, so both were better choices.

"If that is what you want," said Stella.

"I did do a lot of bartering back in my home world; therefore, I would be ideally suited for this role," suggested Blue.

We discussed for a bit and decided that Blue was the best choice to make the deal on our behalf. The whole team would be there as well, in case things went sideways and we needed to fight our way out of this.

Once we figured out *how* we'd make the deal, we debated about *where* we'd do it. In the end, we picked the woods where Liv and Bree had taken on the cultists as the location. It was remote enough that we wouldn't be disturbed, and we could use the boulder the cultists were going to use as a sacrificial altar to lay out our tribute.

"We'll get the supplies we need for the summoning and the tribute, but we'll get Bree and Liv to hunt the deer for the tribute once the sun goes down," said Stella.

We broke up the meeting and Stella and Blue left to go shopping. I retired upstairs to the office and hit the Internet, hoping to find some lore on how to kill the Coyote. I knew this was a longshot, but I hated the idea of making a deal with this thing and maybe I'd get lucky.

***

At sunset, the whole team was in the kitchen having dinner, or breakfast in the case of the nocturnal members of our team. We brought Bree, Olivia, and Alteea up to speed on our plan.

Olivia was pissed off that we were rewarding this thing, but eventually conceded that we didn't have much choice.

After dinner, Bree changed into her panther form and Olivia changed into some old clothes. That surprised me as Liv usually hunted nude as to avoid getting blood all over her outfit and ruining it. I

180

figured that she must have decided to wear clothes this time as to not be standing around naked while Blue negotiated with the Coyote. She also had her sword, Mr. Slicey, sheathed over her shoulder, which was another thing she usually didn't do when she hunted. Blue shadow-travelled them out to the woods. They were to call us once they had the deer.

It turned out to be a long wait and we didn't get a call until after midnight. Stella and I gathered up the supplies for the summoning and the tribute and Blue opened another portal.

We stepped out into the darkened woods. I spotted the freshly killed deer lying on the altar and Bree and Liv were just off to the side of it. It was a cool but clear night which was a welcome break from the heat we'd been having.

"Took you two long enough," I said, shaking my head.

Liv looked a little sheepish and said, "Yeah, Bree ate the first one we caught …"

Bree was now in her standing Were form. She growled softly and rubbed her furred belly. I rolled my eyes. I should have expected that.

We dumped our tribute on the rock. To amuse the Coyote, Stella had bought a Rubik's cube and a puzzle book. The deer covered the venison part and there were three different pouches of pipe tobacco to cover the last requirement.

On the far end of the rock, Stella had laid out the birch bark, herbs, and feathers needed for the summoning ritual.

We all gathered around the altar and I said, "Okay, when we're finished, Alteea use your powers to light the summoning ingredients and then fly up to one of the trees and film everything." I got a couple of puzzled looks at that and explained, "If this does go south and turns into a fight, we have a chance of making a bounty claim if we get it on film." The team nodded, and I continued, "This turning into a fight is something we want to avoid at all costs. As much as we don't like it, making the deal is the best play here. Blue will make the deal and Stella will be her advisor. The rest of us need to keep our tempers in check and do nothing to mess this up, understand?"

I looked over at Liv and she slowly nodded. "If it turns ugly, then we hit it with everything we've got hard and fast. Go for the kill and don't give it a chance to disappear. Once again, the fight option is a worst-case scenario and hopefully that doesn't happen. Everyone clear?"

I got nods all round and finished with, "Alteea, light it up."

Our pixie pointed at the pile of summoning ingredients and a thin stream of fire ignited from her hands. The pile started burning and Alteea cut the flames. She engaged her glamor and darted up to a nearby tree. As a precaution, I thickened the air around me as a shield.

Blue stepped closer to the burning pile and yelled, "Coyote! Coyote! Coyote!"

For a few seconds nothing happened, and then it appeared in its old man form in front of us. The Coyote had a cocky grin across on his face that got wider as he saw the tribute.

The huge bright silver aura around him was awe inspiring. The largest aura I'd ever seen before was Elizabeth's, Master of the English vampire court, but this one was even bigger than hers. As much as I wanted to take this thing down, I prayed to Odin that this didn't turn ugly. This thing was way out of our league. In a strange way, this fact made me feel better about making a deal. If we'd tried to banish or kill it with a spell at this moment, my knees would have been trembling so bad I doubted I'd still be standing.

He nodded approvingly and looked us over with an amused twinkle in his eyes. His gaze stopped on Liv and he said, "Olivia, nice to *see* you again."

I groaned to myself as I knew it was a crack about Liv having to regrow her eyes last night. For a brief moment, I thought she didn't catch it, but that hope went out the window …

Her face erupted in anger, her fangs descended, and she screamed, "SEE THIS, MOTHERF—"

Thankfully, Bree dropped one of her big dark paws over Olivia's mouth and cut the rest of her tirade off. Bree also wrapped her other arm around Liv's midsection and pulled her back. It worried me that our resident angry Were was the calm one in this situation.

The Coyote chuckled at Liv's reaction and turned his attention to me. "You wish to make a deal? Took you long enough. For an experienced hero and hunter, you really took your time figuring this all out."

My temper started to flair, but I forced it down. It was trying to goad me, and I wasn't going to let that happened. I took a deep breath and though clenched teeth said, "We wish to make a deal. Blue will be our spokesperson."

His eyes widened at that. My anger dissipated as it felt good that we had actually surprised him for a change.

The Coyote turned to Blue and said, "Very well, what are your terms?"

Blue's tail flicked back and forth, and she said, "You leave us alone and do not interfere with our lives for the next fifty years."

The Coyote laughed at that and said, "Is there a bigger tribute somewhere around here that I don't see?" He pointed at the items laid out on the rock and said, "For this, a year would be generous of me."

"A year?" exclaimed Blue. "Stella, pick up the stuff, this god isn't serious about bargaining …"

Stella took a single step towards the tribute and the Coyote said, "Wait! Let's not be hasty … three years seems fair."

Blue mockingly laughed at that and countered, "Three years? The deer alone should be worth three years. For all of this, thirty-five years is fair."

The Coyote rubbed his chin but didn't answer. He turned his attention to the tribute and eyed it critically. He frowned as his eyes lingered on the pipe tobacco and said, "How do I even know your tribute is worthy?"

Blue's tail went still for a moment and she said, "The deer was freshly killed, so surely that isn't the problem?" The Coyote nodded and she continued, "The Rubik's cube and the puzzle book are right there, and you can examine them if you wish …"

The Coyote picked up the Rubik's cube and played with it for a moment and then flipped through the word puzzle book and nodded in grudging approval. He turned his attention to the three pouches of pipe tobacco and said, "The only unknown is the tobacco," he paused for a moment and a pipe suddenly appeared in his hand, "how about we take a break from these negotiations and have a little sample?"

A concerned look appeared on Blue's face and her tail flicked in sharp, agitated motions. "You are welcome to try some. I'm sure you will find no issues with the quality."

The Coyote opened one of the pouches, took out a wad, and filled the pipe. A small flame appeared at the tip of his finger and he lit the pipe. He inhaled a couple of times to get it lit and then offered the pipe to Blue. Blue shook her head and raised her hands in a stop motion. The Coyote frowned and said, "Why don't you want some? Is there something wrong with this tobacco that I should be aware of? Are you too proud to smoke with me?"

Blue's shoulders slumped. "There is nothing wrong with it," she said and held out her hand.

The Coyote passed her the pipe and she took a tiny puff from it and offered it back to him. The Coyote cocked an eyebrow at her, and she said, "Fine," and she took a long haul off it.

I expected Blue to start hacking and coughing from doing that, but she calmly exhaled like she'd been smoking a pipe all her life. I wondered why she had been so hesitant to share the pipe with him.

She handed back the pipe and the Coyote took a long pull on it and smiled as he exhaled a cloud of smoke. "Now, I believe we were about to agree that five years of me not interfering in your lives was a fair price for this tribute."

Blue giggled, which wasn't the reaction I'd been expecting and said, "More like twenty-five years … you now know that this is good shit."

I blinked at that last part as I never had heard Blue swear before. I wondered what was going on with her. I grew concerned that the Coyote had cast a spell on her or was messing with her in some way. I took a closer look at Blue and noticed that her purple eyes somehow seemed more vivid than usual and she was swaying slightly as she stood there.

The Coyote also seemed a bit confused and taken aback by Blue's behavior, which relieved my concerns that he was responsible for Blue's current state. He said, "Seven years is more than fair …"

Blue laughed. She half walked and half stumbled over to the Coyote and with a huge smile put her arm around his shoulders and pulled him close, "You know what? I like you. You remind me of my old grandpa with your cute little wrinkles … though you are a little pale and could use more blue in your skin. Because I like you, I'm going to offer you fifteen years as the price."

Stella gasped at this and Liv giggled behind me.

Blue had slurred a few of her words in her last offer. It was almost like she was drunk. It dawned on me what was going on—the tobacco must be a narcotic to her. It was the only thing that made sense. I suddenly became very nervous that our future was being negotiated by a stoned alien.

"Blue, are you okay?" asked Stella with concern.

Blue waved her off.

"Eight years," countered the Coyote.

"Eight? I thought we were friends here ... Twelve years is the lowest I'm willing to go!"

The Coyote rubbed his chin. "Nine years." Blue shook her head and he added, "Ten years. That's my final offer."

Blue said something sharply in her native language and shook her head.

Ten years was more than I expected us to get and I was worried that Blue was going to play hardball over a year or two. "Blue, ten years is good, take the deal."

She looked at me and frowned but then slowly nodded. "Fine, ten years." She turned to the Coyote and added, "You are robbing me at that price, you old goat!"

"Ten years then," and with that he offered his hand to Blue.

Blue and he shook on it.

"It's been fun," laughed the Coyote, and then he and the tribute disappeared.

I exhaled, relieved that it was over.

Stella turned to Blue and said, "Are you okay, Blue? I've never seen you like this."

Blue smiled and slowly blinked at Stella's question. She nodded and said, "I'm fine. The tobacco hit me harder than I expected. There is a name for it on my home world that would roughly translate to 'Satan's smoke' or 'the Devil's weed.'"

"Oh my God!" exclaimed Olivia, "Blue is stoned; that is awesome!"

"Are you sober enough to open a portal?" I asked.

Blue nodded and opened a portal to home.

Epilogue

We came out of the portal beside a 7-Eleven. I glanced around in concern as Bree was still in her Were form and Blue hadn't bothered using her holographic disguise but, thankfully, the lot was empty. I was also confused at why we were here. "This isn't home, Blue."

"I know. Do you have your wallet with you?" I nodded and she added, "Good, go in and get me a large bag of BBQ chips and a bottle of hot sauce. I'm craving a snack."

"Blue has the munchies!" laughed Olivia.

Bree let out an amused growl at this too.

A moment later, a car pulled into the lot. The driver took one look at our group and slammed on his brakes. He tossed the car into reverse and peeled rubber as he tore out of the lot.

The fleeing driver made up my mind. "I'll get your snacks, but open a portal and send Liv, Bree, and Alteea home while I do that, okay?"

Blue shrugged and opened a portal.

A few minutes later I returned to Blue and Stella. Blue took the goodies from me and opened the bag of chips.

"Um, any chance we can go home now?"

Blue shook her head as she poured the hot sauce into the bag of chips. "Lab first. I sent Bree, Liv, and Alteea there as I assumed they wanted to visit the Food-O-Tron." She paused as she stuffed a handful of hot sauce covered potato chips in her mouth and added, "Mmm, so good."

Five minutes later, after a quick stop at the lab to pick up the rest of our team, we were all back home and gathered around the kitchen table. Everyone seemed to be in a good mood.

Blue grinned and said, "I never realized how much I missed bartering. This world is too civilized with its set prices for things ..."

"You did great. I figured we'd be lucky to get five years Coyote-free and you doubled that," I said.

Blue tipped her head at me and went back to eating her chips.

Alteea had a puzzled expression on her little face as she looked at her phone and Liv asked what was up.

"The Coyote doesn't appear in the video. It looks like we are all just talking to ourselves ..."

She turned the phone around and sure enough, she was right.

"I was afraid that might happen ... the Coyote is a god after all," I said.

Stella nodded and added, "It is a good thing it didn't turn into a fight; no video proof, no bounty."

Liv lowered her pint mug of blood and said, "Bounty or no bounty, I still would have enjoyed kicking that thing's ass."

I shook my head at her and said, "Trust me, Liv, if you could have seen its aura, you'd be having second thoughts about getting into a fight with it. It made Elizabeth's aura look tiny ..."

Liv blanched a little at that and the whole table went quiet. The mood had gotten somber, so I added, "Look, we did good tonight. We have ten years before we have to worry about how to deal with the Coyote again. By that time, Walter's friend who works for the Mages council will have his god-banishing spell finished and we will have a decade of experience working together; the poor thing won't have a chance. For now, we put a stop to it indirectly killing anyone else around here. We made a ton of money and we are all in one piece." I paused as everyone nodded and perked up and then said, "And the best part is I have some great pictures for our Christmas party."

Everyone laughed at that, except for Liv who just rolled her eyes and flipped me the bird.

Blue said, "You forgot that we also took on a number of new creatures and now know how to better deal with them if we ever have to go against them again."

I nodded at that. This whole episode with the Coyote and the wide range of Enhanced Individuals we fought certainly had been a learning experience.

Bree finished the last of her cheeseburger and said, "There is one downside to this whole Coyote thing being over ..." We all looked at her in confusion and she explained, "Before it showed up, business had been slow. Now that the Coyote is gone, we are probably back to sitting around with our thumbs up our butts again."

I shrugged and said, "I'm sure something will turn up soon enough."

Not a second after I'd said that my phone rang. I wondered who could be calling me this late. I glanced at the display and saw Rob's name and groaned.

"Hey, Rob, what's up?"

"Hurricane, we need your help. We have a Wererat that has attacked a sanitation worker in Stoney Creek. SWAT is tied up with a shooting in Ancaster and EIRT won't be on scene for at least forty minutes."

I got the rest of the details from him and hung up. Liv was already on her feet and putting her sword on her back. Bree was taking off her clothes to change into her Were form. They both heard every word of the conversation. I filled the rest of the team in.

A thought suddenly hit me, and I yelled, "Coyote, we had a deal! This better not be something you've caused!"

Everyone went dead still and then the TV in the living room came on. Shaggy's song *It Wasn't Me* started blaring from the surround sound.

The Coyote was a dick, but I had to admit he had style and I couldn't help but laugh.

I shot a look at Liv and she blurred off and turned off the TV.

I focused back on the problem at hand, "Okay, people, we have a Wererat to deal with. Gear up and let's take this thing down ..."

A minute later, Blue opened a portal. I warily eyed Blue and the portal for a moment as Blue still seemed a touch unsteady on her feet. I had no idea if the portal would take us to Singapore or Stoney Creek but figured wherever it led, we'd deal with it. After these last two frantic weeks, I knew there wasn't anything this team couldn't handle.

The End

Author's Note

I hope you have enjoyed reading the Bounty series as much as I have enjoyed writing it. I would greatly appreciate your honest review from wherever you purchased this book.

If you are a fan of the series and want to keep up to date with news about my work, please visit my website at http://www.markusmatthews.com or my Facebook page at https://www.facebook.com/TheBountySeries/.

Also, if you want to give feedback or have questions, you can e-mail me at me@markusmatthews.com. I'd love to hear your thoughts.

Lastly, thank you for reading and supporting the series. I can't express how much that means to me.

- Markus Matthews (April 2020)